Rachel SINCLAIR
REASONABLE DOUBT

By Rachel Sinclair

Kansas City Legal Thrillers

Bad Faith

Justice Denied

Hidden Defendant

Injustice for All

L.A. Defense

The Associate

The Alibi

Reasonable Doubt

The Accused

The Hate Crime

Secrets and Lies

Until Proven Guilty

Vinci Books

vinci-books.com

Published by Vinci Books Ltd in 2026

1

Copyright © Rachel Sinclair 2017

The author has asserted their moral right to be identified as the author of this work in accordance with the Copyright, Designs and Patents Act 1988. This work is a work of fiction. Names, characters, places and incidents are the product of the author's imagination or are used fictitiously. Any resemblance to actual persons, living or dead, places and incidents is entirely coincidental.

All rights reserved. No part of this publication may be copied, reproduced, distributed, stored in any retrieval system, or transmitted in any form or by any means, including photocopying, recording, or other electronic or mechanical methods, nor used as a source for any form of machine learning including AI datasets, without the prior written permission of the publisher.

The publisher and the author have made every effort to obtain permissions for any third party material used in this book and to comply with copyright law. Any queries in this respect should be brought to the attention of the publisher and any omissions will be corrected in future editions.

A CIP catalogue record for this book is available from the British Library.

Paperback ISBN: 9781036703226

The EU GPSR authorised representative is Logos Europe, 9 rue Nicolas Poussion, 17000 La Rochelle, France
contact@logoseurope.eu

Chapter One

I MET WITH DILL DEWITT, the husband of Leland Dewitt IV, a prominent gay socialite who lived in an enormous mansion located just off the Country Club Plaza. I had no idea how this particular case fell into my lap, especially since Dewitt had been on the cover of the *Kansas City Star* just about every day since the internationally famous artist, Jackson Michaelson, was found murdered in the back of a downtown art gallery.

Jackson was considered to be the hottest artist in New York City at the time of his murder. He had had showings in Prague, Paris and London which were sold out, as wealthy patrons from around the world paid top dollar for his paintings, sculptures, installations and sketchings. He was also extremely active in the gay community, giving millions to charities that focused on bullying, HIV awareness and teen suicide.

I pulled up to the house and immediately saw the throngs of reporters waiting just outside Leland's gate. I drove through the gate, with the reporters banging on my window, asking me to speak with them. I just shook my head. There was no way I would make a statement. I didn't know what to say, for one. Also, I made it a point never to speak to the media about a case.

I drove up a long driveway and hit a circle drive with a large fountain in the middle. Leland's home was one of those turn-of-the-century mansions with 20 rooms. I understood his home had a temperature-regulated wine cellar, a movie theater, a recreation room, an outdoor pool complete with old-world statues and a hot tub that seats 10, an entire room dedicated to clothes and shoes, and a kitchen as large as that in a restaurant.

This was a murder made for the media. Leland Dewitt IV was only 32 years old but was one of the richest men in the city. He was from old money. His great grandfather, Leland Dewitt, was a robber baron. He made his fortune around the turn of the century during the height of the industrial revolution. He supplied lumber for railroads and shipyards and died in 1960 at the age of 81. He was a billionaire at the time of his death.

Leland Dewitt IV and his brother Roger were the sole heirs after Leland Dewitt III and his wife, Loretta, were killed in a TWA plane crash in the 1970s. Which meant that both Leland and his brother were billionaires in their own right after the crash.

Since Leland Dewitt was the suspect in this murder, and the victim was an internationally known artist, I knew the media would be all over this case like flies on shit. I didn't particularly want this case for that reason alone. I never wanted the spotlight. I turned away from it whenever it tried to shine on me. Since I had such a chaotic and impoverished upbringing, I didn't feel secure having the spotlight on my face.

I went to the front door, an enormous wood structure, and rang the doorbell. I heard the sonorous chimes and waited for somebody to open up the door and let me in. Which happened a few minutes later.

A tall and thin man with a mustache, dressed in a suit, answered. "You are here for Mr. Dewitt, correct? You are Damien Harrington?"

"I am."

"Dave, let him in," a high-pitched male voice admonished from behind the door. "Honestly, David, do you always have to act so butlery?"

The man, who I assumed was David, stepped aside and I walked in. Leland was standing in the enormous foyer, with the 30 foot ceilings, Greek columns and marble floor. To the right was a large marble staircase that led to the second floor, which overlooked the foyer and an atrium around 20 feet away from the foyer.

"Come in, come in, handsome," Leland said as he approached me.

Leland was a slight man, only around 5'5" and probably weighed 120 lbs. His hair was light blonde and shaggy, his face was tanned and slightly worn, and he had big blue eyes. He was dressed in plaid shorts and a pink golf shirt, with a sweater wrapped around his neck. He had bare feet.

He walked right up to me and extended his hand. I shook it and he beamed. "Me and Dill were just sitting out by the pool, waiting for you. Follow me. It's such a hot day, I knew it was pool time."

I followed him through the house and through two enormous French doors which led to the pool area. The pool was enormous and kidney-shaped, and the terrace that surrounded the pool was, just like the rest of the house, made of marble. There were statues surrounding the pool and an island in the middle of it that featured a wet bar.

In the pool was, apparently, Dill. He had dark hair and sunglasses and was floating in the middle of the pool while he sipped a red drink from a straw. He saw me, smiled and waved. "You must be Damien," he said, still waving. "Thanks for coming out here to see Leland."

"Well, come on in," Leland said to Dill. "You need to talk to Damien too."

At that, Dill rolled off his float and swam to the side of the pool. He went around to the pool steps, stepped onto the terrace and toweled off. "Thanks for coming," he said again. "Sit down."

I sat down at one of the tables surrounding the pool, across from Leland and Dill. Leland was sitting very casually – his right leg crossed over his left knee. He had put on a pair of sunglasses. Dill, for his part, hadn't bothered to put on a shirt. He was sitting to the right of me, dressed only in his swim trunks. On the table was a pitcher filled with tomato juice.

"A Bloody Mary?" Leland asked me. "David might be a stiff, but he makes one helluva good drink."

I nodded. Why not? It wasn't usually my habit to drink on the job, but when in Rome…

Leland poured me a glass and I took a sip. I had to admit that David really did make a mean Bloody Mary. I considered myself to be a bit of a Bloody Mary connoisseur and this was one of the better ones I had tried. It was spicy without being unbearable, and it tasted unbelievably fresh.

"This really is an excellent Bloody Mary," I said.

"Well, David squeezes actual tomatoes. Me and Dill buy them at the Farmer's Market on Saturday afternoon, and David uses them to make the drink. That's really the secret to truly delicious things, by the way – use fresh ingredients and you get a fresh taste. That's pretty basic, but sometimes the most basic ideas are still the best ones."

I took another sip. "Does David squeeze and ferment the potatoes to make this vodka, too?" I asked as a joke.

"No," Leland said. "But I admit, I like the high-dollar stuff. I get this stuff called Magnum Grey Goose. $800 a bottle."

"Well, that would do it," I said. "If you're going to spend that much for vodka, it better taste damn good."

"Right?" Leland said. "Well, drink up. You're going to need it after you get through with my story." He shook his head. "Poor Jackson. He was so young. So full of life. He really had the tiger by the tail, that one. The tiger by the tail. He certainly didn't deserve…" At that, he choked up. He bowed his head, shaking it, while Dill scooted over and put his arm around Leland's shoulders. "He didn't deserve what happened to him. The world will be deprived of a great, great man. Imagine if Beethoven was cut down at the age of 27. We wouldn't have ever gotten the Fifth Symphony, the greatest masterpiece the world had ever known. Now, Jackson is dead at 27, and who knows what masterpieces he had yet to create?"

"Oh, that's right," Dill said. "That's so true. In a parallel universe, Jackson is still alive and creating, and the people of that other universe will be enjoying many more years of his work. But in this universe, he's cut down in his prime. In his prime." He sighed. "I wish I could teleport to that other universe so I could see just what Jackson would create when he got to be old and grey."

Leland smiled. "Dill really believes that stuff, by the way. He really believes in other worlds, parallel universes and worm holes. I think he's been watching too much *Dr. Who*, but to each his own. Anyhow, in this world," he said, shooting Dill a look, "Jackson has joined the 27 Club."

I nodded. I was familiar with the 27 Club. The term referred to the fact that so many of our geniuses, both musical and artistic, died at the age of 27. That club included Amy Winehouse, Kurt Cobain, Jimi Hendrix, Janis Joplin and Jim Morrison. It also included the great New York artist, Jean-Michel Basquiat, whose 1982 painting, which was Untitled, set a record high for any US artist at an auction, selling for $110 million.

As if he read my mind, Dill said "You know Basquiat died at Jackson's age. His art is selling for hundreds of millions of dollars. Jackson might have that kind of legacy, too, you know."

"Yeah," Leland said. "I wouldn't be surprised if Jackson's art commands that kind of price tag in about 20 to 25 years." He shook his head. "And you know a movie was made about Basquiat. I fully expect a Hollywood producer will want to make a movie about Jackson's life and death. That's how beloved he had become in such a short, short time."

I nodded and took another sip of the Bloody Mary. I thought about how nice it would be to not have to worry about money. Not having to worry about working for a living, just living for traveling the world and playing tennis in personal courts, and sitting on the veranda sipping Bloody Mary drinks made with freshly-squeezed tomatoes. I was comfortable enough - I was still living off the millions I got from that wrongful death case a year or so ago - but nothing like *this*.

"And how did you know Jackson?"

"I was one of his earliest and largest patrons," Leland said. "I found out about him 10 years ago, when he was 17 years old and living on the streets of Hell's Kitchen. He was literally a starving artist back then, but I saw some of his graffiti he created around the city, and I was just blown away. I had an eye for guys like him and I set him up in a loft in the Village and paid his living expenses so he could just create art without having to worry about where his next meal was coming from or whether or not he could sleep in an actual bed."

"Don't worry," Dill chimed in. "Leland's interest in the boy wasn't sexual. At least, that's what Leland tells me."

"Well, I wasn't exactly a dirty old man at the time I met him," he said. "I was only 22 when I met Jackson, but he really wasn't my type. Too blonde, too skinny." Leland shook his head. "No, I wasn't sexually attracted to him. I just saw his graffiti work around the city and I knew talent when I saw it. He was definitely talented."

"Of course he was talented," Dill said. "After all, he became the toast of Europe when he went over there. The *bon vivant*."

Leland rolled his eyes. "He's always using foreign words wrong. Dear, *bon vivant* means a social and luxurious person. Jackson certainly wasn't that. I mean, he was. He was a social guy. He had to be. But luxurious, no. He wasn't. He always told me he was more comfortable sleeping on a hard floor than on a luxury bed. That was why I used to go to his loft, and this was after I lined up wealthy patrons for him, mind you, and saw he slept on the floor. A blanket on the floor, with a pillow. That was all." He shook his head. "I guess that came from the fact that he lived on the streets, from the time he was only 16 years old. Could you imagine that? Living on the streets at 16? I'm surprised he didn't end up joining a gang."

"Oh, no gang would have wanted him," Dill chided.

"He was too gay, too sensitive, too skinny, too everything. He did get along by being a rent boy, though, to several different men over the years. Funny, that. He never let anybody actually get him an apartment, though, until Leland. I guess because Leland was interested in him professionally and not sexually."

"I guess," Leland said, obviously not convinced. "I don't know why the boy let me take care of him. But Dill is right. Jackson let me set him up in an apartment. He let me give him a monthly allowance. He let me introduce him around to my friends. I was very connected in the New York art scene and he totally allowed me to hook him up with all my wealthy friends. I mean, not hook up in the sexual sense, but hook up in the professional sense."

"Anyhoo," Dill said. "So, yeah. That's the story in a nutshell about how Leland and Jackson know one another."

"Now, let's see," I said, looking through my file. "In your statement to the police, you told them you didn't remember going into the living quarters of the gallery. The night that Jackson was killed. Is that right?" In Leland's gallery, he explained to me that he had an entire studio apartment attached to the back of the gallery – complete with a kitchenette, dining room, and a couch that pulled out into a bed. That was where Leland was apparently arrested the night of the murder.

"Oh, yes, that's right." Leland nodded his head. "I was blotto that night. It's not often that I drink to excess like that, but I did that night. The crazy thing was, I seemed to be semi-coherent to everyone around me, including Dill. Nobody knew I was three sheets to the wind. I think that it's also because I have been prescribed Ambien for sleep. I took one right before midnight that night."

Dill gave Leland a look and then shook his finger at him

like he was being particularly naughty. "I know. I always tell Leland about that. I always tell him not to mix Ambien with alcohol, but does he listen?"

"I know, Daddy, I know," Leland said with a roll of the eyes. "Anyhow, I try to take Ambien an hour before I go to bed. And I planned on sleeping in the back of the gallery that night." He shot a look over to Dill. "Dill was being a pill and I didn't feel like going home. I set up an entire bedroom in the back of that gallery for just those occasions when I don't want to go home. And that happened to be one of those nights."

"And, let's see, it looked like Jackson's time of death was-"

"2 AM, the morning of April 9. I know. That's what the police told me when they brought me in for questioning."

"Right. 2 AM. So, what happened on the evening of April 8, then?"

"Well, it was Jackson's Kansas City debut. It was a First Friday, you know, when all the art galleries are open late and have little parties for the people. And there was a lot of excitement about Jackson being in town. A ton of excitement about him. Our gallery was filled with people that day, from the time the First Friday got going to the time we closed. First Fridays are always packed, you know. There's always thousands and thousands of people that come to Crossroads and go through the galleries and appreciate all the wonderful art that each gallery has to offer."

I nodded. I had never actually been to a First Friday, but it was one of Sarah's favorite things to do. She was the art aficionado, not me. In fact, I had never even heard about Jackson Michaelson, but Sarah knew all about him. She had been a fan of his from years back and was devastated to find out he had been murdered. But she was extremely impressed to know I would be defending Jackson's alleged murderer. That is, as long as I was convinced that his alleged murderer, Leland, didn't do it. If I thought he did it, Sarah wouldn't be speaking with me for awhile.

"This will make your career, Damien," Sarah had said.

"That's all I need," I had said. "To be known as a celebrity attorney." I rolled my eyes. "I'll see what he has to say before I agree to represent him."

"Okay," I said. "So, it was a First Friday, and Jackson was the star attraction."

"Yes. The star attraction. Our gallery got so much foot traffic that day, I tell you what. I usually buy at least a case of wine for the guests, but I knew I would need more wine, so I bought four cases. Four cases, and they were all gone by the end of the evening. Not to mention about twenty wheels of Brie cheese and tubs and tubs of fig spread. Thank God for Costco." He smiled. "I mean, I got money to burn, but I don't always like to spend it so much. I like a bargain as much as the next guy."

"Nothing wrong with that." I drew a breath. "So, there were thousands of people in your gallery that evening."

"Tens of thousands, probably."

Dill snorted.

"What? Listen, each First Friday attracts at least 10,000 people, and I swear to God, every last one of those people ended up in my gallery at some point."

"And what was Jackson doing?"

"He was holding court. You know, he was dressed in ripped jeans and a t-shirt, five o'clock shadow, his hair hadn't been combed in God-knows-how-long, but he didn't care how he looked. Nobody else did, either. They were fascinated by him. He was going around the gallery, talking about the inspirations for his paintings and just selling himself and his art. I don't usually sell a ton of work on those First Fridays, but I did that night. Even at $50,000 and up, his art was selling like crazy."

"Selling like crazy? How many paintings did you sell that night?"

"I sold 20. I had displayed 25 and sold 20. We're talking the most expensive painting was $100,000, and most of them were between $50,000 and $75,000. I considered that to be a very successful night."

"And how much did Jackson get of that?"

Leland shrugged. "I just give him all the money. I don't take a commission from him. Why would I? I have more money than God. No, I just give him all the money."

"And how much did the gallery collect from people that night?"

"Well, we ended up doing $1.4 million in sales."

"Wow. $1.4 million. And Jackson got to keep all that money for himself?"

"Every dime. But you know, money meant nothing to him. Zero. He gave most of his money away. AIDS charities, anti-bullying programs, all sorts of animal rights organizations. He gave most everything away. Oh, I mean, he kept some money for himself. After all, he has to eat and he does still have that loft in New York. The same loft I got for him back in the day – he still lives there. He insisted on buying it from me and I let him. So, he has the upkeep of that loft. But, other than that, he never spent much money. The kid was a saint when it came to charitable giving."

Dill nodded. "A saint," he said, echoing Leland. "What kind of a kid would just make millions of dollars a year and still sleep on the floor of an old loft and give most of the money away?"

I nodded, thinking hard. Was his charitable giving tied to his murder? Or was it something else?

"So, he was very generous with his money."

"Too generous. But that was Jackson. See, he had a hard upbringing. He was living on the streets at the age of 16, you know."

Dill put his arm around Leland. "Dear, he knows that. You already told him that."

"Oh, right, I guess I did. But he was." Leland's voice got low. "You see, I think, although I never did find out for sure, but I think his stepfather used to do stuff to him. Molest him. I didn't know about all of this, but I found out soon enough, that his family had more money than my family does."

"Oh? What do you mean?"

"Just what I say. Jackson's family was extremely wealthy."

"But they let him live on the streets?"

"Well, they didn't *let* him do anything. He lived on the streets and evaded detection for many years. He told me he got good at it. His family reported him missing, and you know, his face was always in those newspapers. You know the ads, where it shows the kid when he went missing and then shows an age progression. I'm sure you're familiar with these ads. Everyone has seen them."

"Yes, I am," I said. "So, his family put his face on these ads?"

"Yeah. They even hired a private detective to find him. But Jackson was always too smart for all of them. So he lived on the streets for years, hiding in plain sight, while his family looked for him, high and low."

"That's where his career as a rent boy came in," Dill said.

"He never let them give him money or any of that, but he allowed them to take him in from time to time. He would stay with this john or that john whenever he thought the police were getting wise to where he was. And these johns, they never turned him in, because they all knew why he was running. They all understood it so they never turned him in as a runaway."

"And his parents lived in New York City, too?"

"Oh, no. I mean, his father was an international financier in Lower Manhattan. His mother was from old money. He lived with his mother and stepfather out in Connecticut, and his stepfather was, shall we say, a-"

"*Bon vivant*," Dill said with a smile.

"Yes, a *bon vivant*. He used that term right that time. A *bon vivant*. He loved to party and loved all the luxuries that life can bring. And he apparently loved Jackson a little too much." Leland shook his head. "I didn't mean that. Of course he didn't actually love Jackson at all. If he loved him, he wouldn't have done what he did. Anyhow, the stepfather was just an all-around awful person. He was a sexual predator and went through his wife's money like water. He had mistresses and also had boys on the side. I always say there are no bisexuals in the world, but I think I might be wrong. The stepfather seemed to be somebody who loved men and women about the same."

I carefully made notes while I listened to them speak.

"The stepfather, what else can you tell me about him? Is he still married to Jackson's mother? Is he still living in Connecticut? Is there any way possible he might have killed Jackson?"

Leland sighed. "Yes, he still lives in Connecticut. No, he's not still married to Jackson's mother. He and Jackson's mother, Marie, were divorced five years ago. As to whether or not he killed Jackson, I don't know. I don't know what kind of motive he might have had to do that."

Dill piped in. "I do. I know what kind of motive he would have."

"Enlighten me, dear," Leland said.

"Pretty simple, really. Jackson was getting more and more famous. That means newspapers are talking to him. Reporters are interviewing him." He turned to me. "Did you know Netflix was going to produce a special about him? About his life?" He nodded his head. "That's how famous Jackson was getting."

"A special? Like a documentary?"

"Yes, a documentary. One of those things where they visit the hometown and talk to the people who knew him growing up and then talk to the people who know him now. Show his art work, you know the drill. I'm sure you've seen a Netflix documentary before. It's always the same standard format."

I nodded. "Yes. I have seen Netflix documentaries. Well, that would definitely give the stepfather reason to kill Jackson, wouldn't it? If that documentary gets produced, there's a good chance the stepfather's secrets will be revealed. So, I'm going to have to find out the stepfather's name, where he works and all that. I'll either send my investigator to speak with him, or I'll do it myself."

"Yes," Leland said. "That's a good place to start. His name is George Mason. He lives in Greenwich, Connecticut. He works at Goldman Sachs as an investment banker."

"Are you sure he still works there, honey?" Dill asked.

"Yes. I'm sure." Leland turned to me. "That's actually the first person I thought about when I was arrested for this. I thought maybe George was behind it all."

"Good," I said. "I'll be sure and speak with him. Now, can you think of anybody else who could have done this?"

Leland bit his lower lip and then took a sip of his drink. "Dill, honey, could you do me a favor?"

Dill looked at Leland suspiciously. "What?"

"I need to speak with Damien alone. Could you check on David and see if there's anything he needs?"

Dill rolled his eyes. "You promised me you wouldn't keep secrets." He crossed his arms in front of him. "Or don't you remember promising that?"

"Stop being such a drama queen, Mary," Leland said, using the gay slang term for somebody annoying or effeminate. "And see if you can give David a hand."

Dill didn't move a muscle. "You're going to tell him about Mystic Anna, aren't you?" Dill looked at Leland accusingly. "You're completely wrong about her. She wouldn't do something like this."

Leland rolled his eyes. "Will you just please give us a bit of privacy?"

"Okay," Dill said. "But you better not tell him what I think you're going to tell him."

"I'll tell him whatever I want," Leland said. "It's my life on the line, you know."

"Now who's being a drama queen?" Dill still didn't look like he was going to move.

"With all due respect," I said to Dill, "Leland isn't being a drama queen when he's telling you his life is on the line. It absolutely is."

"You mean," Dill said, "they're going to try to give him the chair?"

"Actually, in Missouri, it's lethal injection. But no, they aren't seeking the death penalty for Leland. At least, they haven't certified him yet for that. But they might upgrade the charges and seek the death penalty in the future. Even if they don't, he'll probably be sentenced to life in prison without parole if he gets convicted for this. So he's facing very serious time. If he knows something about somebody who might have done this, I need to know about it."

Dill suddenly looked very worried. "Well, he won't go to prison because he didn't do this. Right?"

I looked over at Leland who was trying hard not to also look worried.

"Leland hasn't yet told me he didn't do it. That said, even if he blacked out from the Ambien and the alcohol, I doubt very seriously he killed Jackson. I've done research on the topic of Ambien blackouts and I've found that a person won't do something on Ambien that he wouldn't do while he's conscious. In other words, if Leland didn't have cause to murder Jackson and Leland doesn't have violent tendencies, it's unlikely he murdered Jackson."

"Well, then, if he didn't murder Jackson, he won't be convicted." Dill seemed pretty satisfied with that answer, even if that was an answer he made up himself. "So, I'm not worried."

I looked over at Leland. "Go ahead and tell me what you were going to tell me. It looks like Dill is pretty set on not leaving us alone to speak, but I need to know everything you might know about somebody else who might have done this."

"Okay, then," Leland said. "I'll go right ahead and tell you."

Dill gave Leland a look, but Leland studiously ignored him.

"And?" I said to Leland.

"Her name is Mystic Anna. She's Dill's psychic. I

personally think she's the most likely one to have killed poor Jackson."

Chapter Two

"OKAY," I said. "Tell me about Mystic Anna."

Dill piped up. "There's nothing to tell about her," he said. "She's a fine person. She never would do something like this."

"Oh, shut up," Leland said. "You never want to think she does anything wrong." He turned to me. "Dill relies on her for everything. He's just afraid that if she gets sent up the river that he'll curl into a ball of goo and die. He literally can't make a single move without her say-so."

"Well, you're just trying to get her out of the way because you don't like my relationship with her."

"You have no relationship with her. She's a charlatan who takes all your money. Or should I say she takes all of my money." He addressed me. "Dill doesn't actually work for a living. I take care of him and all his needs. He's my husband, so it's only right. But he's absolutely on the nose when he says I don't like the way he relies on her for everything. He can't even eat a bowl of cereal in the morning without calling and consulting her." He lowered his voice. "He pays her a half-million a year."

I cleared my throat. "A half-million a year?"

"A half-million a year."

Dill rolled his eyes. "As if you'd miss that money. That's pocket change to you."

"Can I ask what you did before you met Leland?" I asked Dill.

"What do you mean?"

"Did you work? Did you have your own money?" I didn't quite know what to think of the two men. I got the impression Dill was the *bon vivant* and latched onto Leland for his money. Not that that meant anything, but perhaps that would give me another lead on who might have done it. I had to clear Dill, in my mind, of murder.

Maybe Dill was jealous of Leland's relationship with Jackson? Threatened? Maybe he believed Leland would one day leave him for Jackson? That would be motive for murder, especially if there was a tight prenup and Jackson might be left with little to nothing in the event of a divorce.

"Why are you asking all these questions?" Dill whined. "You're making me feel like I'm under suspicion."

"I just wanted to know."

Leland sighed. "Dill was somebody I met up in New York. He was working at Lips New York as a drag queen. His drag name was Helen Heels."

"And that's how you met? At the bar?"

"Yes, that's how we met." Leland nodded his head. "He was serving cocktails and lip-syncing to Christina Aguilera tunes. Now, can we please move on to Mystic Anna?"

"Certainly. Tell me about her."

Leland glanced at Dill, who was still staring daggers at

him, his arms crossed in front of him. "Mystic Anna is Dill's personal psychic. She works out of her New York City home. I've been there with Dill." Leland shook his head and made a face. "Her home looks just like you might think. Crystal ball, incense, beaded curtains in the doorway, the whole nine. I was surprised she wasn't wearing a scarf around her head."

"There's a reason for all of those things, if you must know," Dill said indignantly. "The crystal ball actually helps her see the future. The incense helps her clients relax." He rolled his eyes. "And she happens to really like crystal beads."

"Whatever. Anyhooo…Dill relies on Mystic Anna for all his big decisions."

"She told me to marry you, didn't she?" Dill asked.

"A broken clock is right twice a day," Leland said dismissively. "As I was saying. Mystic Anna fancies herself to be some kind of latter-day Jeane Dixon or Edgar Cayce. You remember who those people are, don't you?"

"I do remember something about Jeane Dixon. Didn't she make a bunch of predictions in the *National Enquirer?*"

"Yes," Leland said, with another roll of his eyes. "She would make predictions like 'Charles and Diana will have marital problems,' long after everyone knew they were having marital problems. Her predictions, the ones that came true, were ones that didn't take a rocket scientist to figure out. Most of the things she said didn't come true, though. She was a real charlatan, if you ask me."

"Yet she was a wealthy charlatan. Didn't Nancy Reagan rely on her advice?" I asked.

"She did," Leland said, with a nod of his head. "And yes, she managed to make her charlatanism into a cottage industry for herself. A sucker's born every minute and Jeane Dixon reached those suckers."

I looked over at Dill, who looked like he was getting more and more pissed by the second. He was glaring at Leland and shaking his head. But he didn't say a word.

"And Edgar Cayce, he was famous for being a seer too, right?"

"Right," Leland said. "Anyhow, this Mystic Anna wanted to be taken seriously. She has this blog where she makes predictions for the coming year. Most of them were bullshit, but she predicted the death of poor Jackson."

"Yes she did," Dill said triumphantly. "She did. She predicted it just last month."

This piece of news got me interested. "Really? Let me see that blog post."

Leland snapped his fingers and David came out. "Could you bring me my Apple?" Leland asked him.

David disappeared and came right back out with a silver Apple laptop in his hands.

"Thank you," Leland said. He logged on, and, in a matter of seconds, he brought up a blog page. "Here," he said, "look at this."

The page was black with a picture of a woman as the banner. It seemed to be a pretty typical psychic website – there was a tab where you could find out your astrological sign, and another that promoted a book on doing star charts for people. Still another was a blog post about developing individual psychic powers. Mystic Anna was also selling different psychic implements, such as tarot cards, candles, incense, and stones, runes and crystals. All of which were purported to be blessed by her individually.

I clicked on another tab that was marked "predictions," and, sure enough, among the other predictions about obvious things – North Korea would continue to be belligerent, there would continue to be mass shootings in America, that sort of thing – there was another list of famous people who she predicted things would happen to. This celebrity couple would welcome a baby girl, and that celebrity couple were going to break up; etc. Right in the middle were predictions about which celebrities would kick the bucket, and I saw Jackson was in the middle of that list.

I looked over at Leland, who was nodding his head knowingly. "You see. She said he would die. She had to make that true so everybody who comes to her website would think she's the real deal. Like Jeane Dixon."

I shook my head. "That's pretty far-fetched, isn't it? I mean, you know there's these on-line betting pools where you can bet on who will croak during any given year. Most of the time, people bet on obvious celebrities kicking the bucket – old people, sick celebrities, ones with drug problems. But every so once in awhile, somebody correctly predicts the death of a young and healthy celebrity. I think that means they get extra points in the game or something like that." I wasn't entirely clear on the rules of the Ghoul Pool game, but I knew a little about it, and I knew that obvious celebrities are worth much less than not-so-obvious-ones. "What I'm trying to say is that sometimes people get lucky when they predict the death of a random young person." I hated to use the term "lucky" in this situation, but, then again, that's what it was – it was a lucky guess on Mystic Anna's part.

Dill nodded and smiled. "You see? Damien isn't buying your cockamamie story."

Leland raised an eyebrow. "Except for one thing, Dill. You forgot what else makes me think Mystic Anna is a suspect in this murder."

Dill shook his head. "Whatever, Mary." He rolled his eyes.

"What is that other thing?"

"Well," Leland said. "I know all about the ghoul pool. I thought about that angle myself. And Jackson had a drug problem, yes he did. So, it wouldn't have been a stretch to predict he would die so young. But Mystic Anna is the personal psychic for Dill, and she told him personally, in one of his sessions, that he mustn't socialize with Jackson. She detected a dark energy around Jackson and said he would meet his end within a month. That was three weeks ago that she told him that."

"And? I'm still not getting why you think she killed Jackson."

Leland lowered his voice. "She said he had dark energy around him. She was afraid for Dill. She told Dill that if he continued to hang around with Jackson that bad things would happen to him. She didn't want to lose her gravy train with Dill, and she was apparently afraid Jackson would harm Dill or even kill him. So she killed Jackson herself."

I had to suppress my feelings that this whole thing was hokum, but I thought it in my head. "She thought that Jackson would kill Dill, and-"

"And Dill gave her a half million a year for all kinds of various bullshit. Readings, candles, blessed crystals, on and on and on. She keeps telling him that if he didn't pay her for these things that he'll lose everything. That he'll get sick, lose me and never have love in his life again. Dill is very taken in by Mystic Anna. If you ask me, it's no different than any other kind of addiction. Dill is Mystic Anna's bread and butter, and no way is she going to risk losing his business. If she thinks somebody will threaten Dill's life, she'll take care of it."

That angle actually started to make a weird kind of sense to me. "And she framed you because-"

"Isn't it obvious?" Leland said, giving Dill the side-eye. "I finally told Dill that I've had enough of Mystic Anna. Dill's been paying Mystic Anna all these years because we have a joint checking account, and, really, there's more money in there than either of us know what to do with. I didn't really care if Dill wanted to see her or not. I figured it was a harmless thing. Silly but harmless. But the two of us started seeing a marriage counselor this year, and it turned out that I really hated how much of a hold Mystic Anna has over Dill. We can't go on vacation without him consulting her. I ended up telling the therapist that I really couldn't stand Mystic Anna, and the therapist encouraged me to cut Dill off from her. Which I have done. Just this past week."

"So, she killed Jackson and framed you to get the both of you out of the way. That's what you're trying to tell me, right?"

"Bingo," Leland said.

I still felt skeptical, but, at the same time, it was something I would have to check out. While I was in New York, I could also see the stepfather. I had a feeling the stepfather would be an invaluable witness for me. Not to mention the fact that the stepfather was also, in my book, a likely suspect.

Besides, Jackson's home was in New York. I could pay for Garrett to come with me and the two of us could probably run down most of the people Jackson knew in that city. That could give me a good idea as to who might have done this crime.

"Okay," I said. "I'll go up to New York and check it out. I should go up there, anyhow, because New York is where all the witnesses will be."

"Go and do that," Dill said. "Mystic Anna has nothing to hide."

"Hmph," Leland said with a roll of his eyes. "We'll just have to see about that. Anyhoo, you be sure to give all my love to those vultures out there. If they could come in here and peck my eyes out, they would, trust me."

"I know all about the media. You must leave all that to me. I won't say anything to them, of course. I can't possibly comment on an impending investigation. So don't worry about all that."

"We won't."

I got to my feet. "Thanks for the Bloody Mary," I said. "It was honestly the best I've ever had." Which wasn't surprising, considering the tomatoes were freshly squeezed and the vodka was super high dollar. "I'll show myself out."

"You do that. And if you need somebody to show you around, Dill here would be more than willing. I can't, of course." He motioned to his ankle, which had the electronic monitor on it. "As much as I would love to go with you and Dill, I don't love the idea of waiting for my trial while wearing an orange jumpsuit. That shade of orange does nothing for my complexion. Nor for anybody else's, either."

I raised my eyebrow, wondering if I had a choice on whether or not to take Dill. Something told me he would try to interfere with my questioning of Mystic Anna, which wasn't what I needed at that moment. I needed somebody to let me do my job, which was to ask questions and go wherever my investigation led me. "I'll think about that."

He looked at me for a second or two, his finger on his cheek. He finally nodded. "I think you need something from Dill and me. I think you do."

"Well, yeah, of course I need something from the two of you. I need both of your honesty and testimony. Not to mention help with my investigation."

"No, I think you need something else. In fact, I know

you do. I've done my own investigation on you, and I know a few things."

I inwardly groaned. "You know a few things about me. Like what kind of things?"

"I know about your friends in prison. And I think I know a way I can help."

Chapter Three

IN SPITE OF MYSELF, my ears perked up when Leland said he had a way of helping. Nick, Tommy and Jack were all up for parole and all were due to have their hearings in a month. Connor, of course, wasn't eligible. As much as I stayed up nights doing research on Connor's case, looking at every Law Review article, case law and statute I could find, I still didn't see a way around the fact that Connor would probably die in prison. As tragic as that was.

"Well, the guys are all hopefully getting out on parole in a month or so," I said.

"But not Connor, right?"

I sighed. "Right. The other guys had their sentences commuted to 20 years. They originally got life in prison with the possibility of parole. Connor's sentence wasn't commuted, though, because he actually pulled the trigger on the security guard."

Leland nodded. "What if I told you I have blackmail material on the governor?"

"What kind of blackmail material?" I was curious. I wouldn't necessarily use the material. But maybe, if it was good enough, I would. If it was good enough that maybe I could force Connor's sentence to also be commuted, I would certainly use it. I would do anything to make sure our band of brothers was together again. They were all worth that much to me.

"Well, you know Governor Weston is such a good Christian, family-values guy, right? He's all in the culture wars. God forbid a trans person uses the wrong bathroom. God forbid a gay couple wants to get married. All of that." Leland rolled his eyes. "You know that about him, right?"

That was right. Our governor was one of the holy-rollers. Which probably meant he had either a dead girl or a live boy in his closet. That was the saying, anyhow – the surest way to derail a political career is to find a dead girl or a live boy who's involved with the politician, whoever he happened to be. This was especially true with "family values" types like Governor Weston.

"I'm listening," I said.

"What if I told you I have proof that Governor Weston likes his boys on the side?" Leland asked me.

"What kind of proof?"

"I've got a dick pic sent from his cell phone. He sent it to Jackson himself." Leland looked delighted with his revelation. "Truth be told, that was most of the reason why I chose you to be my attorney. I knew you could use that piece of information and could use it wisely. Plus, you're a hottie." He laughed. "No, really, I checked out your credentials, and you have one of the most impressive profiles of any lawyer in the city. But I also knew I could help you out a lot when I told you about what I'm telling you."

"Where is his cell phone now?" I could hardly contain my glee. I would still visit Mystic Anna and the stepfather and whoever else I happened to find up in New York, but, right at that moment, I was dying to see if this dick pic thing was true. I didn't really doubt it, because politicians were always getting into trouble by being indiscriminate with their sexual proclivities. Yet it all seemed too good to be true.

"The police have Jackson's cell phone, of course," Leland said. "But not that one. That was a secret one Jackson had. Jackson liked to get nasty with his rich friends and he used a special cell phone to give and receive nasty messages." Leland put his finger to his mouth. "Shhh, though, the cops don't know about this cell phone."

"Well, I need to see this phone. I want to see if it's true the governor sent these dick pics, but, also, the cell phone will give me some other clues on who might've killed Jackson. After all, if there were some prominent men like the governor who Jackson could've brought down, that widens the suspect list. Who knows? Maybe the governor himself was involved with the murder."

"Oh, I don't know about all that. What I do know, though, is that Governor Weston would probably do anything to keep this quiet. He thinks the cops have the cell phone that has the dick pics and he has no idea I have it. So use that information. I'll get the phone to you, and you can decide how to use it against him."

I thought about all the politicians brought down by sexual dalliances. Anthony Weiner with his dick pics and Eliot Spitzer with his prostitutes. The governor of Alabama resigning because of a sex scandal. Dennis Hastert and his wrestling boys. Larry Craig tapping his foot in a bathroom.

On and on and on, really. Politicians had been brought low by sexual proclivities probably since the dawn of time. And this one, seeing as it involved a boy, would be especially juicy.

I hadn't yet heard a word about it. I knew, however, if I could somehow corroborate the governor had sent these dick pics to Jackson...Connor would definitely have his sentence commuted.

I cleared my throat. "How do you know he sent these dick pics?" I asked Leland.

"Well, he has a birth mark right on his upper right thigh. That birthmark is clearly visible in the picture. You can't miss it. It's the size of a quarter and is shaped a little like the state of Texas. You're a lawyer. You can threaten him with some kind of legal action that would mean you can force him to submit to a physical exam to match his dick up with these pics, can't you?"

I nodded. "I could. I could threaten to bring him into this murder case, which means that I really could get a court order for a physical examination to prove the dick in these pics belongs to him. I mean, how do we know he wasn't behind the murder of Jackson, really? He might be. That's a long shot, but people have killed for less."

Leland waved his hand in a dismissive gesture. "Oh, I don't believe in all that, not at all. I know he had an alibi for the night Jackson was murdered because he was at a fundraiser that night. That's how he got to know Jackson, by the way. They're both active in animal charities. The governor was at a charity ball the night Jackson was killed."

"But maybe he hired somebody to kill Jackson. That's possible."

Leland nodded. "You go with that, Damien. I don't

think that for a hot second, but go ahead and tell the governor that you'll finger him as a suspect, which means you can get a court order to show the dick pics are him. I have a feeling he'll do anything you want at that point."

"Plus," Dill piped up. "I need to be the voice of common sense here. Why, on God's green earth, would the Governor have Jackson killed and then just leave the incriminating cell phone at the murder scene? They would try to recover it before they killed him, or they certainly would have tried to find it. As it was, it was in a drawer in one of the night stands." He rolled his eyes.

Leland and I looked at each other. I personally felt embarrassed I didn't use my brain on that one. Guess this Bloody Mary was stronger than I thought.

"Good point," we both said at once.

I sighed. This was a dangerous proposition and slightly scary. I was skating on thin ice, really, considering what I did with Gina Degrazio. She hadn't yet turned me in for suborning perjury, but she was a volatile one and could squeal on me at any time. She had nothing to lose because of the double-jeopardy clause. She couldn't be tried again for the murder of her husband, so she knew that, if she really wanted to, she could make my life a living hell. I would need the governor on my side in case that ever happened and I was brought up on charges that might result in my disbarment.

In other words, it was best not to piss off the governor. What if I tried to blackmail him and he called my bluff? He would be forever my enemy and I couldn't count on him to save me if something went wrong. In fact, he probably would make sure that I was disbarred if ever my case came up in front of him.

If this all went south, I would no doubt be disbarred just for trying to blackmail him. Plus, blackmailing was illegal. I could certainly go to prison for doing such a thing.

Yet, the prospect was intriguing, too. If it worked, Connor might get out with the other guys.

High risk, high reward.

"Let me have the phone," I said. "And you know that, by taking this phone from you, I'm essentially withholding pertinent evidence from the prosecutor's office. That means I need to blackmail Governor Weston and get this phone over to the police as soon as possible. If that is what I'm going to do."

"Of course," Leland said. "But there's nothing from me on this phone, so I don't think the police will be too interested in it." He shrugged. "What can I say, they have a hard-on for me, and not in a good way. But do with it what you will. I don't think there's anything on there incriminating for this murder, either. You can look through it if you like, though. I still think you need to stick with checking out Mystic Anna and the stepfather. Start there. See what you can find out from them. Don't go running on some wild goose chase because you find out some rich guy had a thing for Jackson."

"I'll decide what's relevant. In the meantime, give me the phone. I'll think about what I want done with it. What I need to do with it. I like your idea about blackmailing, but if it goes sideways, I'll be behind bars and you'll have to find another attorney to try your case. Fair warning on that."

"I understand." He nodded his head. "Do what you need to do, then give that phone to whomever wants to see it as evidence. Just don't get too bogged down in it."

Dill rolled his eyes. "I think you're the one who has the

hard-on, only yours is for Mystic Anna. Why do you want to believe the worst about her?"

"I just think she's up to no good, that's all."

"Well, then, go ahead and talk to Mystic Anna," Dill said. "And talk to George Mason, Jackson's stepfather. Go up to New York and see what you can find out. See what you can run down up there. I have a feeling you'll crack this case."

"He better crack this case," Leland said. "I don't want to live the rest of my life being the boyfriend of some enormous guy named Brutus. I'm too pretty for jail."

I had to smile at that one. Leland was a good-looking guy, in a feminine sort of way. He probably wouldn't last very long in prison. That much I knew.

"Well, I'll get David to give you that phone. I hope it helps you."

"Thanks."

In ten minutes, David was back, a phone in his hand. He gave it to Leland, who handed it to me. "Here you go. Do what you can with it, and then give it to the police or whatever you need to do. Then I hope you can get up to New York and find out what you can find out from everyone up there." He patted me lightly on the shoulder. "I trust you, by the way. I trust you can do a good job on my case."

"I will, I promise."

As I left the mansion with Jackson's phone in my hand, I could hear my heart pounding. What would I do with this piece of evidence? Was I really going to risk going to prison and having my law license stripped, all on the off chance I could possibly see one of my best friends freed from prison?

I nodded when I got to the car and found the picture in question. It was accompanied by some text messages as well. I saw the birthmark that Leland was telling me about, and it was certainly distinctive. Just as he said it was. It did kind of look like the state of Texas.

I closed my eyes and listened to my heart pounding.

I knew I would risk it. If it worked, I would finally see the one thing I never thought I would – Connor freed from prison.

For that, I would risk anything.

Chapter Four

I MET with Garrett that evening. I mainly wanted to make sure he would come with me to New York. Other than that, I would have to lean on Sarah to take care of the kids while I was gone.

Sarah and I had finally got to the point where I was ready for her to move back into the house. We had gone through many, many hours of marital counseling. I screamed at her during these counseling sessions and she cried. Somehow, the therapy worked and we both saw one another's points of view. I also decided I was to let go of my rage about her leaving me and Amelia when we both needed her the most, and I just had to trust her not to do it again.

But it still bothered me that she was so weak that she couldn't handle the crisis with Amelia. I wondered what she would do if something like that happened again. God forbid Amelia had some kind of a relapse. But I had to admit that I never stopped loving her, and she was the mother of my children. That had to mean something.

He showed up at our usual dive bar in Midtown. I was drinking a beer when he sat down. "Alright, buddy," he said. "What do you got for me?"

I took a deep breath. I was still wrestling with the whole dick pic thing. It was scary to think that I could very well end up in prison for doing this. I wanted to run it by Garrett to see what he said.

"I think I have a way to get Connor out of prison."

He nodded his head. "I'm listening."

"It turns out I might have some blackmail material. It's related to this murder case I'll be trying. Maybe you've heard about it. It's the case of Jackson Michaelson, the artist."

"Yeah," Garrett said. "I've read about that in the papers. God, the newspaper is on it like flies on shit."

"Of course the media is on it. The suspect is a very wealthy heir to a lumber company established in 1901. He's a billionaire. The victim was a hot artist selling out shows from here to Prague. I've read in the paper that his artwork is currently selling for millions of dollars."

"Millions of dollars?"

"Yeah. That's what happens when a hot artist dies young. That happened with that artist, Basquiat. He died at the age of 27 and one of his paintings sold for over $100 million. There's every reason to believe Jackson's work will someday be just as valuable."

Garrett nodded. "Who are the suspects?"

I shifted in my seat. "We'll talk about that in a few minutes. In the meantime, I need to run something by you."

"Shoot."

I took another deep breath. "Well, apparently Jackson and our dear Governor Weston knew one another."

"Yeah. Go on."

"And apparently Governor Weston likes boys."

I saw a huge smile creep up on Garrett's face. "Go on."

I got out Jackson's phone. "Here," I said. "Here's a picture of the junk belonging to Governor Weston, our family values governor."

Garrett looked at it and then burst out laughing. "Really? How do you know that's the governor's junk?"

"Well, I don't know. That's where you come in. I need you to do what you can to confirm the number associated with this text belongs to the governor. From there, according to Leland, we can prove the penis belongs to him because of the birthmark on the upper right thigh. As you can see, that birthmark is quite distinctive."

Garrett looked harder at the picture. "Yeah. Kinda looks like the state of Texas, doesn't it?"

"It sure does. I'm reasonably sure this picture is the real thing, just because Leland told me it was. He was very close with Jackson, so I would imagine Jackson probably told Leland all his dirty secrets."

"Oh, I see." Garrett nodded his head. "I get what you're going for. You want to blackmail Governor Weston with this dick pic so he'll commute Connor's sentence. Is that what you're thinking?"

I nodded. "That's what I'm thinking."

He leaned back and took a swig of his beer. "You do know that if this doesn't work, you-"

"Will be in prison, probably for quite a few years. I'll lose my family, my license to practice law and my freedom again. Yes, I know that to be true."

"Yeah. Blackmailing a government official like that, the feds won't fool around with that shit. Extortion carries at least a 10-year sentence."

"Try 20 years. In the federal pen. So, yeah, this is a huge risk. I know that. You in or you out?"

"I'm in," Garrett said with a smile. "For no other reason than I'd love to see that sanctimonious prick squirm. Hell, I'll even be in the room with you when you do it. That'll expose me to 20 years in prison, too, but it'll be worth it just to see that bastard's face turn white."

"You got something personal against our governor?"

Garrett shrugged. "Nah, I just hate fucking hypocrites. I would love it if each and every one of them could be brought down low. That bastard is as hypocritical as they come, too. He's all Jesusy and all that, always wagging his finger at everyone else. Always talking about morality, family values and the whole nine. I just want to see his face when you do this."

I smiled. "Well, I understand that, but, Garrett, I can't involve you too much in this. The only thing I want you to do is investigate and make sure the phone number that texted Jackson belongs to the governor. Find a hacker who can figure that out. I know you know some guys who can give you that information. Find that out and report that to me. I'll take over from there. I won't expose anybody else to this liability if I don't have to. There's really not a reason for both of us to end up in prison."

"Alright, buddy," Garrett said. "Maybe you can sneak in a video camera of his face when you tell him what you got on him. That would really be enough for me."

"No promises. Okay, well, do that for me, and I also wanted to know another thing."

"What's that?"

"You coming to New York with me? Assuming I don't get arrested for blackmailing our governor?"

"Yeah, buddy."

"Good. I'm going to need some backup on this. I need to question every witness up in New York that I can. Maybe you can do some undercover investigation while I track down some of the leads Leland gave me."

"Sure. What leads you got so far?"

"Well, his stepfather molested him when he was a young boy. And, apparently, Leland thinks this psychic lady had motive to kill Jackson, too." I laughed when I saw Garrett's face when I said that. "Apparently she thought he was evil and would kill Dill, Leland's husband. Also, she had predicted Jackson's death just a month before he finally bit it. I'll talk to her because I agree there were just too many coincidences to not at least take a look at her."

"Okay, sure. The stepfather, he molested Jackson when he was a boy? Why kill him now?"

"Well, Netflix was preparing to make a documentary about Jackson. The theory is that the stepfather's nefarious deeds would come out in that documentary, which would ruin him. The stepfather is an investment banker at Goldman. He's a rich bastard, probably a country club bastard. Needless to say, he wouldn't want his perverted ways to be known to his rich friends, so that gives him reason enough to kill Jackson."

"Yeah. I also think we need to take a look and see if anybody ended up buying a bunch of Jackson's paintings. Everybody knows that art is worth much more when the artist is dead than when he's alive. Maybe somebody wanted an early cash-in on their investment."

"Good thinking. I was actually thinking that myself. At any rate, we have some people we can look at for this, and if we go up to New York, we might find even more people."

Garrett reached out his hand and I shook it. "Let's do it."

"Yeah. That's if I don't end up in prison, of course. Well, jail awaiting prison. I would imagine I could make bail, but I'll have on an ankle bracelet. That would mean I couldn't try Leland's case."

"You're so matter-of-fact about all this. Why does this guy mean this much to you?"

I took a deep breath. "They all mean that much to me. Nick, Jack, Tommy and Connor. We were a band of brothers when I was 12 years old, up until the age of 18, when they went to prison. I went to prison, too, but I was completely innocent. But, yeah, I didn't have a family. My mom was a druggy whore and there was no dad around. Well, there was a dad around, Steven Harrington, but he beat the crap out of me. Sent me to the hospital a few times. It was the same for them. They came from the same situation. We all basically lived on the streets together, evading the child protection services and just having each other's backs. Each of those guys saved my life at least once and I did the same for them. They would all take a bullet for me, even now. I would do the same for them. So, yeah, if I get the chance to save them, I'm gonna do it. I'll stick my neck out for each and every one of them."

Garrett nodded his head. "I understand. I really do."

"Yeah. This is even more important to me because Connor was the baby of all of us. We were all 18 when we all got busted and sent to the joint, but Connor was only 16. He's Jack's baby brother. They're all getting out, at least I hope that they are, but Connor…" I shook my head. "As of now, he's scheduled to die in prison. So, yeah, it's a huge risk I'm taking in getting him out, but if it works, it all will be worth it."

"I'll find out that information for you. How are you gonna get to see the governor, though?"

"Trust me, when I call him and tell him what I have, he'll meet with me. You've seen all those politicians whose lives and careers were ruined for less than this. If I decide to go to the media about this, he's finished. His career is finished, his marriage is probably finished and he'll be disgraced. He has a lot riding on this. Yeah, he'll see me."

"Okay, then, I'll find out what I can find out."

We finished our beer and then walked out to our cars. "I'll talk to you later," I said.

"Later."

TWO DAYS LATER, Garrett called me. "It's his cell phone," he said. "I got two different hackers to confirm that to me."

My heart was pounding when he told me that. "Good," I said. "Okay, then."

I was happy Garrett confirmed that for me, but, at the same time, I was apprehensive. Man, this whole thing could backfire on me big-time. If I didn't play my cards just right, things could go sideways in a hurry.

This wasn't quite the same thing as the dead hooker in the senator's bed in *The Godfather II*, but, to me, it seemed just as dangerous.

Yet, I knew I couldn't possibly back down.

But that night, Sarah knew that something was up. I was genuinely afraid that I would never see Amelia and Nate again after that night, and she cornered me after dinner to ask me what was going on.

"Nothing," I said with a shrug. "Why do you ask?"

"I'm your wife," she said. "I've known you for over 10 years. I know when something is wrong and something is definitely wrong."

"Sarah, I-"

"Out with it."

I took a deep breath. "If I weren't around, you would take good care of our kids, wouldn't you?"

She closed her eyes. "Of course I would."

"Would you? I mean, if something happened to me, and Amelia's sickness came back, could you care for her?"

She shook her head rapidly. "We've been through this in counseling. Again and again. I've tried to apologize for leaving her when she needed me the most. I've tried to make amends to you for doing that. I don't know why I acted the way I did, other than the fact that I had PTSD from it all. You know that."

"Yeah. That's right. I do know that. But I asked you a question and I want an answer. If something happened to me and Amelia got sick again or Nate gets sick, will you be around for them? Will you be around for their doctors' appointments and be in their hospital rooms? Can you take them to chemo if that's what they need? Can you be emotionally able to handle their sickness? I need to know that question."

"Why are you talking like this? Why do you think you won't be around?"

I shrugged. "Because you never know when you might be hit by a bus." *Or go to prison for blackmailing the governor.* "If something happened to me tomorrow and I don't come home, can I trust the kids to you?"

She cast down her eyes. "I need you. I need your strength. I can't imagine not having you around."

"In other words…"

"No. I don't think I could handle the kids if you weren't around."

I sighed. I knew that to be true. I had the feeling. "Okay, then. Okay."

"What? What are you saying?"

"I'm saying I don't think you and I will work after all. I'm saying that I'll have to see an attorney and make sure there's a proper guardianship in place for the kids in the event that I'm not around anymore. That's what I'm saying."

"But, Damien, I was going to move back in. We talked about this."

"Yeah, but, Sarah, I've never gotten over how you reacted when Amelia was sick. I never got past that. I don't think I can ever get past it. I'm sorry, but I really need a woman who will be there, through good and bad, sickness and health, thick and thin. I need somebody strong for the kids. Life has no guarantees and you just never know when your number will be up. I need to know that if my number comes up sooner than I anticipated, the kids will be okay. That's what I'm saying."

Sarah's head started shaking back and forth, back and forth, back and forth. "Damien, you can't do this to me. You just can't."

"I can't do what to you? Listen, I'm going to talk to Harper about the possibility that she can be guardian to the kids if something happens to me. She has two girls at home and I think I can trust her with Nate and Amelia. What I don't want is for them to end up in foster care. And I certainly don't want them to be in your care." I nodded. "Amelia has to be monitored for another 4 and a half years. Constantly monitored. Bone scans, blood work, CAT scans, physicals. I think I can trust Harper to make sure she gets the care she needs."

Sarah started to cry. "Damien, you're going to be around. I don't know where this is coming from."

"It's coming from the fact that..." I would have to lie to her. I couldn't possibly tell her what I was about to do. "It comes from the fact that I had a dream last night that I was shot. And I woke up and started to think about my life with you. I started to think about what happened when Amelia got sick. I started to ponder about what would happen if I really were shot dead in the street and Amelia's cancer came back. And I knew I would have to confront you."

"Oh, that's just a dream, Damien. Don't be so silly."

"I'm not being silly. Not now. I was being silly when I thought you and I could ever get back together and try to recreate our family again. That was silly of me. Right now, I'm thinking clear-headed. I'm thinking more clear-headed than I have ever thought. Now I know that giving guardianship to Harper will be complicated, legally, because you are still the kids' mother. I'll just have to figure out a way around it. Although, I must say that, if something did happen to me, I think you would willingly give her guardianship of the kids."

I looked at her face and knew I was right. There was no way Sarah could ever be a mother to our children if I weren't around. In fact, she had a hard time being mother to them right now. She wanted me back, but the kids...not so much.

Why didn't I see that before? How could I have been so goddamned blind?

"Damien-"

"Go back to your apartment, Sarah," I said. "I'll call my divorce lawyer again tomorrow and get the papers filed. Don't worry, you were married to me when I got that $4 million windfall from that wrongful death case. You're entitled to half of that, plus half of everything else we have around here. You'll be more than taken care of."

"Damien, please. Please don't do this. I mean, we've been doing so well."

"Yeah, we have been doing well. You and I have been doing well. And, I must admit, if nothing happened to me, I think the kids would be okay. I know what to do for them. I know how important they are. How important their health is. But if things fell apart, I couldn't rely on you to do the right thing. And, I'm sorry, I need a woman I can count on."

"But you can count on me," she said.

I shook my head. "Go, please. Just leave." I put my head in my hands. I had to focus on the task at hand – extorting our governor without getting put in prison – and I just needed to be alone to think about it.

She opened her mouth and shut it again. I pointed to the door and she slumped her shoulders and opened it gingerly. In a second, she was outside the door and I went to the window to watch her get into her car.

As I watched her drive away, my feelings were mixed. I was sad, angry and relieved all at the same time. Sarah and I had been together for a long time. We knew each other so well. I felt empty, but, at the same time, I knew it was time to move on.

If Sarah couldn't be a mother to our children, I would have to find somebody who could.

Chapter Five

A FEW DAYS LATER, I was heading to Jefferson City to meet my destiny. I had carefully laid out all the plans, and I knew how I would approach it. But not before I had a talk with Harper about possibly being a guardian to Nate and Amelia if something happened to me.

Like Sarah, she was curious on why I asked about this. But she didn't pry.

"Sure, Damien," she said. "I love your kids. But Sarah's their mother. I don't think you can just draw up guardianship papers like that without her consent."

"Trust me, if something ever happened to me, she would give her consent. She doesn't want our kids and she can't meet their needs. I think I can rely on you to make sure Amelia gets to all her doctor's appointments and all of that. As for Nate, he's no trouble, yet, but you never know. He's just a typical 9-year-old with typical 9-year-old problems. Which means he has no problems, really. Amelia is the one I'm worried about."

"She hasn't had a relapse, has she?" Harper asked, a concerned look on her face.

"No, thank God," I said. "But whoever cares for her has to stay diligent about that. It's a lot of monitoring and praying, really. I think you can handle it, though."

She put her hand on my shoulder. "I can. But what does Sarah think about it?"

"Sarah admitted to me that she couldn't handle the kids if I weren't around. That's all I needed to hear."

Harper narrowed her eyes. "Is there a reason why you're asking this right now?"

I shook my head. "No. Things just came to a head last night, that's all."

"I'm sorry to hear that."

"It is what it is." I took a deep breath. "In the meantime, I thank you for doing this for me. If you don't mind, I would like to have my family lawyer draw up some papers and we can get them signed."

So, we did that, which made me feel better about going to Jefferson City to do what I needed to do. Not that it would be any easier, even knowing that Nate and Amelia would be in excellent hands if something went wrong.

I didn't have nerves of steel. I was human. So, when I was driving to Jefferson City, my heart was pounding a mile a minute. I felt more terrified during this time than I ever had in my entire life. Even when I was in prison, or growing up on the streets, or being beat on by various men in my mother's life – none of that compared to the feeling I had as I approached the governor's mansion.

I had Governor Weston's schedule. That was another thing Garrett managed to find for me. I knew when the governor would be in his mansion, and I had the story at my fingertips on how I could see him face to face.

It was really pretty simple. I had scheduled a meeting with his Chief of Staff, Henry Rollins. Once he learned I was the attorney for Leland Dewitt, he made an appointment for me in a hurry. Of course, I wouldn't go through the Chief of Staff. I would have try to convince him that I needed a face-to-face with Governor Weston. I had the feeling he would let me do that.

I knew Governor Weston had to privately be sweating this whole thing out. Jackson was found murdered, and Governor Weston had to know what that meant. He had to at least suspect that Jackson's cell phone was in the possession of the authorities. He had to be freaking out. The fact that I was the attorney for the man who was accused of killing Jackson meant Governor Weston would want to speak with me. He would want to know what had happened to that phone.

That was how I knew Henry Rollins would let me speak with Governor Weston face to face.

I got into the mansion, and was immediately led to the office of Henry Rollins.

Or so I thought.

I was surprised to find I was actually led to the suite of Governor Weston. "The Governor is expecting you," the escort, whose name was Cheryl Mills, told me. "Have a seat, and he will be right with you."

I nodded as I sat in the chair right outside the Governor's office. My hunch was right. The man was obviously terrified.

"Thank you," I said.

Not ten minutes later, Cheryl Mills opened up the door and I walked into the governor's office. She shut the door behind her.

The governor stood up, his hand outstretched. "Mr.

Harrington," he said as I shook his hand. "Damn glad to meet you. Sit down, sit down."

I sat on one of the leather seats facing the enormous desk. I tried to calm my jumping heart, but it was difficult to do.

"Thank you for seeing me on such short notice," I said, and then I cleared my throat.

"Yes, yes," he said. "Well, I found out you're representing the guy who killed Jackson Michaelson, so I knew I had to speak with you. Damned shame about that poor kid. Damned shame."

"It is." I cleared my throat again. "You might be wondering-"

"I am. Wondering about why you wanted to see me. But let's not talk about that. I need to know one thing."

"What is that one thing?"

"Was there a cell phone confiscated? A cell phone that belonged to Jackson?"

"Well, yes," I said. "There was. The authorities-"

"They don't have it. They have one of his cell phones, but not the other. I need to know if there was another cell phone the authorities just don't know about." He looked at the far wall. "That phone has some sensitive information on there. Jackson and I were…friends. Anyhow, I've been making phone calls to the police investigating this, and they seem to think there was only one cell phone. They described it and I know it's not the one I'm thinking of."

I suddenly knew this whole thing would be easier than I imagined it would be. I guess I should have considered the thought that the governor was already on pins and needles about the phone. I somehow thought he would put up a fight about it, but I now knew he wouldn't.

"Well, actually, that is the reason why I came to see you. I have the phone. I have it in my possession."

I suddenly saw a look of relief spread across his face. "You have it? Let me see it."

I got the phone out of my pocket and held it up. I didn't want him to snatch it away from me. Then again, I made sure to make a backup of the phone before I came to the office, so, even if he did snatch it away, I would still have the evidence.

He nodded. "I would like that phone," he said. "If you don't mind."

"Actually," I said. "I can't just give it to you. It's evidence the police will need."

"I understand that," he said. "You can give it to me, and I'll make sure it is safely turned over to the proper authorities."

I shook my head. "I can't let you do that," I said.

He stood up. "Listen, I know for a fact that you currently don't have any kind of blemish on your record. You are a respected attorney in good standing at the Missouri Bar. However, I have the power to make sure something happens to you. Something that will ensure you never practice law in Missouri again."

I cocked my head. "What does that mean?"

"It means that I can unseal your juvenile records and send them to the Missouri Bar. I've seen your Bar application. You lied on it. You specifically wrote that you had no juvenile adjudications. I know you have. You had two adjudications for stealing cars. As I see it, you'll have a difficult time explaining to the Missouri Bar why you didn't disclose your juvenile record."

I took a deep breath. "Okay, so I'm going to have to

answer a few questions about that. I'm sure I could beat that inquiry down."

"Don't be so sure." Governor Weston was determined to play hardball. "I have the power to make sure your little peccadillo will end up with you being completely disbarred. Don't be naïve. I'm the governor of this state and I have a lot of power. Now, are you going to give me that phone or aren't you?"

Steady, Damien. You've come this far. You can't give up that phone without getting what you need out of this. "I will. But only if you do something for me first."

He crossed his arms in front of him. "What is it that you want?"

"Connor O'Brien. He's serving a life sentence without the possibility of parole in Cameron. I have all his prison information right here in my briefcase."

"What about him?"

"I want a commutation of his sentence." That was fine to ask for this. That wasn't against the law. What was against the law was what I said next. "You grant a commutation of his sentence and you'll get that cell phone."

For the next ten minutes, the governor stared at me. Intimidating me, or at least trying to intimidate me. The minutes ticked by and I stared back at him. I had to let him know there was no way I would give him what he needed unless he gave me what I needed first.

He finally spoke. "Mr. Harrington, I believe you are attempting to extort me."

"I am." I nodded. "I'll admit it."

"You understand that if I called the authorities in here, you'll be carted off to join your friend Connor in Cameron?"

"I do understand that."

"Yet you are still going to put the conditions on me that I commute this Connor O'Brien's sentence, in exchange for Jackson Michaelson's cell phone?"

"I am. That is the condition. If you don't commute Connor O'Brien's sentence, I will turn this cell phone over to the authorities investigating Jackson's murder and make sure they know exactly what is on there. Your entire career, your reputation, your marriage, everything, will be in shambles."

He stood up again. "This is bullshit. I won't commute this Connor O'Brien's sentence. I don't give into such tactics. Now, you either willingly give me that cell phone, or I'm going to call the police right this second. They'll come here and arrest you for extortion. You'll lose everything. Your freedom. Your career. Your family. Your life."

It was my turn to stand up. "Go ahead," I said, my face three inches from his. "You go ahead and call the authorities. You think you can somehow get the cell phone from me if that happens. The authorities will come in here and arrest me, and then, when I'm in handcuffs, you'll just dig into my briefcase and get that phone out of there. Well go right ahead. I have a backup copy of this phone in my office under lock and key. I have instructions to an individual that he is to give that phone to the police if something happens to me. So, you might succeed in destroying me. But you'll go down right along with me."

He narrowed his eyes. "What did your friend do? He's serving LWOP, he must have murdered somebody."

"It was felony murder and it was really an accident. He and some other guys held up a liquor store, there was an off-duty armed security guard on the premises, that guy pointed a gun at Connor and Connor shot him. He died in the hospital from an infection he picked up there." I got

Connor's papers out of my suitcase and handed Governor Weston the file on him. "You can read about it right here."

"I can't just commute the sentence of a murderer. I'll be crucified in the media. I'm up for re-election next year. I commute your friend's sentence and I might as well just step down right now."

I cleared my throat again. "I hate to state the obvious, but if the news about what's on Jackson's cell phone gets out, you won't be able to run for re-election. You'll be forced to resign. You've seen this scenario, time and again. This is a scandal. The media will be on this like you won't believe." I shrugged my shoulders. "On the other hand, if you commute the sentence of somebody who was only 16 when he was convicted for an incident that was more of an accident than anything, you might get some flack, but it will blow over. These sex scandals don't blow over. They just get worse and worse. Especially since it involves another man."

He sat down and I knew I had him. I had to suppress a smile.

"Let me look at that file."

"It's right there in front of you," I said. "Read away. I've got nothing but time."

He got out a pair of glasses and opened Connor's file. I sat back and just let him peruse it. I saw him nodding his head from time to time as he flipped through the pages.

I sat quietly for the better part of an hour while he studied everything about Connor O'Brien. "Let's see, it looks like he's been a model prisoner," he said. "He has been in some fights but it looks like it was all self-defense. According to this file, it looks like he's accepted responsibility for killing that security guard and has exhibited remorse. He has written letters to the widow of the victim and to his children." He nodded. "Now, I want you to know one thing. If this was a serious thing, and by serious I mean your friend was found guilty of pre-meditated Murder One, there is no way in hell I would ever consider commutation. I would just take my lumps and let the cell phone scandal sink me, rather than let a violent murderer back on the streets."

I nodded. "That's not the case here. Connor is not a violent man. He was a mixed-up kid and he panicked. That's all."

"That's how I read things as well." He steepled his fingers. "And that's how I'll play it to the media. I'll tell the reporters who ask about this that I'm commuting his sentence because he was only 16 years old when he was convicted and the death was an accident. That's how I'll spin this. You and I will have to be on the same page, because I'm going to tell my Chief of Staff and all my cabinet that the reason why I met with you this afternoon was to discuss this commutation. We discussed this commutation and nothing else. You hear?"

"Of course," I said, my heart leaping. "Of course."

"Now, you need to give me that cell phone."

"No. You need to sign the commutation papers first." I got into my briefcase. "I have the papers all drawn up for you to sign right now. I used the proper language. All you have to do is sign and seal this and then file it. You do all of that, and you'll get the cell phone and the copy of the cell phone."

"And how do I know you will actually give me the cell phone and the copy and there's not another copy out there?"

"Because why would I do that? Once you give me what I want, I no longer have a reason to have leverage over you."

"Bullshit. You might make multiple copies to blackmail

me at will. You know how powerful my position is. You can hold that bullshit over my head for years to come." He shook his head. "I don't know about all this. I don't know if it's worth it. If I commute the sentence of your friend, how do I know you won't keep coming at me with requests?"

I sighed. "I guess there has to be an element of trust here. You'll have to take me at my word when I tell you that I have only this phone and one other copy. You'll just have to trust that if you give me what I ask for, you will get what you seek. You can keep this entire cell phone incident under wraps." I shrugged my shoulders. "Or, you can refuse to commute Connor's sentence and you can be guaranteed that cell phone will end up in the wrong hands. The ball is in your court, as I see it."

He shook his head. "Are you this much of a bulldog in the courtroom?"

"Hell yes," I said. "I know when I have a good hand and I know just how to play my excellent hands. I have a straight flush right now."

He looked defeated. "Give me those papers you drew up," he said.

I handed him the papers and he read them. He nodded. "The language is right," he said. Then he got out a pen and signed it, and sealed it. Then he pressed his phone. "Ms. Mills, please come in here. I have some papers I need for you to file."

Cheryl came in, and Governor Weston handed her the papers. "Make a copy of this and file it," he said.

She nodded. "Will do," she said. Twenty minutes later, she came back in and handed him a copy of the paperwork that showed she filed it. He handed it to me, and I tucked it into my briefcase.

"Now, give me that phone," he said.

I handed it to him. "Here. Now you have to know the police need this phone as evidence. So, please go ahead and scrub it as you wish. If you could please make sure the proper authorities get it after you do that, I would be much obliged."

He nodded. "You play hardball, Harrington." He nodded again. He seemed to be in a much better mood now that he had that cell phone in his hand. "I would never want to go against you in a court of law."

"Be thankful you don't have to." I stood up. "Well, I think our business is done here. If you don't mind, I need to make sure the commutation goes through. Once it does, I'll give you the phone copy I have. You can destroy that if you wish."

"I understand," he said. "Hope you don't mind if I tell you to show yourself out."

"Not at all."

I left the office and made my way out of the mansion.

It wasn't until I got to my car that it hit me. Connor would get out with the other guys. The paperwork specified that Connor was to be released as soon as possible. In the criminal justice system, that meant he would probably be in the prison for only a few more months. He might even be out before all the others.

Connor would be free and I dodged a bullet myself.

As I drove home, I felt a level of happiness that I had never before experienced.

Yeah, I took a huge risk, but, boy, did it pay off.

Chapter Six

"DAD," Amelia said as I drove her to Harper's house. "I still don't know why me and Nate can't come to New York with you and Tom."

I tousled her head. Harper agreed to watch the kids while I went to New York to do what I could to track down alternative suspects for Jackson's murder.

As soon as I got the Connor issue behind me, I knew it was time to focus on Leland's case. I did so with a lightness I didn't know was possible. All this time, I worried, constantly, about Connor. I didn't worry about the other guys so much – I knew they would be fine. They all were model prisoners and I knew they would be paroled. But Connor…I woke up nights thinking about how he would react when he was left alone in prison. I knew he survived behind bars because he had Nick, Jack and Tommy in there with him and they all had each other's backs. I knew those guys were Connor's emotional support. Without them, he probably would have a hard time surviving in the joint.

He was getting out, though, and that was the best thing

that could have ever happened. Once I got that out of the way, I had the mental energy to do whatever it took to make sure Leland didn't go down for Jackson's murder.

"Kiddo, I think you know why. It's a little thing called school. You remember that concept, don't you?"

I looked in the back of the car, where Nate was sitting, playing on his iPhone. Ever since I kicked Sarah out, and I sat the kids down and explained to them their mother and father were, in fact, going to be divorced, Nate decided not to speak to me anymore. He was close with his mother and he blamed me for kicking her out.

Amelia, on the other hand, solemnly told me I did the right thing. "Sarah's not for you, dad," Amelia said, with a maturity that went far beyond her 7 years on this earth. "You deserve better. I do, too. Don't forget, she ditched us when I got sick. You need to find somebody who won't bail when your kids get sick. You did the right thing."

"I hate school," Amelia said. "I would rather go to New York with you. I've never been there before."

I sighed. "Well, again, kiddo, as we talked about last night, I'm going to be busy up there. I need to track down a bunch of witnesses. Harper has somebody who is her nanny, her name is Sophia, and she's awesome. You're going to love her. And love Harper, too."

I looked back and hoped Nate would look at me, but he didn't. He continued to study his cell phone. I sighed. I hoped Nate would forgive me because I knew how much he still loved his mother. I knew he would get over it in time, and I just needed to give him the space to do that. I learned enough in our family therapy sessions to know what I needed to do.

"Hey, sport, what do you think about all this? You

looking forward to staying with Harper and her kids?" I was looking in my rear-view mirror as I spoke.

Nate shrugged. "I guess."

Amelia glared at me. "He means that he's mad, too, that we don't get to go with you."

"That true, Nate?" I asked him. "You mad at me because I'm not taking you guys?"

"Nah, I don't care," he said. "It's all good, whatever you want to do, Dad. I'm just along for the ride."

I looked over at Amelia, and she shook her head, a glare on her face. "Don't believe him. He's mad, too."

I got to Harper's house and Amelia and Nate reluctantly got out of the car. "I still don't understand why Mom's not watching us," Nate said.

How could I explain to Nate that Sarah wasn't really a mother to them? That I couldn't trust her to take good care of them while I was gone, even for a short period of time? I had finally come to the conclusion that some people just weren't meant to be parents, and Sarah was apparently one of those people. Wish I would have seen that when I first met her, but, then again, if Sarah and I had never gotten together, I would have never had my two beautiful children. For that, I would always be grateful to her. That was the one thing I had to remember whenever I laid awake at night, tossing and turning and feeling more and more angry with Sarah. I had to remember that, without her, I wouldn't have Nate and Amelia. They never would have existed. That thought always made me feel less angry at Sarah.

Harper was standing at the door, a big smile on her face. "Nate, Amelia, come in, come in," she said. "I have my spare bedroom all ready to go for you, Nate, and Amelia, you'll share a room with Abby. Don't worry, she's very neat and, as far as I know, she doesn't snore."

Abby put her arm around Amelia and the two of them disappeared up the stairs.

"Thanks for doing this, Harper," I said. "I owe you."

"You owe me nothing. I'm $1.8 million richer because of you, or did you forget about that?" She smiled. "Anyhow, it's not a problem, not at all."

Harper was referring to the fact that I settled a wrongful death case for $18 million last year, and I gave her $1.8 million of it, just because I wanted to. Harper didn't actually work that case, but I wanted to let her know how grateful I was for her giving me a chance.

Harper was having me for dinner and Axel wasn't around. She wanted to pick my brain about my new case and wanted to find out what she could do to help out. I would have her second-chair this and help me prepare for it. I would share my fee with her, too. Leland, thus far, had paid me a $50,000 retainer and I billed $350 per hour. I would also charge him for travel expenses to New York. It was good that I had a client who happened to have an endless supply of cash. I knew what it was like to have broke clients and chasing down money from these clients wasn't something I ever wanted to do. With Leland, that wouldn't be a problem.

After we had our roast with potatoes and salad and Amelia and Abby went to the den to watch television – Rina was apparently staying with a friend that night – and Nate went to his designated room, Harper and I sat around the dinner table and chatted. "So," she said. "Tell me about your Leland case."

"Well, let's see. The first thing is that the media has been on this like flies on shit," I said. "It seems like this is front page news, day after day. Have you read the papers about this?"

She shook her head. "Oh my God. That poor kid. Poor Leland, too. They're dragging him through the mud, aren't they? Is it true that Leland killed Jackson because Jackson was having an affair with his husband Dill?"

I tried to suppress a laugh. That was how the media was playing it. They were portraying this as a crime of passion and vengeance. I heard that Leland had caught Jackson and Dill together in bed. I heard that Jackson, Dill and Leland were in a throuple and that Dill and Jackson had just informed Leland they were going off together. I even heard that Jackson had talked Dill into getting a sex change because Jackson wanted to be married to Dill and he also wanted to be married to a woman. Something about Jackson wanting to be married to a woman because it would be better for his career. Or something of the sort.

"No, there was no affair. None whatsoever. There are, however, a cast of other characters I'm looking into in New York. I'm starting with a psychic that Dill has been paying a half million dollars a year, and I'm also speaking with Jackson's stepfather. From there, I hope to figure out if there are others I can talk to. I hope to figure out who really did this by the time I get back from New York."

She nodded her head. "Well, if you need any help, you know who to ask."

"I do."

"So, what's going on with the guys? Nick and all them?"

I shifted in my seat. I didn't tell Harper about my blackmailing Governor Weston. I certainly didn't want Harper to know about that. I always was afraid she would end up embroiled in my messes, and the less she knew about them, the better off everyone would be.

"They're coming up for parole in a couple of weeks. And Connor..." I took a deep breath. "He's getting out, too. In fact, he's the only one I'm certain will be getting out. The Governor commuted his sentence down to 17 years, which means it's a formality that he'll be out within a few months."

Harper smiled and raised her water glass. "Congrats. How did that happen? He was LWOP, right?"

"Right," I said, nodding my head. "Harper, I would like to ask one thing of you on this. Please don't ask me any more questions about it."

"Okay," she said. "I will respect that." She smiled. "God knows we all have our secrets. I respect that you have yours and I have mine."

"Thanks." I felt bad for her. She had to be intensely curious. I would be if I were her. "Anyhow, I fully anticipate that all the guys will be out within a few months. I'm going to hire all of them to do something for me. Either that, or I'm going to ask around and see who can hire them. All I know is that it's going to feel really good to have them around again. They're really my family. My kids and those guys – those are the only family I have."

My mother was still alive and was living in a trailer home in Raymore, out in the country. But she wasn't my family. She never was. Even so, I sent her $100,000, in the form of a certified check, when I got my large settlement. I knew she would probably just spend that on drugs, drinking and gambling, but I felt I should still do it. She never called me to thank me for it. I didn't care – I hadn't spoken to her for years, and I doubted I would ever speak with her.

No, the guys were still my only family. Them and Amelia and Nate.

Harper put her hand on my shoulder. "I don't think I've seen you this happy," she said.

"Ironic, isn't it? I just filed for divorce from Sarah, but

that's been a done deal for awhile. I just haven't wanted to acknowledge it. But, yeah, I am happy right now. I'll be even happier if I can win this case for Leland. I really think the guy is innocent. I just need to prove it."

Harper and I talked some more about things unrelated to the case or to the guys. I left that evening feeling the kids were in good hands. I also knew Harper was right about one thing.

I *was* happier than I had been in a long while.

Chapter Seven

THE NEXT DAY, Garrett and I were on the plane, heading for New York City. I had everything mapped out – the home of Mystic Anna would be my first place to go. After that, I would speak with Carina Maxwell, the director of the Netflix documentary about Jackson. After that, I would speak with George Mason. From there, I hoped to get a broader array of people who might have had motive to kill Jackson. I knew Carina could give me some names of people who Jackson knew, and I hoped she would have some kind of an idea about anybody who might have had it in for Jackson.

Garrett and I were in First Class and we both were drinking a Bloody Mary. Delta Airline's Bloody Mary wasn't nearly as good as Leland's but, then again, I doubted that Delta paid $700 for its bottle of vodka, and I doubted they freshly squeezed the tomatoes, either.

For what it was, it was delicious.

"So," he said. "What happened with our holier-than-thou governor?" he asked.

"It went down easier than I thought. You probably won't be surprised when I tell you he was clearly panicking about that cell phone before I ever got to see him. In other words, I had him right where I wanted him. He would have gotten down on his knees if I asked him to."

Garrett chuckled. "I don't doubt that. You're a good-looking guy, Damien. And we now know the Governor likes boys."

"Ha ha. No, really, he was more than anxious to play ball. I probably should have pressed even more – maybe asked for a pardon for all the guys. But I didn't want to press my luck."

We fist bumped and Garrett sipped his Bloody Mary. "Now, we have appointments to meet Mystic Anna and Carina, but we don't have an appointment with George Mason. Right?"

"Right. I couldn't fit into his busy schedule, but that's okay. I managed to score an invite to a cocktail party where he'll be. I'll ambush him there."

"How did you manage to get that invite?"

"Leland knows everyone. He lived in New York for most of his life."

"And what brought him to Kansas City again?"

"He was tired of living in such a huge city. He wanted to move to a smaller city, but one that has just enough going on that he wouldn't be bored. Kansas City fit that bill. I have to admit he's right about that. I've always said Kansas City is probably one of the most underrated cities in America."

"True that. But he doesn't miss all the plays, symphonies, galleries, 24-hour restaurants and all that?"

"He says he doesn't. He and Dill fly to New York several times a year, so they get to see plays and all that when they go. And he says he's just done with all the stress and noise of New York. You should see his house in Kansas City. I wouldn't miss New York, either, if I were him."

I looked down and saw the bright lights come into view. "Looks like we're about to land at JFK." I booked a room at the Four Seasons, and I was looking forward to staying there. I liked luxury as much as any other guy.

The plane landed, we got our bags and our Uber, who took us right to the hotel. As I walked through the marble lobby and looked up at the ceiling, some thirty feet above me, I knew I would have a good time staying here.

We got to our suite, with its view of the city down below, and I relaxed in a leather chair with a glass of Scotch. "This is the life," I said. "I mean, I love my home, and I love being around my kids, but sometimes you just have to have the time to sit back and relax. Just relax and not think about all the bullshit in your life. You know?"

"Don't I know," Garrett said.

THE NEXT DAY, Garrett and I traveled down to Brooklyn to see Mystic Anna at her home. Her neighborhood was a typical working-class enclave, with trees lining the street and identical pitched-roof homes built around 1900. I walked up to the porc and knocked on the door.

Mystic Anna opened up. She was around six feet tall, with wild curly brown hair and big blue eyes. She was dressed in a long pink and green dress that ran down her ankles. On her feet were silk shoes in blue.

"Hello," she said in a low voice. "Mr. Harrington."

Garrett looked at her, an amused look on his face. "She really is psychic," he whispered. "She knew just who you were." Then he laughed a little. I looked at him and shook my head. I told him not to crack jokes while we were here, but I knew that was hard for him to do.

Mystic Anna gave Garrett a weird look. I couldn't tell if she was pissed or just concentrating on him. Then she looked at me. "I'm very sorry to hear about your wife," she said. "Although I don't think you loved her anymore, it's still hard to deal with." She motioned for us to walk in. "Come on in."

I raised an eyebrow. I didn't tell her about Sarah. I imagined she found out about her somehow, though. "Thanks for the words," I said. "And, yes, it's true I didn't love her anymore. But we aren't here to talk about my relationship with my wife."

"No. You're here to talk to me about Dill Dewitt," she said. "And his husband, Leland."

"Yes," I said. "That's what I'm trying to talk to you about. Leland and Jackson Michaelson, actually."

When I said the name "Jackson Michaelson," she crossed herself. "Jackson Michaelson had much darkness around him. Much darkness."

"Darkness? Did you consider him to be evil?"

She shook her head. "No. Not evil. He just had a dark energy surrounding him. Addiction. Molestation. He was always running from all of these forces trying to bring him down."

I followed her through the house. She led us into a room with red walls and a beaded curtain. A crystal ball was on the table in the middle of the room, and, on the other table, there were two Tarot spreads. She sat down and started to shuffle her Tarot cards.

"Sit down," she said. "I want to do a reading for you."

I sat down and shook my head. "No, thanks," I said. "I don't like to know my future. I like to be surprised."

She ignored me as she shuffled the cards. "This spread doesn't predict your future," she said. "Celtic Cross. I just want to get a feel for you. I need to know how sincere you are about this case."

I rolled my eyes but kept quiet. I knew well enough that I shouldn't offend a potential witness. I would play along as much as she needed me to. I needed her to feel comfortable with me.

"Okay, go ahead. Tell me what you need to tell me."

She started to lay down the cards in the shape of two different crosses which were connected. The middle cross had three cards and the outer cross was four cards. In the middle, one card was laid over another one. Mystic Anna looked hard at the spread, nodding her head.

"You've had a hard life. Much darkness." She shook her head. "Prison, wrongfully imprisoned."

I looked over at Garrett and shrugged. Dill probably told her all about me.

But did Dill know about my prison sentence?

"Your mother, very unstable. Very mentally ill. Addicted, abusive, sexual dysfunction."

I took a deep breath. Either she spoke with people who knew me, somehow, or she was a goddamned lucky guesser.

She went on. "Your father," she said, nodding. "A wealthy man. A powerful man. Supplied your mother with drugs. Wasn't around in your life, ever."

I raised an eyebrow. I had no idea who my father was. Mom never told me. Not that Mom and I ever talked about things like this. I always assumed he was a junkie, just like she was. I mean, if he was a wealthy guy, why the hell did she live in a trailer with no money all her life? Why was she still living in that same trailer?

Mystic Anna nodded. "Your mother never told you about your father. There was violence surrounding your conception. Very shamed, your mother is. Never was able to get past what your father did to her. You really should give her a break."

I wanted to ask her to quit with the Tarot reading, but something made me intrigued by all of this. It was something I probably needed to ask my mother about. I hadn't spoken with her in years, but I suddenly felt the need to have a conversation with her.

"Your daughter," she continued on. "Challenges behind her but a bright future in front of her. You're very worried about her, but you needn't be. She will continue to thrive. Her sickness is in the past."

I found myself feeling a sense of relief as she spoke. She was right about that. I *was* very worried about Amelia. Thus far, she had a clean bill of health. Her scans and blood work all showed she was in remission. According to this Mystic Anna, Amelia would continue to be healthy.

I was believing this woman and what she was saying. In spite of myself, I was believing in her.

I shook my head. No, I had to keep on my mission on why I was there. I was there to question her. She was right on the money about certain things – that my mom was a piece of work, my daughter was sick, I was divorcing and I was wrongfully imprisoned. But somebody must have told her all these things. Somehow, somebody told her, and she was using this information to bring down my defenses.

"Okay," I finally said. "This is enough. I need to ask you questions about Jackson Michaelson, Leland Dewitt and his husband Dill. You-"

She nodded. "Sure. If you want the rest of the reading, I'll be happy to give it to you. Now, what do you want to know?"

"Dill Dewitt paid you some half million a year, is that right?"

"Yes, that's true. I've blessed crystals and candles for him, time and again, and I've been giving him daily readings over the phone. I haven't just taken that money from him without giving him value in return. If that's what you're accusing me of doing."

"Well, I need to know what you know about Jackson. You told Dill you felt Jackson had darkness surrounding him. That you were afraid for Dill if he continued to be associated with Jackson. Plus, you predicted Jackson's death. You predicted it not even a month before he was actually found dead."

She stared at me, her blue eyes penetrating. I almost felt she could see inside of me and I felt uncomfortable. I hoped I didn't show how uncomfortable I was, though.

Her cheek, right below her right eye, started to twitch.

She finally spoke. "Yes, that is true. I sensed Jackson had darkness within him. I didn't even know Jackson, though. I only gave Dill a reading on Jackson because Dill requested I do that. He was worried about Jackson and his hold on Leland. He gave me a painting that Jackson made and asked me if I could read Jackson's energy by laying hands on that painting. It was extremely easy to read Jackson's energy from that painting, because that painting just radiated with Jackson's essence. Just radiated with it." She shuddered. "And it was dark, his energy. He had a lot of pent-up rage. If you just take a look at his paintings, you can see that for yourself."

I had looked at Jackson's paintings, and I could see what

Mystic Anna had meant. At least when I looked at his recent paintings, I saw fear, death and hell in them in many different ways. His earlier work seemed a bit lighter, but even the early paintings weren't exactly Monet's *Water Lilies*. I knew something about artists, having taken a few art appreciation classes in my day, and his work was reminiscent of Francis Bacon.

"You have the painting Dill gave you?"

"I do."

"You got that painting for free?"

"Yes, I did."

"Have you had it valued since Jackson died?"

"No. I have not." She crossed her arms. "I would not kill a man just to cash in on his death."

"I believe you." I moved on, feeling off-balance. This woman literally seemed to read my mind. "Now, let's backtrack a bit. You said Dill wanted a reading on Jackson? That he was worried about Jackson?"

"Yes." She nodded. "He felt threatened by Jackson. He was always afraid that Leland would leave him for Jackson. He didn't like that Jackson was addicted to heroin, and he was always afraid Leland would return to his own heroin addiction because he was around Jackson so often. Those were two of the things Dill was frightened about. He wanted me to do a reading on Jackson, and I told him the truth – that Jackson's aura was very dark and very frightened."

This was the first I heard about Leland having a problem with drugs. I wrote that down. Dill was looking good for the crime at that point. I would have to rule him out, and I made a mental note about that.

"And what about your prediction that Jackson would

soon die? That was a pretty lucky prediction, don't you think?"

She sighed. "I will let you in on a secret. I'm very good at reading people's pasts. I'm excellent at reading auras and what they've gone through. I am not one to predict the future. The future is tricky for any psychic, because the future is not something set in stone. Everybody has free will and the ability to affect their own future. There are just too many variables."

"But you told me my daughter would continue to be healthy. That's predicting the future."

"That is something different. I told you that because whether or not your daughter is healthy is less predicated on decisions and free will. Either she will remain cancer-free or she won't. I'm telling you she will remain healthy. But with something like whether or not somebody will die, or about anything else that will happen in the future, that is something difficult for most psychics." She pointed at the final card on her Tarot spread. "Even this final card, the outcome card, can be changed by your free will."

I nodded my head. "Thanks for your honesty about that, but why do you make predictions on your website?"

She smiled. "Because maybe I'll end up getting lucky on one of my predictions. That will bring more attention to me and to my website."

"But all those other predictions that don't come true. Won't that make you less credible?"

She cocked her head to one side. "The most famous psychics in the world had far more misses than hits. Far more. I know Dill spoke with you about Jeane Dixon, astrologer to the stars. Almost none of the things she predicted came true. Yet, once in awhile, she would hit it right, and that was the prediction everybody remembers.

She predicted the Kennedy assassination, which put her on the map. The same could happen for me. So, I put the predictions out on my website, hoping one will come true. It just so happens this one did. And, if you knew Jackson, it certainly was not a stretch that his life would be cut short. Not a stretch at all."

"But you didn't know Jackson, right? That's what you said."

"Yes, that is correct." She nodded. "But I could tell all just by examining his painting. And Dill told me all about him. I also did a reading for Jackson, which was possible because I was surrounded by his energy, and I saw what was within him. I saw he had a powerful addiction. I have known people who have struggled with heroin addiction, and if they do not get their addictions under control, they're not long for this world. It wasn't a stretch that he would die."

I looked over at Garrett, who was, thus far, absorbing this entire exchange between Mystic Anna and me, not saying a word. I gave him an expression that said *what do you say about this?*

He cleared his throat and shook his head. I got the impression Garrett was just hanging back and wasn't going to say anything. I had the feeling he would have plenty to say when we left this place, however.

"Do you know anybody else who has expressed concern about Jackson to you?"

"No," she said. "Only Dill."

I finally decided I got the information I needed from her. "Thank you for speaking with me. I'll just show myself out."

She pointed at the door. "If you need anything more, you are welcome to come and speak with me again. I have nothing to hide." She glanced down at the Tarot spread still on the table in front of her. "But would you like to hear the rest of the reading?"

I looked at the last card, which had a picture of a sun, and shook my head. "Nah. No offense, but I think I heard enough." I glanced over at Garrett, who nodded his head. "Let's go, huh?"

At that, we both left Mystic Anna's home.

We got into my rental car and Garrett nudged me. "What was that all about in there? All that stuff about your mother and your father?"

I shrugged. "I don't know. She certainly made some lucky guesses."

"You gonna talk to your mom about that? About your rich father who apparently raped your mother?"

I started to feel uncomfortable by Garrett's questions. "I didn't hear that from her. I didn't hear my father raped my mother."

"She said you were conceived in violence. What do you think that means? And your father was a wealthy bastard. Do you believe all that?"

I took a deep breath. "No. That woman in there is a quack. Yeah, she saw my mother is an addict. She saw I was wrongfully imprisoned. She saw my daughter was very sick. I still think Dill fed her all this information somehow."

"How does Dill know about that stuff?"

"Leland knew my closest friends are in prison and that Connor was LWOP. Leland did his research on me and my background before he hired me. Dill got that same information. He must have told Mystic Anna all about these things."

"But how would Leland know about your daughter? And your mother? I can see how he would find out about the guys – there are plenty of newspaper articles written about the robbery you guys went down for. It doesn't take a rocket scientist to figure out you have friends in prison. From there, Leland just has to make a few phone calls to find out if your friends are still in prison. But how would Leland know about your daughter and your mother?"

I shrugged. "I don't know. I suppose there is a way Leland could have figured those things out."

Garrett shook his head. "That woman gave me the creeps. Seriously. When she started in about all those things about you that were on the money, I started to get chills. I never believed in shit like that. But I don't know about that woman. I think she might be legit."

"She might be." I watched the road ahead. The Brooklyn Bridge was coming up and I was happy to be getting as far away from Mystic Anna as I could. "But come on. How could those stupid cards tell her anything? I still think she's a charlatan who has cheated poor Dill out of a lot of money. I was, however, interested in what she had to say about Dill being jealous. The media has it that Leland was jealous. What if it was Dill the entire time? Think about it – Dill was aware of Leland's Ambien activities. Dill was aware that when Leland took Ambien with alcohol, he did things without being aware of them. What if he deliberately made sure Leland was drinking himself into a stupor and was taking Ambien, and then he went in and killed Jackson while making Leland think he might have done it?"

Garrett shook his head. "I was thinking the same thing, but I don't know."

"What don't you know? He's legally married to Leland. That means that if Leland goes to prison, Dill gets to live the high life and do whatever he wants without worrying about Leland putting constraints on him. I think we might have to look into how Leland and Dill's relationship is. See how strong it is."

"Well, that's an interesting theory," Garrett said. "I'll try to figure out if there are any holes in it. At that moment, I can't really see anything. Dill was jealous, thought Jackson and Leland were having a fling or whatever. Maybe you're right. Maybe Dill secretly hates his husband and wants him out of the way so he can do what he wants. We'll just have to figure that out."

As I headed back to our hotel, I knew I had another avenue to explore.

I just didn't know how Leland would feel about my investigating his own husband.

Chapter Eight

THE NEXT DAY, I went to the New York offices for Netflix, which was located in the Flatiron District. While I went to the Netflix offices, Garrett was out on the streets, asking Jackson's friends and acquaintances questions. Hopefully he would provide me with more leads.

The Netflix building was gleaming and modern, a brand-new geometric building with floor-to-ceiling windows. The Flatiron District was a trendy area of Manhattan, with a blend of old and new buildings and more than its share of home and design stores, boutiques and restaurants.

I took the elevator to the 10th Floor. I got to Carina's suite, gave my name to the receptionist, and waited for Carina to come out.

She did in about twenty minutes. Tall and blonde, with a straight walk and confident gait, Carina looked like she could have been a model if she really wanted to. She could have done me in if I let myself go there – she was obviously intelligent and creative, considering she was a director and producer of documentaries, plus she was a knockout. That was an intoxicating combination.

But she wouldn't do me in. I had a job to do, and Carina wouldn't trip me up.

"Ms. Maxwell," I said when she came out to greet me. "Thanks for making the time to speak with me about this."

"Of course," she said, her voice low and throaty. "I would do anything to help. This was actually my first documentary, and it really sucks that my subject died before the documentary could be produced. I've been told that, because he was murdered, that would make my documentary even more successful, but I can't say I care about that. I really got to know that guy, and, even though he had his issues, I really befriended him. He was a good guy. So, yeah, I'll do whatever I can to help you figure out who might have killed him. Assuming Leland Dewitt didn't, of course."

"Well, of course, I'm assuming Leland Dewitt didn't do it. That's why I'm here speaking with you."

I followed her into her office and she sat down across from me. She swiveled in her chair while she watched me carefully.

She finally hunched her body forward. "Okay," she said. "Ask away. I know you have questions about the people that I've met while filming this documentary, and I have some pretty good ideas on who you're looking at for this."

"I know you know about the stepfather, George Mason," I said. "Did you meet him?"

She pinched up her face when I brought up that name. "The abusive stepfather," she said. "Yes, I met him. He hit on me the first thing, too." She shook her head. "George Mason was a typical smarmy sociopath. I'm sure you know the sort. You're a defense attorney and I'm sure that people with personality disorders isn't something exactly unknown to you."

"That's very true," I said. "But what made you believe that George Mason was a sociopath?"

"Jackson told me about how George treated him when he was just a young boy. When Jackson's mother was away, which she often was, because she was traveling a lot, George used to molest Jackson. He was only 10 at the time." She shook her head. "And he's just generally a bad person. He makes shady trades, engages in insider trading, which is part of how he has gotten so wealthy, and has no compunctions about ripping off anybody for a buck. Men like him are destroying this country from the inside out. Greedy, selfish, venal, cruel. Those are all words to describe that man."

"He is all those things?" I asked. "Would you also agree he could possibly be a murderer?"

She bit her lower lip, and I thought about how I would like to do the same – bite her lower lip. They looked tasty, like a plum. I felt embarrassed by how distracted I was by this woman. It had been a long time since I had felt this distracted about somebody.

"A murderer…" She swiveled in her chair. "I guess I can't come right out and say 'no, he is not a murderer' tells you everything you need to know about George Mason. I can honestly tell you I don't know if the man is capable of murdering somebody in cold blood. I honestly can't tell you whether or not he's capable of doing that and then deliberately framing somebody else for his crime. He certainly could have. I don't want to tell you differently."

"Anything else you want to tell me about Jackson's stepfather George?"

"Yeah there is," she said. "The reason why Jackson was

on drugs was because of George. At least, that's what Jackson told me."

"What do you mean? Do you mean Jackson started to take drugs because he wanted to forget about what George did to him? Or do you mean George directly got Jackson onto drugs?"

"The latter. From what Jackson told me, George had a drug problem. George takes cocaine to get him up and heroin to bring him back down. He sometimes does speedballs – both heroin and cocaine at once. George got Jackson hooked on heroin. Jackson also has tried cocaine, because George gave him coke on more than one occasion. Jackson had no interest in using coke because he didn't like the way it made him feel. But heroin was a different story – he told me heroin was something that made him feel relaxed and comfortably numb."

"So, George molested Jackson and got him hooked on drugs. Sounds like a prince of a guy."

"Oh, he is a prince of a guy. A crown prince of a guy. Personally, that guy turns my stomach. He makes me sick. If he killed Jackson, I want him to fry for that. I really do."

"And he hit on you, too?"

"Yeah, he did. He did. I've made a vow never to be alone with him, because he behaves like such a wolf when we're alone. He acts like he's never seen a woman before, I swear. Or maybe he's just acting like somebody who thinks that, because he's wealthy and powerful, he's entitled to just take what he wants, when he wants. I'm not really sure. What I know is that he has scared me, on more than one occasion, because I felt like he was about to rape me. So, that was the end of my ever being alone with him."

I nodded. "I guess I need to talk to George and see if I can find out where he was on the night Jackson was murdered. I need to see if he has an alibi, but I also need to find out if he happened to fly into Kansas City at the time Jackson was murdered. I need to rule him out, because I have the feeling this guy is looking pretty good to me right now."

"By looking good, what do you mean by that?"

"I mean he's looking like he might have killed his stepson, Jackson. I'm thinking that might have been what happened."

"Well, try to figure it out," she said. "And if you need anything else, don't hesitate to come back and speak with me. If you want, you can also take a look at some of the raw footage I shot on Jackson's documentary. That might tell you something you need to know."

"Sure," I said. "I would like that." I opened my mouth, wanting go on and ask her out for a drink, but I changed my mind about that. I was quite sure this woman was hit on all the time. No reason to add my name to that list.

I left and then got out on the street. I called a cab to take me back to the hotel. From there, I would meet Garrett. I hoped he had some type of news for me. Maybe some other avenue to look at.

When I got to the hotel room and stepped in, I knew that perhaps my hunch was right. Or maybe not. What I knew was that I found a note from him, asking me to meet him at the hotel bar.

"I figured out a few things," the note said. "Meet me downstairs at the bar."

I went down to meet him, hoping that he could give me another lead.

Which he did, but not at all what I was thinking about.

Chapter Nine

I GOT DOWNSTAIRS to the bar, and saw Garrett was waiting for me. "Hey," he said, when he saw me. "This place is not at all the place where I would choose to hang out, but it is what it is, huh?"

I looked around, looking at the high ceilings, the wood paneling, the red velvet chairs, the enormous fireplace, and the bartender in the tuxedo, and I knew what he was talking about. This place was definitely not as grimy as the places where he preferred to hang out.

"Yeah," I said. "I guess I should get a gimlet here, instead of my usual scotch and water. Looks like this place might make a good one."

He grinned. "Yeah. I don't know about you, but any place that charges you $15 for a damn beer is not the place for me. Then again, you can't beat the location or the convenience."

The waiter came around and I ordered a vodka gimlet. There was just something about this place that made me crave one of these cocktails.

"Okay," I said. "Now, you were gone all day today. What did you find out about our victim, Jackson?"

"Well," he said. "I found out a few things about Jackson that maybe you didn't know."

"Oh? What did you find out?"

"I found out how it was he got hooked on drugs, for one thing," he said.

"I did too. I found out his stepfather got Jackson hooked on heroin. The stepfather used to do drugs with Jackson when he was young, and that was how he got started."

"That's not what I found out." He shook his head. "What I found out was that Jackson actually wasn't involved in drugs until the age of 15. He never wanted to take them before that time, because he saw what it did to both his mother and his stepfather."

"Go on. I found out the stepfather was involved in drugs, but I didn't know the mother was."

"Oh, she was. But you know, she's a wealthy socialite. She's not down in the muck and taking street drugs. Her vice is prescription pills. Vicodin, OxyContin, Percocet, that sort of thing. She takes those drugs and washes them down with vodka. I spoke with Jackson's best friend at his prep school, Elise Hoffman. She used to hang out over at Jackson's apartment, I mean Jackson's mother's apartment, in the Upper West Side. She said Jackson's mother was perpetually out of it. That usually the mother was in her bedroom, too wasted to get out of bed, but sometimes she was hanging out with them and flying high." He shook his head. "Marie was an addict, even more than George was."

"I guess that makes sense," I said. "She has the money to do it. It sounds like she was bored with her life and wanted to escape. Plus, she was married to bad men."

"Well, it was more than that. From what I understand,

Marie was also suffering from bi-polar disorder. At least that's what it sounded like. She would stay up for days on end, locking herself in her art studio, feverishly painting. She would also spend her days shopping and gambling, losing hundreds of thousands of dollars at the casino and spending literally millions shopping. Then she would crawl into bed and not come out for days. Elise said Jackson told her that was just how Marie was – she had super high highs and super low lows. That was another reason why she took drugs – she was self-medicating. She couldn't seem to come to terms with her illness so she took drugs to take her out of reality. At least, that's what it sounds like to me."

I took a sip of my drink. It was the perfect blend of tart and bitter, with the vodka mixing in with the lime juice. "Go on."

"Well, according to Elise, Jackson was very anti-drug when she knew him. Then something happened. He got into an accident on his bicycle when he was riding it in the street. A car smashed into him. He broke his collarbone and his arm in two places. He had a show scheduled and the art dealer was expecting some new work from him. He didn't feel he could wait the six weeks it was supposed to take for his arm to heal, so he didn't follow his doctor's orders."

"What does that mean?"

"It means he went to another doctor and paid him to take his cast off early. He bribed this other doctor and got his cast off. He needed to get these paintings into this dealer so that's what he did. But he was in a lot of pain and ended up taking prescription pills because he couldn't stand it any more. You can imagine where that led."

I sipped my gimlet while Garrett spoke, my mind turning. Carina told me the stepfather got Jackson addicted. But Garrett was singing a different tune. I wondered what the truth was. Not that I thought Carina deliberately lied to me. She wouldn't have a reason to lie. But maybe she misunderstood about what exactly led Jackson to take drugs.

"What's his doctor's name? The one who helped Jackson get his cast off?"

"Dr. Melber," he said. "He's a Doctor Feelgood type who practices on the Upper West Side. Anyhow, at some point, even Dr. Melber told Jackson he couldn't have any more painkillers. That was when he turned to street drugs. And, get this, from what Elise told me, Jackson was scoring drugs for his stepfather."

"Really? I heard it was the other way around."

"No, I guess it wasn't. At any rate, that was one of the reasons why Jackson ended up running away. His mother wouldn't let him take painkillers because she didn't want him getting addicted. He did it anyway, which pissed her off. Then when Jackson started on the street drugs, she put her foot down and threw him out of the house. Turns out he didn't run away."

"But her husband George was taking street drugs, too."

"Yeah, that's what I heard from Elise as well. But that was a different thing, according to Elise. Marie actually encouraged George to take drugs. I guess because she was hoping George would overdose and leave her alone. She certainly didn't want him divorcing her because that would mean she would have to pay him money for alimony and property division. She just hoped George would take care of all that for her and keel over from using the speedballs."

"Sounds like a match made in heaven between George and Marie, huh?"

"You might say that. The two of them actually hated each other. Marie also hated Jackson's dad, Hugh. Hugh was old money and the only reason why she married him was because her father wanted it. Her father saw Marie's marriage as something that consolidated wealth and power and he could give shit less about whether or not she actually loved the guy. Then he was killed in a plane crash, and, from what I found out by asking people who actually knew Marie and Hugh, Marie was more than happy this happened."

"Okay. What else did you find out about Jackson and George today?"

"I told you the most important things. I talked to Jackson's heroin dealer, too. He's another rich kid, well, I guess he's technically not a kid now, he's in his late 20s, but he was definitely a kid when dealing to Jackson. He was 17 at that time and went to Jackson's same prep school. I guess he made a lot of money dealing to the rich kids at his school. Those kids have an endless amount of money and a lot of them have an endless amount of addictive tendencies. It's a perfect storm for him."

"What's that guy's name?"

"His name is Alan Taylor. What's interesting is that he's also involved in the art world. He still deals drugs, from what Elise tells me, although he's cagey about that when he talks to me. He talks around his answers, instead of telling me directly that he does or doesn't deal drugs. But he's also a legitimate art dealer. He has a gallery in SoHo, and get this – he owns 13 of Jackson's paintings. I guess what happened was that Jackson, when he first got kicked out of the house, had no money to pay Alan anymore for his drugs. Alan told me he was always an art connoisseur, always an aficionado, and knew raw talent when he saw it. So, he allowed Jackson to pay him for the drugs by giving him paintings."

I cocked my head. "Oh, really? What are those paintings worth at the moment? Has he had them appraised or anything like that?"

"I don't know. I asked him if he had them appraised and he said he hasn't had the chance. But I would imagine that those 13 paintings, especially since they were some of Jackson's early work, are probably worth quite a lot of money these days. You might go down and talk to him about all that. It would be worth your while to interview him."

"Will do." I nodded my head. "Good work."

"Yeah." Garrett took a sip of his beer. "You think anymore about Mystic Anna and about what she said to you about your birth father?"

"No. I haven't thought about that at all. I think she's full of shit." I really didn't think that Mystic Anna was full of shit, but, at the same time, I didn't want to believe I came into the world because my mother was raped. I didn't want to believe that violence was why I was born, but I also didn't want to grapple with the reality that I treated my mother like shit all this time because I was disgusted about what she was, when, really, I needed to have compassion for her. Being raped was a devastating experience and having a kid through rape had to have been an enormous blow. If that was the case about my mother, I would feel terribly guilty for being as shitty to her as I had been.

So, at least while I was in New York, I wouldn't think about what Mystic Anna had said about my father. I would have to wait until I saw my mother and ask her directly about it. I couldn't afford the distraction of trying to figure it out right at that moment.

"You gonna ask her about it, at least?"

"I haven't talked to her in years. So maybe it's time to pay her a visit. Anyhow, that's neither here nor there. I need information about this Alan Taylor. Give me the address to his art gallery and I can see him in the next few days. Tomorrow evening is that cocktail party where I'm cornering George. Try to make an appointment for me to see Alan."

"Will do."

Garrett and I sat around and had a few more drinks before we went off and ended up at the Shake Shack for dinner. We might have been staying at a 5 star hotel, with a 5 star restaurant, but both of us had a hankering for a good burger, and the Shake Shack was where we could get that.

Tomorrow was another hoity-toity event, as the Goldman cocktail party was being held at the Butterfly Soho. I had looked that place up, and I saw that this was another place where the beers would be $15 and the cocktails would be $25 and up.

Tonight, though, it was good old-fashioned burgers and fries.

And they were delicious.

Chapter Ten

THE NEXT EVENING, I got into my high-dollar suit, shined up my shoes and headed down to get a cab to the Butterfly Soho. This was a dark bar with dark paneling and dark wood floors and was dimly lit. The men and women were standing around, drinking martinis and chatting. They had closed down part of the bar for this cocktail party, and there were private waiters and waitresses coming around with little hors d'oeuvres on their tray. One waiter had little avocado toasts on them, another had bacon-wrapped shrimp. I went up to the bar and found out the function was an open-bar affair – I tried to pay the bartender for my drink, but he waved it away.

"It's covered," he said.

"Thanks." I took a sip and looked around.

To my surprise, Carina Maxwell was there. I took a deep breath, wondering if she was there on a date with somebody. It would make sense that she probably had a date. After all, she wasn't working for Goldman and I thought most of these people either worked for Goldman or was there with somebody who did.

She saw me and raised her glass. I walked over to her and she smiled and put her hand on my shoulder. "Hey," she said. "Damien. Long time, no see."

"Yeah," I said, smiling back. "It's been, oh, a couple of days at least, huh?"

She nodded. "What brings you here?"

"I need to speak with George," I said. "I tried to get an appointment with him but he was always busy. So I scored an invite to this fancy party so that I could speak with the elusive Mr. Mason. Is he here? I've been looking around but I don't see him anywhere."

I had seen pictures of George, even if I had never met him, so I knew who I was looking for. I felt I could recognize him if he were around.

"He's actually right over there," she said, motioning to the corner. George was sitting in a booth with some other men and women. "You're going to have to somehow get him alone to talk to you. Even then, however, I doubt very seriously you'll get a straight answer from him about anything."

I nodded. "I'm happy to see you, because I wanted to follow up on a few things you told me." I glanced at the man standing next to her. "Is there any way you and I can go somewhere and talk?"

"Sure," she said, and she nodded to the guy. "It was good meeting you, Tim" she said. *Ah, I guess she's not with that guy. I wonder if she's there with any of the other guys.* "Let's go outside," she said. "Don't worry, George will still be there. He's not going anywhere once he's drinking."

We stepped outside on the street and she was right – it was a nice evening. Early May was probably the best time to visit New York – it was before the sweltering humidity and well before the days when snow covered the ground and the temperature was freezing.

"So," I said. "I have to ask you, because I'm really curious – what brings you to this function? Do you know anybody that works at Goldman?"

"Well, yeah, I know some of the traders there," she said, "but I'm really here for business, not pleasure. My boss wanted me to come to this party and find this guy who is quitting Goldman so he can go to Venezuela and work with the poor. His name is Frederico Cantalone, and my boss wants me to do a documentary on him. The guy is a multi-millionaire, he lives in a loft in TriBeCa, he has it all, but he wants to help his fellow man. That's the kind of story that would make a good documentary, kind of a highlight of the super-rich and the super-poor. The juxtaposition. So, I was at this party to see if I could speak with him and see if he's interested in being profiled like that."

I felt myself relaxing when she was speaking. It felt weird that I was hoping, really hoping, she wasn't there on a date. When she told me she wasn't, it was music to my ears.

"Oh, so you're just trying to hook a documentary subject, then." I nodded. "Are you going to go on location, then, to Venezuela? Is that something you do?"

"Sure, sure," she said. "But I'm trying to stay close to home. I'm a bit tired of living out of a suitcase, so I'm getting more into the production end of the upcoming documentaries."

"I see." I looked at her and she appeared to blush. "And what about your husband? I'll bet he likes you staying close to home, huh?"

She looked at me quizzically. "I'm not married," she said. "I'm not even seeing anybody right now."

I raised an eyebrow, slightly embarrassed that I used such a transparent way of finding out her marital status. Still, it paid off, so I guess it was worth the humiliation.

"Oh, okay," I said.

"Well, you wanted to see me for some reason, right?"

"Right. I wanted to ask you about something you told me when I was in your office."

"What was that?"

"You told me George got Jackson addicted. I found out from another source, however, that Jackson actually got addicted when he got hurt riding his bike. He got prescription pain pills when he broke his arm and didn't allow his arm to heal properly because he had a show upcoming and needed to have his arm out of a cast. So, he bribed a doctor named Dr. Melber to get that cast off early and write him pain pill prescriptions. At some point, Dr. Melber cut him off, and that was what made him turn to heroin. At least, that's what my source tells me."

She looked like she was genuinely confused when I spoke with her. "That's not what Jackson told me," she said. "I wonder if he was lying about that. That's weird." She shook her head. "I wonder why he would lie about that."

"I don't know. Maybe he wasn't lying. Maybe my source has it wrong. That's possible."

"I guess. I mean, he told me about that bicycle accident when he was 15, but I assumed he was already addicted to drugs before he got into that accident. Are you saying he didn't become addicted until after this accident?"

"That's what I understand. I have to do my own shoe leather work on this one, but my investigator found a girl who was Jackson's best friend in prep school, and that's what she said. She said he became addicted because of pain not because his step-father got him involved with drugs. I also have the name of the dealer who started to deal drugs to Jackson. His name is Alan Taylor and it sounded like he was the dealer the kids went to when Jackson was in his prep school. I guess he still deals drugs to the upper crust but also owns an art gallery. Interestingly enough, he has several of Jackson's pieces – 13 to be exact. I guess at some point, Jackson didn't have money but still needed drugs. Alan accepted art in exchange for drugs. I guess the guy is sitting on a Taylor mine right about now."

"Yeah, that's true," Carina said. "Maybe you need to look at this Alan Taylor for this, huh?"

"Of course. That goes without saying. He has motive to kill Jackson, especially if he happens to be hurting for money at the moment. I'm quite sure he's aware that artists' paintings shoot up in value after their death. I have no doubt about that. Plus, he's a drug dealer, which means he's not above doing something illegal. Now whether or not I can make the leap to him killing Jackson, or having him killed, is another matter entirely. Just because you're willing to break the law and deal illegal drugs doesn't necessarily mean you're willing to kill somebody. That's quite the leap."

She nodded. "Even so, take a look at him." She put her hands on my collar, straightened it and then patted me on the shoulder. "It's weird that Jackson told me about how his stepfather got him addicted. I just don't know why he would lie to me about that."

That was something to keep in the back of my mind – figure out why Jackson would lie about how he got addicted. In the meantime, however, I was focused on Carina and what she was doing. Her hand kept touching mine and she smoothed back my hair on more than one occasion. She was giving me body-language signals that she was into me and I was noticing them.

"Um," I said, feeling my the blood rush to my face. I was sure I was blushing and the fact that she smiled and giggled lightly as she looked at me told me my hunch was probably correct. "I-"

"You need to get back in there and talk to George, don't you?" she asked.

"Oh, yes, yes," I said, feeling embarrassed that I was close to asking her out on a date. "George, yes."

She giggled again and, when I turned to go back into the bar, she linked her arm through mine. That was the clearest signal yet she was into me and I made a mental note to capitalize on her signals to me.

Right after I went and saw that sleaze George.

I looked over and saw George sitting by himself. I didn't know where the other guys went, the guys who were sitting with him, but I felt lucky that I could corner him.

I went over and sat down across from him. He gave me a look like he didn't quite know who I was but then shrugged his shoulders. "Ron, go and get me another drink," he said, his words slurring. "A vodka straight. Make it a double this time."

He was sweating profusely and his eyes were glazed. His pupils were dilated.

The guy was high as a kite.

"Mr. Mason," I said, "my name is Damien Harrington and I need to speak with you about your step-son, Jackson."

"Jackson." He nodded. "Why you want to talk to me about Jackson? Is there something wrong with him?" His head bobbed back and forth, and he hung his head slightly. "I haven't talked to that boy in years."

I studied his face, trying to figure out if this guy was toying with me. Jackson's death had been well publicized. It was a big deal just because Jackson had attained such celebrity at such a young age. Even if this guy wasn't in touch with Jackson at the time he died and also wasn't in touch with Marie, Jackson's mother, he still would have at least heard about his stepson's death.

I decided to play his game.

"Jackson's fine," I said, "I just saw him a few days ago. He's fine."

He nodded. "Good. So, what do you want from me? Why are you talking to me?"

I cleared my throat. This guy was either a really good actor or he honestly had no clue his stepson was murdered.

I would have to figure out how it would even be possible that this guy hadn't heard about Jackson's death. He had to have been hiding under a rock to not know.

"Mr. Mason," I said, "have you been in town for the past week and a half? Been looking on the Internet during that time?"

He shook his head. "No. I just got back in town. I was in the Poconos with my new girlfriend. Got a cabin up there, unplug while I'm there. Need that time to clear my head. Why?"

I leaned back. "Excuse me," I said, "I'll be right back."

"Hurry back," he said. "With my vodka."

I went over to Carina. "Carina, can you do something for me?"

"Sure," she said. "What do you need?"

"Talk to the head of George's department," I said. "And ask him if George has really been on vacation for the past few weeks." I lowered my voice. "He's talking like he doesn't even know Jackson is dead. I don't know how that's possible."

"I'll be right back," she said and then went over to a tall man standing in as middle of a small group of people. He was drinking a glass of wine and I saw him nodding his head and pointing at George. For his part, George looked labout to pass out. The tall man shook his head and looked disgusted. Carina smiled and then excused herself.

She came over to me. "Okay. Yes, George was in the Poconos for the past two weeks. He goes up there once a year and is unreachable while there. I guess his cabin is rustic. It has electricity but no Wi-Fi or anything like that."

"And when did he get back?"

"Yesterday." She looked over at him. "And, from the looks of it, he probably has been out of it for quite some time. He was at work today but his drug problem is an open secret and, according to the guys he works with, his drug use actually is an asset. It makes him more aggressive in his trading and deal-making and I guess he's taken a few risks nobody else would take. These risks have paid off for him which makes him extremely valuable to the company." She shook her head. "I guess this company puts the bottom line above everything else, so they really don't care how much a person is into drugs as long as that person makes them money."

"Sounds about right," I said. "Listen, can you possibly do me another favor?"

"Sure, what do you need?"

"Go over there and tell George about Jackson's death. He needs to know, anyhow, and I really need to see his reaction when you tell him." I put my hand on her shoulder. "I hope I'm not asking you to do something you're uncomfortable with."

"Not at all," she said. "I'll talk to him and see his reaction."

I wanted Carina to do this, because I knew that, as a documentary film-maker, she had a good grasp on reading people. If his reaction to finding out that his step-son was dead was authentic and he honestly didn't know Jackson was dead until just now, then I could conclude George had nothing to do with killing him. I could cross him off my list.

On the other hand, if he was playing a game with me, which he might be, his reaction to finding out Jackson was dead wouldn't ring true. Carina presumably could figure that out for me.

I looked over at Carina who was talking to George and I saw him put his head on the table. She put her arm around his back. He lifted his head and there were tears in his eyes. I blinked, wondering if they were crocodile tears.

Then he looked over at me and pointed. "You," he said, his words slurring. I looked around and saw people were staring at me and looking back at him. The tall guy who Carina was talking to earlier started to walk over to George, but George abruptly stood up and walked unsteadily over to me.

He got two inches away from my face and pointed at me. "You just told me Jackson was fine. You said he was fine. Well, he's not fine, he's dead." He spread his arms. "Why would you fuck with me like that? Huh? Why would you talk to me about my stepson, a stepson I haven't talked to in years? By the way, I don't even know you. I've never seen you before in my life. I don't know what you're game but it's shitty what you just did."

Carina came over to me and shook her head. "George," she said.

"Yeah, I don't want to talk to you, either. You're that witch who's doing that documentary about Jackson. I'm sure it's filled with lies about me. I'm sure it is. I don't know why you nominated yourself to be the keeper of bad news." Then he looked at both of us. "Unless both of you are playing some kind of fucking game with me. Mind-fucking me about this." He pointed to both of us. "Listen, I don't think I'll believe that about Jackson until I prove it to myself."

The tall guy was over, next to George, and he looked at George sadly. "It's true," he said. "I thought you knew. We all thought you knew."

"How would I know?" George was swaying and looked about to topple over. "I've been off the grid for a couple of weeks. How would I know?" Then he put his head in his hands. "So, it's true. It's true. Goddamn it." He stumbled away from me and several people tried to put their arms around him to comfort him, but he waved them all away. "Leave me alone."

At that, he disappeared out the door.

I turned to Carina. "Well? What do you think? Is that guy putting on a really good acting job or is he really stunned and grieving right now?"

"I think he honestly didn't know Jackson was killed until just now," she said. "And if he's doing an acting job, it's an Academy Award-winning one. So, yeah. I think he's on the level."

I sighed. "In other words…"

"It seems like a dead-end for now." She put her hands on my collar. "Sorry about that."

I looked around. "Not a problem."

She cocked her head. "You wanna get out of here?"

"I thought you would never ask."

Chapter Eleven

CARINA and I ended up on a rooftop bar, sitting right by a small fire in a pit that was giving off warmth, which was a good thing, as the temperature had dropped. I looked on the horizon, seeing the lights of Lower Manhattan twinkling back, felt the crispness in the air and looked at one of the most beautiful woman I had ever seen. I felt incredibly lucky.

17 years ago, when I was serving time in prison for a crime I didn't commit, I never would have thought something like this would be possible. I still had to pinch myself whenever I managed to snag a perfect evening, such as this one was turning out to be.

"Anyhow," Carina said as she sipped her glass of Pinot Grigio. She had a playful look on her face and a twinkle in her beautiful blue eyes. "I couldn't help but think you weren't exactly comfortable with that crowd. I mean, you fit in with them – you dress the part, you look the part, and you're extremely intelligent and articulate – but I got the feeling you're not quite one of them."

"Am I that transparent?" I asked her.

"A little. I mean, I make documentaries for a living. You have to remember that. Reading people is what I'm good at. I hope I don't offend you when I say I can tell that you are not to the manor born. Not that that's a prerequisite for that crowd. Plenty of those traders in there came from nothing. George wasn't one of the self-made ones, but plenty of them are. But most of them, not all, but most, have a certain mind-set that makes them fit in with that crowd."

I felt drawn to her intelligence and intuitive nature. I was also genuinely curious about how she could see right through me. After all, I went to an exclusive law school – the University of Chicago. I was an attorney. I had more education than most people in the world. Yet I still stuck out like a sore thumb when I was around wealthy people. Why?

"What mind-set is that? That those traders have?"

"Oh, it's a mind-set people have when they feel the key to life is collecting things. Money. More and more, a bottomless pit of need. You know, when you make a million a year, or more, and still complain about how it's not enough. A lot of those traders have that mind-set, so they all seem to have each other's numbers. They're on each other's wave-lengths. You're different. I can tell." She took a sip of her wine. "That said, they're not all like that. Some of those guys are genuinely good people, but I think trading attracts people who just want to make as much money as possible."

I studied my scotch neat as I thought about her words. "I'm different how?"

"You really care about people. I think you think of that greed mind-set the same way I do – it's all so stupid and superficial. I mean, look at George. He has more money than God. He makes $5 million a year. And that man has no soul. His inside is filled with rage, entitlement and depression. He gets up in the morning and does a few lines. He does lines all day in his office and then shoots up heroin at night to help him sleep. Then he gets up the next day and does it all again. I don't know about you but I wouldn't want to live like that for all the money in the world. Mental health, and health in general, is priceless, really. I wouldn't trade my mental health for all the money in the world. I think you're probably the same way."

"I am." I smiled. "But I think you would be surprised about just how right you are about how I don't fit in with the rich jerks at that cocktail party." I felt like I had known her all my life, so I felt confident enough to tell her about my background. "My mother lives in a trailer and I never knew my dad. I ran with a bunch of guys and we got into trouble all the time. They ended up robbing a liquor store and I got roped into it, too, even though I wasn't there. I served 5 years in prison for something I didn't do. They're still in prison but they'll hopefully all be out by the end of this year."

She nodded. She obviously wasn't fazed by what I just told her and this made me even more attracted to her. "Now, you see, I knew you came from nothing. Good on you for making it out of that mess and becoming what you are. I'm sorry to hear about your friends, though."

"Oh, it's okay. Really, it is. They're up for parole this year and there's not a reason why they won't make it." I didn't tell her about Connor and how I got his sentence commuted. She might not have understood that. She probably didn't need to know that side of me – the side that would do absolutely anything, be it illegal or unethical, to save the people I loved. I still cringed when I thought about how I suborned perjury from Gina Degrazio just because I needed to win her case, lest Nick get ratted out by Gina's boyfriend, Joey Caruso. And I was ashamed of blackmailing our governor. But the ends justified the means. As long as the guys got out, the means in getting them out were justified, in my mind.

She leaned forward. "I'm actually really happy I met you."

"And I feel the same."

"You're not married, are you?"

I chuckled. "Technically, yes, I am. I'll be straight with you. But my wife and I are going through a divorce." I felt sad. "My daughter Amelia was very sick with cancer last year and my wife left us while that was going on. We tried to work things out, but I finally just decided she could never be a mother to our children. She could never be there for them when they really need her. So, I finally decided to move forward without her. As painful as it is. I mean, she was the first woman I dated when I got out of prison. We've been together for 13 years and had two kids together. I didn't know how weak she was until Amelia got sick. That was when I saw the real her and it wasn't pretty. Not pretty at all."

I had to wonder about Carina, too. Just like she was probably wondering how I was single, I had to wonder the same thing about her. She was beautiful, intelligent, educated and creative. It seemed she probably should have been off the market herself.

"What about you? Have you ever been married?"

She chuckled. "Yeah, I have been. But it's not quite what you might imagine." She took a deep breath. "I was married to a woman. For ten years."

I felt intrigued and profoundly disappointed, all at the same time. "Oh, you're a lesbian." I nodded, wondering if this whole magnetic attraction thing was all in my head.

She smiled. "No. Bisexual. I just fell into marrying Audrey because she and I were best friends and she was there for me when I really needed her." She sipped her wine. "My father was killed in a mob hit when I was 17 and those guys were looking for me for years. Audrey got me out of the city. Her brother lives in Montana and we lived with him while we were married. She always monitored the situation, trying to figure out when it would be safe to come back into town. She eventually found out the guys after my father were taken care of – most of them were dead, but a couple were in prison for life, so I knew I could return to New York. I owed her my life."

I was finding Carina more and more intriguing. "And where is she now?"

She looked sad. "Well, she finally figured out I liked men more than women, so she divorced me. I never cheated on her or anything like that, but she was absolutely right – I liked men. Don't get me wrong. I loved her deeply. And we were passionate together and all of that. But there was just a part of me that knew being married to a woman was not going to be the story of my life." She nodded. "We divorced earlier this year and I've been single ever since."

I felt a sense of relief. Maybe there was a chance for me after all. "So…"

"So…." She gave me a look and I knew I would be getting Garrett a room of his own that night.

Which is exactly what happened. I called the hotel and got George his own room and Carina went back with me.

The next day, Sarah was completely forgotten. I had met the woman I was supposed to be with.

Too bad she lived 1,200 miles away.

Chapter Twelve

CARINA ENDED up going with me to the art gallery owned by Alan Taylor. I had to rule him out and also hoped to get some more information from him that might lead me to other suspects.

Carina wanted to go, and I wanted her to go. I knew I wanted to spend every moment I could with her because I fully anticipated I wouldn't be seeing her anymore once I got back to Kansas City. Long-distance relationships were not my thing and I would be throwing myself into Leland's case when I got back. That was a shame, because Carina, moment by moment, was wrecking me. I knew when I met her that she was the type of woman who could do me in, and that's exactly what was happening. She was doing me in, with every smile, every glance, every touch.

We headed to the gallery in SoHo. The gallery looked to be one of the most luxurious in the area. The ceilings were a good 20 feet high, the walls were white and the floor hardwood. On all the walls, there was all manner of modern paintings. I didn't know much about art – I only took a few classes on Art History, so I couldn't really appreciate these paintings for what they were. But Carina knew something about art and local artists, and, as she gripped my arm, she whispered, "he's got some really valuable paintings here. Some of the hottest artists are showing here."

It was early on a weekday, so there were a few people looking around, but it wasn't packed. I saw there was an upcoming event, however, so I knew this place would be crawling with patrons in a few days.

I looked up and saw a balding guy dressed in jeans, high-tops, a t-shirt and a suit jacket. Although he was balding on top, the rest of his hair was long, and he wore it in a ponytail. He approached Carina and me. "I see you looking at that painting by Don Butler," he said to Carina. "He's one of the hottest artists in the area. But if you really want to see something, come with me."

He led Carina by the hand and I followed closely behind. "Here," he said. "I guess you found out about Jackson Michaelson. Tragic case. Died a couple of weeks ago in Kansas City, Missouri." He shook his head. "I just put these paintings on display. I have 13 of them. I'm asking a million apiece for them. Believe me, these paintings will be worth so much more over time. His legend is growing with each passing day."

She looked over at me and then gestured to him. *Get a load of this guy,* her look said to me. I nodded back.

I stepped over to him. "I see those Jackson Michaelson paintings there," I said. "That looks like some of his early work."

"Good eye," he said. "This actually is some of his earliest work. When he was just 15 years old, he was already an established artist. He started getting prominent gallery showings when he was just 18. These paintings are from when he was just getting known in the art world at the age of 15. To say these paintings will one day be priceless is an understatement. My asking price of a million apiece is, I have to admit, highway robbery of me. But I'm willing to let them go for that price, so if I were you, I would be all over these paintings. All over them."

I nodded. "Well, thank you," I said to him. "My wife and I will think about it." I put my arm around Carina and Alan just shook his head and walked over to another couple that had walked in the door. He led them to two other of Jackson's paintings and gave them the same spiel. He told them both about how these were early Michaelson paintings, how they would be priceless one day, and how his being willing to part with them for the low, low price of a million dollars constituted an absolute fire sale.

"Is that weird?" I whispered to Carina. "This guy certainly is maniacally trying to get rid of these paintings for some reason. I think we need to look into this guy's finances. I just think it's weird he's trying so hard to get rid of this artwork."

"Yes, that is weird," she said. "I mean, he makes a point. This is some of Jackson's earliest work, so it'll be extremely valuable over the years. The fact that he's trying to unload it so desperately tells me something."

"Let's go," I said. "I need to do a bit of checking on this gallery. I'll come back here after I find out about how healthy his finances are."

Carina and I left and I called Harper. "Hey," she said when she picked up. "Damien. How's it going over there in New York? Are you making any progress?"

"I think I am. How are Amelia and Nate? They giving you any problems?" I had been calling both of them on their individual cell phones from the hotel, and they both seemed to be having a good time at Harper's house. They were getting along with the two girls and they were really loving their dogs, Stella and Sue. Amelia, for her part, spent most of the time on the phone with me begging me to get her dogs just like Stella and Sue.

"Not at all," she said. "They're really no trouble."

"Good. Hey, can you ask Anna to do something for me?" Anna was Harper's hacker. According to Harper, Anna could fine any record on any one at any time. It really didn't matter. Anna could get hospital records, financial records, closed adoption records, closed juvenile criminal records. I knew it wouldn't be difficult for her to figure out what the deal was with Alan Taylor's gallery.

"Sure, what do you need?"

"I need the financial information for an art gallery here in SoHo. It belongs to an Alan Taylor. The name is just 'Taylor's Gallery.' How long do you think that will take to get those records?"

"Not long at all. That should be a matter of public record, really."

"I know it is, but if there is information she can glean that isn't a matter of public record, that would be extremely helpful."

"Will do," she said. "I'll give you a call in about a half hour or so."

Carina and I headed to a coffee shop and waited for Harper's call.

"What are you thinking?" she asked me.

"We'll see. That just seems very weird that he's trying to unload those paintings. Unless he's trying to pass off a fraudulent painting. Maybe he has copies of Jackson's paintings and he's trying to pass them off. I would be taken in by something like that. So would most people."

"Regardless," Carina pointed out, "he's clearly trying to capitalize on Jackson's death. That seems strange to me. I mean, we just walked in and he already was on us, trying to sell those paintings. It just reeks of desperation."

I bit my lower lip. "Desperation. But was he desperate enough to kill Jackson to make those paintings more valuable? That's the question I'm asking."

Carina and I chatted some more about the whole thing for the next half hour. We were in the middle of talking about the possibilities when I got the phone call from Harper.

"I got the information you need," she said. "About the Taylor Gallery in SoHo. And it turns out the owner, Alan Taylor, has some serious debts he needs to pay off. He owes legitimate money to everyone in town and has a personal bankruptcy petition on file. On that petition, he indicates he owes money to several people who Anna looked into, and these people are other prominent drug dealers around town. Does this help?"

"Yeah, that helps. That helps a lot. Thanks, Harper."

"You're welcome. Do you want the name of the drug dealers Alan owes money to? According to Anna, these other drug dealers are pretty big-time."

"Sure, give me those names."

"Antonio Wayfair is one, Christopher Greene is another, and Mario Gonzalez is the third one. Between the three of them, Alan Taylor owes over $3 million."

I nodded my head. "That helps. That helps a lot. Thanks."

I hung up. "Well, it is just like I thought. That guy is

desperate for cash. That's why he's unloading those paintings for so cheap."

"How desperate?"

"He owes $3 million to drug dealers around the city. That's how desperate." I raised an eyebrow. "The question is, was he desperate enough to kill a man to make his paintings more valuable, or was that just a lucky break for him?"

"How much were those paintings worth before Jackson was killed?"

"The fair market value for Jackson's work was around $100,000 a painting," I said, "just based upon what my client was selling his paintings for right before Jackson was killed.

"Okay, so the paintings were worth around $100,000 before he was killed and now this guy is asking for a million apiece. That's a markup of 10 times. Look at it this way – before Jackson was killed, Alan Taylor could unload all 13 of this paintings and still be several million dollars in the hole. He might be declaring bankruptcy, but those drug dealers won't allow him to just discharge his debts to them. They'll kill him if he doesn't pay. I'm sure he'll now get that million-dollar asking price. Collectors are keen on buying paintings from artists who die young, especially when the death of said artist is so well publicized."

"That gives this guy motive for sure," I said. "I'll have to definitely put him on my witness list. Right now, it looks like the alternative suspect I can use for this crime can definitely be Alan Taylor. I'll have to find out more information about him before I'm satisfied he's good for this murder, but, at the moment, he's looking like he might have done it."

I hoped I wasn't jumping the gun on this. I always hated to finger somebody unless I was damn sure. I would have to do more of a background check on Alan and find out specifically about some of the crimes he might have been convicted of. I would also send Garrett out to talk to some of Alan's friends and associates and get back with me on whether or not the guy did it.

"So, for now," I said to Carina. "I need to talk to Alan and ask him questions about Jackson and see how he reacts to my questions. I need to get a feel for him. I like to feel pretty solid when I use my SODDI defense, because I hate to finger somebody and throw suspicion on them if they really didn't do it."

"SODDI defense?" Carina asked. "What does that mean?"

"Some other dude did it. When I defend a murder case, I try to either show another person killed the victim, or try for some kind of justification, like self-defense, or excuse. An excuse is something like 'I caught my wife in bed with somebody else and I just freaked out,' and that might mitigate the charges so that I can get the client off on manslaughter as opposed to murder one. Or I might try for some kind of temporary insanity defense or complete insanity defense. If I can't do any of these things, I try to plead them out."

"Can you use the SODDI defense if you don't have an alternative suspect?"

"Sure. But it's usually less effective when you do it that way. Juries are comprised of humans, and humans, as a rule, abhor a vacuum. That means that, if you don't have somebody to pin the crime on, they'll be more likely to convict. That's why I try so hard to find the alternative suspect."

"I see. So, if you determine Alan is likely to have done it, then what?"

"I call him to trial as a witness and try to break him

down. No, it's usually not like you see on legal shows, where the guy breaks down on the stand and admits to having done it. Usually it's just a matter of catching them in lies, or, sometimes, just making them look bad on the stand. That's how I would use somebody like Alan Taylor – just try to make him look bad enough that the jury thinks it's plausible he did it."

"Well, then, let's go back to the gallery and try to poke and prod him and see if we can figure this out." She rubbed her hands together. "I'm a good partner for you on this, you know. As a documentary film maker, I'm always trying to solve mysteries myself."

We went back to the gallery and saw Alan Taylor again. He was standing in the middle of 5 people. They were all standing in front of one of Jackson's paintings and looked very interested in what Alan was saying. He was talking and they were hanging onto his every word.

"That's a group of investors," Carina whispered. "I recognize some of them. If anybody will have a million dollars just lying around to buy one of Jackson's paintings, it would be one of them. I'll bet Alan can sell a few of Jackson's paintings to them."

Sure enough, I saw Alan shaking hands with several of them, and he snapped his fingers for his assistant. She walked over to the group and led them into an office, where, I presumed, they were finalizing a deal.

He saw the two of us walking through the door and grinned. "You're back," he said. "But you snooze, you lose. I just sold three of Jackson's hottest paintings. Three of his best. But these other paintings I have left will also be worth a mint one day. Going, going, gone."

I looked over at Carina, thinking about how much more relaxed this guy seemed than before. I guessed that selling three paintings, at a million apiece, would go a long way towards his newfound attitude.

"Actually, I wanted to ask you some questions about Jackson. How well did you still know him? I know you knew him when he was young. You dealt drugs to him for many years. But how well did you still know him?"

"I didn't know him," he said. "I hadn't talked to him for years and years. Why do you ask that question?"

"Did you know he was going to Kansas City when he went there?" I persisted in asking him these questions because I didn't think he was telling the truth about how well he knew Jackson at the time of his death. "Listen, I'm going to ask around and find out the truth about how well you knew Jackson at the time he died, so you might as well come clean with me."

"I don't know what you're talking about. I just told you I didn't talk to Jackson for years, so why in the hell would I know about him going out of town?"

Just then, I looked at the paintings on the wall. "You just sold three of these paintings, is that right?"

"Yeah, right."

I counted the number of paintings still on the wall. I counted 10. "So, you'll sell all the paintings Jackson gave you? You won't hold one back for yourself?"

"Don't be ridiculous," he said, "of course I'm going to hold one back. I'll keep one of his paintings for myself. It'll be worth $50 million or more one day. I'm not that stupid."

I nodded. I remembered Garrett's source told me that Jackson gave Alan 13 paintings exactly. "Do you mind if I see the other painting? The one you're not going to sell right now?"

"Yeah," he said. "It's in a huge safety deposit box. I'm

not taking any chances with that one. But here it is. I took a picture of it."

I looked at the picture he showed me, and I immediately knew the truth.

That picture he held back was not from the same period these other paintings were. The 13 paintings he was trying to sell were all similar in theme and scope. I didn't know much about art history, but I knew one thing – artists had different periods in their lives and different periods in their artwork. That meant you could tell the difference between a painting painted during a certain period of time from a painting painted during a completely different period of time. Picasso's Blue Period had paintings completely different from his Rose period and these, in turn, were completely different from his cubism period. Artists typically evolved in their art, as they had different experiences and they matured.

The painting Alan showed me was clearly from a different period from the other paintings. This painting was much more mature than those other paintings and it showed a great deal of depth compared to the others. I knew this painting that he had, that he wasn't selling, was something that would be worth even more than the 13 he received when Jackson was young.

In other words, Alan was clearly lying about not speaking with Jackson for years.

Still, I wasn't quite sure what period this painting would belong to. I studied it, trying to take a picture of it in my mind's eye. That way, I could speak with Leland about Jackson's art and find out how recent this painting was painted. If it was something painted fairly recently, this guy was certainly lying.

"Now, when was the last time you spoke with Jackson?" I asked him.

He shrugged. "I knew him when he was a kid. When he was 17, he and I used to hang out. I don't think I've talked to him since he was around 19."

I nodded and looked at Carina. I didn't want to nail this guy to the wall until I had more information about that other painting. "Hey," I said, "can you email me that picture you have of Jackson's?"

He gave me a look like *what the fuck are you talking about?* "No. Why would I do that? And why do you want it?"

Carina stepped forward. She put her hand on Alan's arm and stroked it lightly. She raised one of her eyebrows at him and her voice dripped out in a purr.

"What Mr. Harrington is trying to say is that this is such a beautiful painting and you have impeccable taste. Such impeccable taste." She continued to stroke his arm and I saw his face changing. His expression was definitely softening with every syllable that came out of Carina's mouth. "We would love to really admire your painting, especially since you're obviously so intelligent that you knew a priceless work of art when you saw it. That's all."

He shrugged. "What harm can it do, I guess." He pointed at me. "I'll remind you this painting is in a safety deposit box. You can't steal it even if you wanted to. But, you're right, it is a beautiful painting and I want to show it off. So, sure, I'll text you that picture."

"Thank you," she said. "Damien, give him your phone number so he can text you that picture."

I gave it to him and he immediately texted the picture to me.

"Thanks," I said, nodding.

"Sure." He looked me up and down. "So, you gonna buy one of these paintings or aren't you?"

"I don't have a million dollars just lying around," I said. "Otherwise I would, believe you me."

"Well, then, take a look around the gallery. Not all of these paintings is that high dollar. I got paintings in this gallery that sell for as low as $20,000. They aren't as exclusive as my Jackson Michaelson paintings or nothing like that, but all the artists I show in this gallery have a strong following." He nudged me. "Who knows, maybe you'll get lucky if you buy one of these paintings and the artist dies on you. That can make you a mint, let me tell you. A mint."

"A mint. Got it." I touched Carina's arm. "Carina, what do you say about you and I getting out of here." I raised my eyebrows. I was dying to text that picture to Leland and see if he could give me some indication on the period it was painted. If anybody would know the answer to this question, it would be Leland. From there, I could figure out if Alan was lying about not having had contact with Jackson since the artist was 19.

We left the gallery and I called Leland.

"Hello," he said, picking up the phone. "Damien. Did you talk to Mystic Anna? What did you think about her? Pretty weird, isn't she?"

I heard Dill protesting in the background about how Mystic Anna didn't do anything wrong and I smiled. They were like an old married couple, even though they were both in their early thirties. As much as I lightly suspected Dill of killing Jackson because he was jealous of Leland's relationship with the young artist, I really didn't think that was true.

"Yeah, I talked to her," I said. "But I'm hot onto something else right now. I saw the stepfather, too, but I really think he didn't know his stepson was dead until we told him about it, so I don't think he did it, either. Anyhow, I want to text you a picture. It's a photograph of one of Jackson's paintings. I need you to tell the approximate period it was painted. You know Jackson's work better than anybody, so you can probably help me out with this."

"Of course I can," he said. "Go ahead and text me."

I texted him the picture while he was on the phone with me and he immediately came out with the period. "This was painted during Jackson's Lolita period," he said. "When Jackson was 25 and 26. Those were the years he painted the distorted pictures of the young girls he met on the streets."

I nodded. "Age 25 and 26. Thanks, Leland. I appreciate it."

"Not a problem. Listen, you'll be back in town soon, right? It looks like I got some notice in the mail about an arraignment. I guess my case went through the Grand Jury and surprise, surprise, they found enough evidence to indict me. Dill said Grand Juries indict ham sandwiches all the time, so I knew this would happen. Hurry back, the arraignment is set for next Thursday at 1:30."

I nodded. "I'll be there." I glanced at Carina, knowing I would hate to leave her. I had never felt this strongly about a woman in such a short period of time. Just my luck she lived out of town.

I hung up. "Well, it was just as I thought."

"Meaning?"

"Meaning this painting was from a specific period. Jackson was 25 and 26 when he went through this period. The bastard Alan was lying to me about not being in touch with Jackson since Jackson was 19. I wonder what else he is lying about."

"Probably everything."

"He's looking good to me," I said. "He's looking awfully good."

Chapter Thirteen

THAT SATURDAY NIGHT, I headed home. I found enough reasonable evidence that I could sell other people to the jury, especially Alan Taylor. My plan was to subpoena Alan and break him down. I had already caught him in one lie, and I knew that, if I sprung what I knew on him, I could show the jury he was lying. From there, I could work to establish motive, means and opportunity.

The motive was clear – the man needed money. He needed lots of money and needed it quickly. What better way to get several million in cash than to bump off your hot artist, thereby skyrocketing the value of all his artwork? I had already seen it in action – he received $3 million in the blink of an eye, just by talking up Jackson's paintings to the art investors I saw in Alan's gallery. That was quick and dirty cash for Alan, and that money went a long way towards getting Alan out of the debt he found himself in.

But he owed even more money to people. Anna emailed me a copy of Alan's bankruptcy petition and the amount of debt owed was in excess of $6 million to creditors all over the world. The drug dealers were the ones he wanted to pay off first, of course, since those dealers would kill him if he couldn't pay them off. I was sure he wanted to get his other creditors paid off too, though, because if he didn't, he would lose his gallery.

That was another thing Anna managed to figure out. Alan Taylor was not that savvy of a businessman as he never bothered to incorporate. Taylor Gallery was owned by Alan Taylor personally, not by an LLC or an S Corporation. That meant his personal creditors could take his gallery and all of the paintings in it. They could take everything he owned.

I knew his game in filing for the bankruptcy. He would never try for an actual discharge. He filed for a Chapter 7, which was straight liquidation, which would mean, in turn, all of his property would be sold by the trustee to pay off his debts. No way did he want that. If I were to guess, I imagined he simply filed for the bankruptcy to stop the creditors from moving against him. Before he would have his first meeting with the trustee, he would simply dismiss his bankruptcy. By then, hopefully, he would have enough cash to get everyone paid.

That meant he was on a time limit. Chapter 7 bankruptcies generally are discharged within 90 days. He didn't want to get to that discharge date, so he needed to get that cash fast to pay off his creditors before he could get to the discharge date.

It was all too lucky for him, really. He needed fast money and he needed millions. If he didn't get fast millions, he would have had drug dealers hunting him down and would have gotten to the end of his Chapter 7 bankruptcy without the money to bail him out. His bankruptcy trustee would sell all of his assets to pay off his creditors.

What better way to get out of his dilemma than to kill his best artist?

It all seemed neat and tidy and I knew I could sell this story to a jury.

I leaned my head against the head-rest and looked over at Garrett, who was reading a magazine. "So, we talked about Alan," I said. "What do you think about my theory?"

He shrugged. "It sounds good, but it's always a trick if you can sell it to a jury. I agree, though, the guy had motive, but we haven't quite established he had means and opportunity. There's the rub. You have to show he hired somebody to do it."

I sighed. "That's true." I found out, the night Jackson was killed, Alan had a fundraiser for his gallery. I had spoken to several different people at the fundraiser, and they confirmed Alan was there as well. But that didn't really deter me. Garrett was right – Alan could have hired somebody.

But one thing nagged me about that – Alan was in debt as it was. He needed quick cash. How could he have raised the money to pay somebody to carry out that hit? That was the hole in the story, and, unless I figured out a way to plug that hole, I was back at square one. That would mean this trip was a wasted one.

But as I looked out the window, and saw the lights of the city gradually getting smaller and smaller, I knew one thing. This trip wasn't a waste. No matter what, even if I didn't manage to find the perpetrator of this crime on this trip, it wasn't a waste. I met Carina, and, even though she lived in New York and I lived in Kansas City, and she had her life and I had mine, the days I spent with her were mind-blowing. The nights were even more so. Her soft skin, her pillowy lips, her long limbs, her hair…everything about her was burned in my brain.

If I had more confidence in my relationship with her, I probably would have proposed some kind of arrangement to where we could see each other once in awhile. Maybe a weekend in New York for me once a month. She could visit Kansas City and see for herself that I didn't live in a cowtown, not that she thought Kansas City was a cowtown. But I convinced myself she didn't want to bother with the long-distance thing, so I didn't even ask her about it.

Now, on the plane, as I saw the city fade into the blackness of the night sky, I regretted I didn't ask her to continue her relationship with me. But, then again, I was still married to Sarah. What the hell was I doing?

"What other ideas do you have for this murder?" Garrett asked me.

"I have no clue. I've hit a wall on this one. Nobody else is popping out at me, except for Alan. I felt like the stepfather would be an excellent candidate, until I met him and he still thought Jackson was alive. So, he's not a candidate anymore. Other than that, I got nothing."

"Well, maybe it will end up coming to you."

"Maybe." I closed my eyes because I didn't really feel like talking. I was too much in my head at that moment. So many things were swimming around in my brain. I thought about the guys and how they would soon be getting their parole hearing. I thought about Connor and how he would be thrilled to find he was getting out with the others. I thought about my mother and how I would have to confront her and ask her who my father was.

And, most of all, I thought about Carina.

THE PLANE TOUCHED down at KCI several hours later and I went to my car and drove to my house. It was too late to get the kids from Harper's, so I just crashed in my bed.

The next day, I went to Harper's to get the kids. Amelia was happy to see me, and Nate hung back a tiny bit, but he, too, looked like happy I was home.

"Daddy," Amelia said, rushing into my arms. I picked her up and she wrapped her arms around my neck. "How was your trip? Did you bring me stuff?"

"Of course," I said, "I always bring you and Nate stuff. It's all at home. I think that you'll like it."

"Hey Dad," Nate said. "Good to see you."

I put my arm around him and he buried his face in my waist. He was getting so tall. His hair was getting a little wild, as it always did between haircuts, and I made a mental note to take him into the barber shop. "Good to see you too, kiddo. You didn't give Harper any problems, did you?"

Harper appeared in the living room. "Hey, do you want to stay for breakfast? I'm making blueberry banana waffles. It's kinda my specialty."

"Sounds good," I said. "You sure you made enough?"

"Of course. I knew you were coming, so I made extra."

I went into the kitchen, got the plates out and helped her set the table. "Waffles are my favorite," I said. "You know, when I was a kid, my mom would try to be a mom once in a great while and she would make me waffles. I remember that like it was yesterday."

Harper smiled. "You see, your memories of your mom weren't all bad."

"No, not all bad." I cleared my throat. "And I'll have to see her soon."

"That's a good idea," she said. "You know, your kids are pretty fond of your mother. I don't know if you know that. Amelia talks about her and so does Nate." She nodded her head. "I think it's possible you have a mental block when it comes to her and maybe you don't see her for who she really is."

"The kids talk about her?"

"Yeah, they do. Amelia said she thinks her grandmother is, quote, hilarious, and Nate has taught me all the card games your mother taught him. They do both say she smells of cigarettes and stumbles around all the time, but they both seem to love her."

"Well, I guess I should probably take the kids when I see her. But not this time, though. I have to talk to her about something serious."

"Oh? Do you care to share?"

"No. I mean, I will, once I figure out what I need to figure out." I shrugged as I set the table. "For now, though, I just need to see her and ask her a few questions I should have asked her a long, long time ago."

The table was set and the waffles were on the Lazy Susan in the middle. I called my kids and Harper called hers. They all four bounded into the dining room and took their seats.

"Mom makes really good waffles," Abby said as she stabbed one. "I really like the ones she makes with chocolate chips."

Rina screwed up her face. "I like the ones with chocolate chips too, Mom. Why aren't these chocolate chip? You said you wanted to make it special for Damien on his first day back."

"I thought Damien liked blueberry better, so I made blueberry," Harper said.

"Hey," I said to the kids, "I just like waffles, in general. I'm really not picky about all that."

"Good for you," Rina said. "But I still like chocolate chips better."

Harper rolled her eyes. "Okay, I guess everyone has a waffle, so let's eat." She turned to me as she cut her waffle with her fork. "Now, Damien, tell me how your trip went. Did you find out anything good to bring to Leland?"

"I thought maybe I did. There are a few holes I need to plug up, but I found somebody promising. Somebody who definitely had motive."

"Do tell."

I told her about Alan, his debt, and how he magically got out of debt because he could sell Jackson's paintings for so much more than if Jackson had still been alive. Harper listened with interest then her face fell when I told her Alan had an airtight alibi for the crime.

"You think he hired somebody to carry it out?"

"Maybe."

She shook her head. "Hits aren't cheap. Especially not when it concerns a high-profile figure. He's in debt to the tune of $6 million, and you're telling me he has millions to hire somebody to kill Jackson? That doesn't ring true to me. Not unless he maybe gave somebody one or two of Jackson's paintings in exchange for the hit." She pointed a fork at me. "Now that would be something you could sink your teeth into. You say Alan has 13 paintings on his gallery wall and one in a safety deposit box. You should really find out if this Alan got his hands on some other of Jackson's paintings that are now mysteriously missing. That would be something I could buy and something you can sell to a jury."

I leaned back. "How could I figure that out, though? Jackson apparently gave Alan these paintings when he was a kid in exchange for drugs. It's not like there'll be a paper trail on these exchanges. I found out from a source who knew Jackson back in the day that Jackson gave up 13 paintings to Alan. I never heard about any other ones."

"But Alan apparently got a painting from Jackson when Jackson was 25 or 26," Harper reminded me. "And you caught Alan in a lie about the last time he saw Jackson, assuming that he got that one painting from Jackson himself and not through a third party. Talk to Leland, see if he knows anything more about any dealings Jackson and Alan might have had throughout the years. Leland might know something. If Jackson gave Alan additional paintings and Alan doesn't currently have those paintings, that's circumstantial evidence that Alan gave those paintings away to somebody. If he didn't give them away, then there would be a paper trail on who purchased them. If, on the other hand, he gave them to somebody – say, in exchange for a hit – there wouldn't be a paper trail. There you go."

I nodded. "I'll definitely talk to Leland about it. You're right, though. If anybody will know about whether or not Jackson gave Alan additional paintings, it would be him."

I looked over at Rina, who was listening to all of this with rapt attention. She smiled at me when I caught her staring at Harper. "What Mom does is cool," she said. "I'm gonna be just like her one day. Just wait and see."

"God forbid," Harper said. "Why anybody would want my life is beyond me."

I chuckled. "Be thankful you have a kid who admires you and what you do. Nate here, he wants to be an actor when he grows up. Can you imagine?"

Nate smiled and nodded. "I'm good, too. I get all the leads in my school plays."

"Well, he certainly has the looks for it," Harper said. "Like his father."

"Ha ha," I said.

"Well, you do." She raised an eyebrow. "I can just imagine when you get back on the dating scene. Women will be lined up for that one."

I nodded, thinking of Carina. I didn't want women to be lined up. I only wanted one woman in line, and she lived 1,300 miles away.

"Let's change the subject," I said, looking at my kids. Amelia was smiling and Nate wasn't. I needed to be sensitive to Nate's feelings on the matter.

We talked some more at the table. I then said goodbye to Harper and the kids and headed home with my kids.

In the car, I was astounded about how much Amelia had absorbed from my conversation with Harper. She was only 7, but I swear she was 7 going on 17. "Dad," she said. "Do you think Harper was right about that guy you saw in New York? Do you think he hired somebody to kill Jackson?"

I sighed. In a way, I hated that I was exposing my kids to the dirtier parts of my job. But it couldn't be helped. They would find out sooner or later. Might as well be now. "I don't know, kiddo. I don't know." I paused. "It's Sunday." I took a deep breath. "What do you two think about dropping in on grandma?"

To my surprise, they both perked up when I said that. "We get to see grandma?" Nate asked. For the first time in a long time, I actually heard enthusiasm in his voice. "Rad."

Amelia nodded her head eagerly. "Oh please oh please," she said.

I looked at the two of them. "We haven't seen her in a long time. Why am I just now figuring out how much the two of you like her?"

"Guess you just haven't been paying attention, Dad," Nate said.

"Guess not."

Chapter Fourteen

A HALF HOUR LATER, I arrived at the trailer park where my mother lived. Olivia Barton, which was my mother's name, lived in a single-wide trailer at the very end of the block. I felt a bit of shame that I still allowed her to live like this, but she always told me she loved it. She was friendly with all her neighbors and told me she was always getting together with them to play cards or drink wine or watch *The Last of Us*. In a way, I was envious she had such a tight circle. I certainly didn't have that tight of a circle. Then again, my neighborhood wasn't like a trailer park. In a trailer park, everyone lives so close to everyone that it's easier to get to know and befriend them.

I got to her trailer and got out of the car with the kids. Her lot neighbor, whose name was Rosy Dalton, waved at me. "Hey, Damien," she said. "Long time no see, huh? You finally going to see Olivia?" She shook her head, but she smiled too. "She's been talking and talking about you and the kids. Wondering why you won't return her phone calls."

I swallowed hard. "Hey, Rosy," I said. "Yeah, I'm seeing Mom. I figured the kids should probably get to see her."

"Well, she'll be tickled to see you. Just tickled."

I rolled my eyes and knocked on the door.

Mom answered right away. She saw the three of us on the other side of her door and put her hand up to her chest in a mock heart attack gesture. "And the dead shall rise," she said. "Damien."

"Hi Mom," I said.

"Let me see my grandbabies," she said as she looked at Nate and Amelia. "Good God, Nate, you're growing like a weed." Then she looked at me and rolled her eyes. "Oh, I forgot you don't even like me to say the word weed."

"Mom," I said in a low voice. "I told you I don't care if you smoke pot. I just don't want you to roll a joint in front of the kids, that's all." Unfortunately, the last time I was visiting Mom with the kids, that's exactly what happened. Mom was rolling joints on the coffee table and didn't stop rolling them when we all got into the living room. She talked to the kids, asking them about their school work, rolling the joints the entire time.

"Oh, Jesus H. Christ, watching me roll a perfectly legal product ain't gonna hurt nothin'."

She looked at the three of us standing in the living room. "Well don't just stand there, sit down guys." Then she hollered out the door. "Hey Rosy, the prodigal son just returned. Why don't you come and say hello, huh?"

"I did," Rosy hollered back. "Does this mean Bunco is off for tonight?"

"Ah, fuck no," Mom hollered back to Rosy. "Like I would miss that." She turned back to me. "I always win about $100 smackeroos when I play those suckers. No way would I give that up."

"Mom," I said, "that's great, but I need to talk to you."

"You do, huh? Well, imagine that. My hoity-toity son wants to talk to his white trash mama. Hell, he even made a special trip to do it. I guess I shoulda rolled out the red carpet but it's in the dry cleaners right now."

I saw Amelia grin, laugh and shake her head. Nate, too, looked amused. I guess they weren't used to grown-ups talking like this around them.

"What's so funny, kiddo?" she asked Amelia.

"You are, grandma."

"Well, it's not like I'm trying to do a *Saturday Night Live* skit or nothing like that. This is just me. What you see is what you get."

Ain't that the truth. I looked over at Nate and Amelia and wondered how I could possibly get rid of them so I could talk to my mother alone. Her trailer was tiny – it was a one-bedroom, only about 600 square feet, so there wasn't anyplace for Nate and Amelia to go. "Let's go on the porch," I said.

There was a tiny stoop right outside the door. It had an awning above it. The stoop wasn't anything more than concrete steps. Considering it didn't smell that much of cigarettes in the trailer and my mother was a chain-smoker, I figured she probably came out on this stoop to smoke all the time.

"What porch?" Mom asked. "Oh, you mean my stoop. Yeah, okay, let's go out there." She looked over at the kids. "Sorry, kids, I guess your dad needs to tell me something top secret. We'll be right back." Then she started to laugh. "Oh, I hope your kids don't watch those slasher films. Whenever somebody says they'll be right back, it really means they're about to be hung up on a meat hook."

We got out on the porch and Mom immediately lit up a

cigarette. "So, what was so goddamned important that you couldn't ask me in front of your kids?"

I took a deep breath. "Who is my father?"

She shrugged. "I told you once before, it was some random guy I picked up in a bar. I know we've been through this a million times. I guess you don't like that answer, and I'm sorry you don't, but that's the truth."

Another deep breath. "Who is he really?"

She gave me a look. "Why you asking these questions now, Damien?" She smiled wickedly. "Your father was a jackal who knocked me up with the seed of the Devil. That's why I named you Damien. Your birth was the same as Damien in those *Omen* movies." She took a drag on her cigarette. "Sorry I didn't tell you earlier, but I figured you would find your destiny sooner or later. Guess now's as good as any other time, huh?"

"Mom...."

She took another drag of her cigarette and looked into the distance. "Why are you just now asking me this?" Her voice was finally serious and I knew I struck a nerve. "Why now?"

I didn't want to tell her I had seen a psychic who told me she was raped by a rich guy who became my father.

"I just wanted to know, that's all."

"After all these years." She shook her head, stomped her cigarette on the ground and then immediately lit up another one. "After all these years."

"After all these years." I put my arm around her. "You know, don't you?"

She shrugged. "I know nothing," she said. "I certainly don't know your father."

"But you know who he is, don't you?"

Another drag on her cigarette. She put her hand on her

hair and looked at her door. "Your kids are awful quiet in there," she said. "We better check on them. God forbid they put on that gas stove and blow up the house." Then she chuckled. "Which would actually be an improvement to this dump."

"Mom, I don't have all day," I said, and then immediately regretted I was pressing her so much. "I mean…"

"Yeah. I know what you mean. It's always the same with you, Damien. Always the same. Always going, going, going. Never stopping for long enough to just enjoy life." She wagged her cigarette at me. "You might think you're so much better than me. You made it out. Good for you. Big shot lawyer, getting your name in the paper all the time. Winning cases, drinking champagne with the muckety-mucks. You probably can't imagine people like me might actually be happy."

"Well, I am happy," she continued on. "I'm happy with my 20-inch television with the old-school glass lens, my pipes that are always rusting out and my bed I found next to the dumpster outside. I have to defrost my piece of shit refrigerator or else everything in there gets iced over. I might not have the money to live in Brookside or Leawood and maybe I can't afford a decent car, a decent bed or a decent refrigerator, but goddammit, I have friends and that's all you really need in life, huh? God knows I proved to the world you don't have to have a relationship with your own son to be happy."

"Mom, I'm not talking about that. I know you're happy. To tell you the truth, I envy you your relationships with your neighbors. That's not why I came here."

"No. You came here to reopen an old wound." She shook her head. "You know when I saw you and the kids coming in the door, I was happy. I thought you wanted to visit with me. Turns out you don't really give a shit about seeing me, you just want to come here and nit-pick me just like you always do."

"Mom, I-"

"Okay, then. Okay. You win." She threw her cigarette on the ground dramatically and, just as dramatically, stomped on it. "You fucking win. Your father is a rich bastard whose name is Biff Tannin the third." She smiled. "No, I'm just giving you shit about that. His name is Joshua Roland, and he's one of the richest men in the city."

Chapter Fifteen

"JOSHUA ROLAND. Where have I heard that name before?"

"Where haven't you heard that name before? Listen, we got several big-time families in this town. The Kempers, the Kauffmans and the Hunts. Oh, and the Blochs, too, I guess. So, yeah, those are the big four families. Right underneath those families are the Rolands. Their money goes way back. The great-grandfather made his fortune in diamonds. Guess he ripped off a war lord in Africa and was lucky to escape with his life back in 1909. Whatever, he made his money in diamonds and then his son got into shipping and lumber. By the time it got down to Joshua, the whole family was richer than Roosevelt."

"How did you meet him?"

"Josh? I was a dancer in a club back then. Nude dancer. Totally nude dancer. Guess you didn't know that about me, did ya?"

"What club did you dance at that was totally nude?"

"It was a club that you didn't hear about. An underground place. Needed a password. Josh was one of the regulars." She shrugged. "You might not know it now, but your old lady was quite the looker back in the day."

I actually could believe that. She was 51 years old and the years of chain smoking, alcoholism and doing drugs had caught up with her. But, underneath the leathery skin, I could see the young girl she once was. The dark haired, green-eyed, olive-skinned young girl. I could imagine she caught some eyes back then.

"I thought you were a hooker back then," I said.

"Nah. I became one after I had you." Then she shrugged. "I mean yeah, I was a hooker, but I found my johns in the club. It was common for us girls to find some of the guys who would ask us for lap dances or whatever and give them a little something-something extra for the right price."

"I see."

"Anyhow," she continued on, "your father, Josh Roland, was one of my best customers. I gave him lap dance after lap dance, always in this private room. Tipped really well, too. If I could have stayed at that job, I certainly wouldn't be living in a dump like this." She waved her hand around. "I mean, I love this dump, but it is a dump, you gotta admit."

"I don't deny that."

"But, you know, I was only 15 at the time. That's why I ended up losing that job. The cops finally raided the place because the entire club was illegal. Kansas City didn't permit nude dancing. They still don't, really. I mean, they do, at that Bazooka's place, but it's a juice bar. What fun is that?"

"Bazooka's can't even have nude girls now. Not since the 2010 ordinance banning it."

"Well, I'll be goddamned. It's still a juice bar, though?"

"As far as I know." I actually represented a dancer who got caught with a DUI several years back, which was how I found out the place couldn't have nudity anymore.

"No nudity and no alcohol. What is this world coming to."

"I don't know. Anyhow, you were saying…"

"Yeah. I was saying. Josh was one of my best clients but I was underaged. I had an ID that said I was 21, though, which was how I got that job." She took a deep breath. "And you know what, I wasn't into him that much. I gave it to the guys willing to pay for it but he wasn't. He took it from me anyhow, though."

"What does that mean?"

"It means he followed me out of the club one night and dragged me into an alley. He beat the crap out of me and raped me by the dumpster." She shook her head. "Raped me by the dumpster. That's really ironic if you think about it. I mean, he treated me like trash, so it was only fitting he raped me next to the real trash."

I looked at her face and saw how devastated she was about it. She tried to hide it, but I could tell the memory was painful for her.

"How did you find out he was my dad?"

"You mean, how did I know he was your dad when I was doing men from the club all the time? That's what you mean?"

"Yeah. That's what I mean."

"I fucking saw him about a month later in the club and went over to him with a pair of scissors and cut off a lock of his hair. By then I had stopped getting my monthly rag and I had the feeling he was the bastard who put that bun in my oven." She started to laugh. "He never even knew I had cut off a piece of his hair. He was that wasted when I did it. For that matter, he was that wasted when he raped me. I took that hair and kept it, and when you got born, I sent it in to the lab and his DNA matched yours."

I sighed. "Mom, why didn't you-"

"Soak him for all he was worth? Hang him out to dry? Trust me, kiddo, I wanted to. Was dying to. I was all set for him to be my meal ticket. My way out of this dump. I knew I could take him for all he was worth, especially since I was only 16 when I had you. Man, that would have been a scandal, huh? Prominent muckety-muck fatcat bastard knocking up an underaged girl. I didn't even need to prove the guy raped me. Just having him declared your father would be enough. Statutory rape, you know."

"Yeah. Seriously, Mom, why didn't you do all that? Establish him as my dad and all that?"

She shook her head. "Nope, I wasn't going to do that. Listen, and listen real good. I love you, kid. Always have. I might not have always showed it so much, because, you know, I've had my issues with the drink and the drugs all my life. Well, I had that problem for most of my life, and, trust me, it got worse after I was raped. There was one thing I wouldn't ever do, and that was give you up. I knew that bastard, and his family, would steal you from me if they knew about you. I was just a 16-year-old living in a trailer, making ends meet as a nude dancer. Your bastard father was part of a billionaire family. What do you think would have happened if I would have come after him for child support?"

She continued on. "I'll tell you what would have happened. He would have gotten custody of you. No way did I want that for you, to be raised by a father that violent and corrupt. Who cares if he was richer than Croesus? I didn't want you nowhere near him. So, no, I didn't do a goddamned thing when I found out he was your dad. And I don't regret that one bit. Not for one single moment have I ever regretted that move."

As I sat there, listening to her, I thought, again and again, to the words of Mystic Anna. How the hell did she know? How could she possibly have known? *I* didn't even know. I also absorbed the fact that my father, the man who gave me genes, my mom's sperm donor, was a billionaire. How weird was that?

"You don't regret not trying to get money out of him?"

"Oh, hell no. I told you, I wouldn't let that bastard get a piece of you. Any piece of you." She shook her head. "In fact, I'm starting to already regret telling you now about it. I know you'll track that guy down and announce he's your dad, just like in the movies. The last thing I want is for you to get sucked into that man's bullshit. Into his family's bullshit. They're always in the news. Josh has been nailed for a DUI three times been busted for drugs several times. His sister is a screw-up too. She's been in and out of rehab and the looney bin a time or three. That family might have money but they got no brains."

I hung my head. I suddenly felt guilty for the way I'd treated her. I had hated her for so many years because I felt she was a shitty parent. I suddenly saw the sacrifice she made for me and it tore me up. I never thought she cared, but I suddenly realized she did.

"Mom," I said softly, "I can help you out financially. I settled a case last year for millions and got over 4 million out of it. I would like to help you."

Her eyes got big and she raised both of her brows. "Woo hoo, look at you. You're a millionaire. Congrats. I guess you joined the ranks of the muckety-mucks yourself, didn't you?"

"I'm hardly a muckety-muck," I said. "I still remember where I came from."

"Son, you've never remembered where you came from. You could give shit less about these people around here and you never did. You were always so anxious to get out of this place, as if it's all so goddamned bad." Another cigarette appeared in her mouth. She lit it and took a long drag. "I'll tell you one thing. I wouldn't trade any one of these people around this trailer park for any one of your fancy friends. Not a one. You can keep your money. I do just fine."

"Mom, you're working at Wal-Mart," I said. "Let me help you."

"And what the hell is wrong with working at Wal-Mart?" Mom shook her head. "It's a good, honest living. I know, I lived the other way, prostituting myself and dealing drugs. That's no way to live. But working at Wal-Mart isn't something shameful. I got friends working there, just like I got friends living around here. I take your money, and I'm suddenly living in Leawood or some hoity-toity place like that, with snooty neighbors and an HOA telling me to take my Christmas lights down on January 1."

She pointed to the Christmas lights still up, even though it was early May. "I'll be goddamned if anybody is going to tell me to take my lights down or make me water my lawn because we can't have brown grass, ever. You go to those neighborhoods and never see a goddamned car in the driveway. You know why that is? It's because their HOA forbids them to park their car anywhere but in their garage."

She had a point. I hated those busy-body HOAs too. "Mom, you don't have to move just because I give you money. You can live here, but you'll have money to see a doctor when you need to and get your sink repaired. I saw there were dishes piled up. I don't know if that's because your sink isn't working or because you just don't like doing dishes. Hell, you can even buy a dishwasher. Or maybe a double-wide in this same complex. You can live the way you want, but you don't have to live quite so desperate."

I said the wrong thing when I used the term "desperate" and I knew it as I said it.

"Boy, who you calling desperate? I know you're not talking to me when you say the word 'desperate,' because I just told you I don't want your goddamned money. I do just fine. I've been doing just fine all these years without your money, and I'll keep on doing just fine. I told you, I like living this way. Keep it."

"Mom-"

"Keep it. End of story." She glared at me. "Desperate." She shook her head. "Desperate. I know you weren't talking about me when you just said that."

I put my hands on my knees. "I'm sorry I offended you."

"Whatever." She shook her head. "And listen, I know you sent me a $100,000 cashier's check last year but I didn't cash it. I figured if you couldn't be bothered to come here and give it to me in person, I didn't need your goddamned money."

I took a deep breath. "I wondered about that. When I saw you still had an ancient fridge, still didn't have a dishwasher and still didn't get new hubcaps for your car, I figured you just blew all that money I gave you."

"Well, I didn't blow that money. I don't drug or gamble no more. Guess you don't know that about me. But, no, I didn't cash that check. You can have it back."

"I don't want it back. I want you to cash it."

"Whatever." Another big drag on her cigarette. "Hey, I read in the paper your buddy Connor O'Brien just had his sentence commuted. Wonder how he managed that. Wonder who got blackmailed or bribed for that to happen." She glared at me some more. "Not that I'm pissed about that. I always did like that boy. Glad he's not going to be a lifer after all."

She had changed the subject, so I knew there was no more pressing her into letting me help her out. At the same time, I kinda freaked out when she mused about who was "bribed or blackmailed for that to happen." That was a lucky guess, or maybe it was a joke, but it hit way too close to home.

"Nobody was bribed or blackmailed. You saw the article. The Governor just decided that because Connor didn't mean to kill that guy, coupled with the fact that he was so young when it happened, plus he's been a model prisoner, it was the right thing to commute his sentence. That's all there is to it."

"Yeah. Well, great. Lucky break for that kid. What about all the others? They getting out too?"

"With any luck, yes they are."

"You getting the band back together, then?" She snorted and dragged on her cigarette. "The five Musketeers. Shit, you cared much more for them than you did your own family, namely me. Why you always felt you had to run off and live on the streets with them, when you had a perfectly good home with me, I'll never know."

"You do know. Steven Harrington beat on me. Remember?"

She shook her head. "Yeah, marrying him wasn't my most shining moment, was it?" She stubbed out her cigarette and lit up another one. "Sorry about that. I kicked him to the curb soon enough, but you still didn't come home. You guys all ended up in that detention center, that Ozanam place, didn't you?"

"Actually, Mom, that was where I met them. In Ozanam."

"Yeah, that's right. That's right. I always forget what came first. Well they were bad news, and they still are, I guess. I mean, you don't end up in prison for life by acting like a choir boy, do ya."

"They aren't in prison for life."

"They were supposed to be. Until their sentences got commuted – Nick, Tommy and Jack. Still don't know how that happened, either. Something tells me you're behind it all."

I cleared my throat. "This conversation is over."

"Yeah, just as I thought. Well, that's fine. You did your good deed in making sure your buddies don't rot in prison. Now you want to do a good deed by me, but I won't let ya. I won't let ya, because I think you're sneaky and got something up your sleeve. I don't quite know what it is, but you want to get me out of this place and into your fancy neighborhood. I'm not buying what you're trying to sell. So, I thank you, but the answer is no."

"That's fine."

"It sure is. Now, do you have any other questions to ask me? Your kids have to be wondering where the hell we are."

"No. No more questions."

"Good. Let's go inside."

We went inside and the kids insisted on staying the day. Mom played cards with them, and, at some point, her neighbor Rosy and some other girls from around the park showed up and they all played Bunco with the kids. I never saw the kids have such a good time.

While they played their games, I fixed Mom's sink and garbage disposal and then went outside and worked on her car. She was out of oil, which meant the engine would blow up at any moment. She also needed brake fluid and three new tires. I went to the auto parts store and got what she needed, and then I changed her tires, topped off her fluids and changed her oil.

When I was through, she didn't even acknowledge what I did, let alone thank me, but I didn't care. It was enough that I knew her car wouldn't break down in the middle of the night and she could do her dishes and use her garbage disposal.

As we drove home that night, I wondered if Mom was right about me. I wanted to force her to live the way I wanted. I wanted to get her out of the trailer park and into a solid home. She wanted to live life on her terms, and I really didn't want her to. That was part of the reason why I kept my distance from her.

I resolved to change how I saw her from that point on. I had to accept her for who she was if I ever hoped to repair my relationship with her.

Which was what I would do.

Chapter Sixteen

I WENT to see Leland the day after I saw my mother. I would have to find out some information about Alan Taylor and his relationship with Jackson. If anybody would know if Jackson gave Alan Taylor more paintings on the sly, it would be Leland. He knew everything there was to know about Jackson's career.

I got to his home and David invited me in. David seemed to be much friendlier to me than he was in the past. Probably Leland had words with him.

"Hello, Mr. Harrington," he said, reminding me of Lurch in the *Addams Family.* "Leland is expecting you."

He led me through the house to the den where Leland was relaxing in a large leather chair. Just like the other day, he had a cocktail in his hand and was sipping it. Dill was nowhere to be found.

"Dill's off gallivanting," Leland said, sweeping his right hand around. "Wanted to get out of the house, so I sent him to Palm Springs to have some fun. Wish I could have joined him, but this stupid ankle bracelet means I can't get out of town when I want to. God, I can't wait to get rid of this goddamned bracelet."

"Soon enough," I said. "In the meantime, I wanted to update you on some things I found out in New York."

"I'm all ears," he said. "In the meantime, I have a cocktail here for you. I'm drinking a vodka gimlet right now and have another Bloody Mary for you. You seemed to really like the last one."

I nodded, hoping he would give me a Bloody Mary. He was right – I did really like that last one. "Thanks."

"Have a seat, kick back your heels, and tell me all you found out."

"Well," I said, taking a sip of the drink, "I visited Mystic Anna, but I didn't get a vibe off of her that she was involved in this. Not that she's not. But I didn't get that vibe."

"Whatever," Leland said. "I don't want you to let her go, Damien. I still think she's up to no good."

Dill was right – Leland *did* have a hard-on for Mystic Anna. For whatever reason, he was convinced the psychic did it.

"Leland, I don't quite understand the obsession you have for her," I said. "I talked to her and just didn't feel like she had anything to do with this. I'm an attorney and I have to go with my gut most of the time My gut is telling me she had nothing to do with it."

Leland finally sighed. "Okay, I'll just tell you why I want you to investigate Mystic Anna so hard. It's because…" He hung his head. "I don't like her. Every time Dill sees her, he comes back so different. He has threatened to leave me several times because Mystic Ann told him he needs to. She hurts people, Damien, with her bad advice. I guess I just want it to be true that she did it."

"Leland," I said, feeling frustrated with him. "This isn't how this works. I don't use the legal system to push a vendetta. If I serve up an alternative suspect to the jury, it has to be plausible. Now, you're telling me you just wanted me to investigate Mystic Anna because you feel she gives bad advice to people. This isn't how this works. This isn't how any of this works."

Leland sipped his cocktail daintily and then looked me right in the eye. "No. I guess that's right. Truth be told, that isn't the real reason why I wanted you to talk to her."

"Oh? Enlighten me."

"I wanted you to talk to her because Dill told me that it was very important you do so. I don't know why, it was just that Mystic Anna told him to get you up there to see her as soon as possible. Guess she had some information for you."

"Me? She didn't know me. How did she even get my name?"

"Dill told her you were representing me. She said she knew you would be representing me. Her crystal told her about that and she wanted to see you. I'm sorry I lied to you about that, but if you knew that I really didn't want her investigated, I was worried you would be pissed for wasting your time."

"I *am* pissed for your wasting my time," I said. Then I thought better of it. After all, because of Mystic Anna, I finally knew who my father was. Perhaps the knowledge that I was the son of a billionaire could come in handy one day. Maybe that was why Mystic Anna wanted to see me so badly – she wanted to tell me about my father. I never really believed in psychics and Tarot, but I had to admit that seeing Mystic Anna was making me re-think all of that.

"Well, sorry. I hope your visit to her was worth your time, though."

"It kind of was. But that's not why I wanted to talk to you today."

"Go fish," he said. "Tell me what you need to tell me."

"Actually, I have things to ask you. How much do you know about the business relationship between Jackson and Alan Taylor?"

"Alan Taylor is the sleazy drug dealer who Jackson knew when he was 15, correct?"

"One and the same. From what I understand, Jackson gave Alan Taylor 13 of his paintings *in lieu* of cash when he needed drugs from Alan. This was all when he was around 15 or 16. Now, I've already figured out that Alan Taylor received at least one other painting that wasn't given to him during this period of time – he has a painting Jackson painted during one of his latter periods. What I need to know is whether or not you believe Alan Taylor got other paintings from Jackson. This a very pivotal question, so answer it carefully."

"Okay. Now, you know about the 13 paintings Jackson gave Alan when he was 15 and 16, in exchange for drugs." He nodded his head. "And I can tell you Jackson gave Alan paintings on at least three other occasions, sometimes several paintings at a time."

My ears perked up when he said that. "Are you sure about that? Why did he do that? At some point, he had a lot of cash to give him, so why was he still giving Alan paintings?"

Leland rolled his eyes. "I guess you haven't been listening, but I told you Jackson gave away most of his money. Jackson didn't like money. He didn't like having a large bank account. Money reminded him of his family, and how messed-up they were. He came to the conclusion that money was the root of their problems. His mom was messed up, his step-father was messed up and his father was dead. Dead in a plane crash, although that was suspicious in and of itself. It was a little Cessna he piloted. The remains of the plane, and the remains of his father, were never found. There was all kinds of talk that his father, Hugh Michaelson, was actually killed by powerful interests who wanted him dead. Jackson figured that if he was broke all the time that he could avoid all the problems his family had."

"But he got paid a lot of money. Like when you gave him over a million dollars for just one show."

"Yes, that's true, but I told you, he gave it all away. Almost every dime. So, from what I understand, he dealt with Alan Taylor by giving him paintings. Alan Taylor isn't stupid, love. He knows a good thing when it comes across his desk. He knew how valuable those paintings are."

"So, how many paintings did he possibly get from Jackson over the years?"

"Oh, I don't know. Easily 6 or 7 more paintings, in addition to the 13 he gave him when he was a kid. Easily that."

"I see. So, I guess it's just a matter of proving it." I took a deep breath. "See, here's the theory that I'm working with right now. Alan Taylor needed cash. He needed it yesterday. He was in hock to everyone in town, including several drug dealers. He filed for bankruptcy. He didn't incorporate, which meant his creditors could have easily taken everything he owned from him. He needed to get money fast, because the last thing he wanted was for his Chapter 7 liquidation bankruptcy to go through. If that happened, the bankruptcy trustee would have held a fire sale. All of his paintings and his entire gallery would be gone. Not to mention, these drug dealers he owed would have killed him."

Leland nodded. "I see. So, he has all these paintings

Jackson gave him. He wanted them to become much more valuable, so he killed Jackson." He pointed at me. "You're good. See, I knew you would figure it out."

"Right. He needed those paintings to get him out of hock to everyone. The only sticking point is that he has an air-tight alibi for the night Jackson was killed. He was holding a fund-raiser in New York. I spoke with several people who saw him there, holding court the entire evening. So he had to have money to pay somebody to do it. A hit like that would easily be $5 million."

"So he gave some of Jackson's paintings in exchange for the hit." Leland nodded his head approvingly. "Bingo."

"Bingo. Now, I have to figure out how to prove what happened. That's going to be the tough part. Right now, I don't have any idea who he might have hired, which is the first sticking point. The second one would be proving that bartering took place, a painting or two in exchange for the hit. I think the second part might be easy enough to prove, once I figure out the first part. But figuring out the first part will be like finding a needle in a haystack. Unfortunately."

"Well, do your magic. If nothing else, even if you can't figure all that out, you can still drag Alan Taylor onto the stand and make him look bad, right? That would be your alternative plan, right?"

"That might be the only thing I can do. I mean, I can certainly send my investigator out to figure out what kind of criminal connections Alan Taylor might have had, maybe mob ties. But if he's smart, he would have hired somebody with no prior connection to him. No way of tracking the hit man down. It's still a long shot that I can prove anything with regards to Alan Taylor, but I can certainly hit him with as much circumstantial evidence as I can."

"Okay, then." He nodded. "That's good to hear. Good

to hear you seem to be on top of it." He seemed dubious. "What else you got?"

"The case is still young," I said. "I'm still in the middle of my investigation. Don't worry, by the time the case comes to trial, I'll be way ahead of the game. Mark my words."

"I hope you're right. Oh, dear, I haven't been able to sleep lately. Even the Ambien hasn't been helping out lately. I may not seem like I'm stressed about all this, but, trust me, it's all I think about. I just can't figure out what happened. That's what freaks me out even more than the actual charges. I've tried and tried to remember what happened and there's just nothing. No memories of that night. I've tried a hypnotist, meditation and shrinks. Nothing." He took a deep breath. "I'm just afraid that I really did it and just blocked it out. That's what scares me."

"But Leland, why would you do that? Did you have a reason why you wanted Jackson dead? I'm sure your shrink told you that even when you are under the heavy influence of drugs or alcohol, you won't do something that is just not in your nature."

He took a deep breath. "Well, you know, you've read all the media stories about me. Scandalous stories. Especially those stories in *The National Enquirer*. They're ridiculous for the most part. But…"

I stared at him, waiting for him to finish his thought. It was entirely possible Leland would end up giving me the keys to the puzzle. "But?"

"Well, okay, I might have been a little bit jealous of Dill's relationship with Jackson. But it's not the way you might think. I don't think they had something going. I don't think that in the least. But.." He sighed. "Oh, God, this will sound so juvenile, so childish. But I discovered Jackson. I got him off the streets snd introduced him around to my wealthy friends. I made him the toast of the town, from Manhattan to Milan. If it weren't for me, Jackson would still be doing graffiti and sleeping on the streets."

I didn't believe that. I didn't think Leland believed it, either. A talent like Jackson would find its way onto the world stage, no matter who became his benefactor. If it weren't Leland, it would've been somebody else. Somebody would have discovered that kid eventually.

Then again, Van Gogh died in abject poverty, so…

"Go on," I said.

"Well, I took Jackson under my wing and gave him his start. And he was grateful for that, don't get me wrong. But he started to call Dill whenever he had a new painting he wanted to show off. He would start calling Dill first. He would send a picture text to Dill before he sent one to me. Dill said Jackson appreciated Dill's input and Dill's opinion over my own. Something about how Dill 'got' Jackson more than I did. That Dill was more on Jackson's wavelength than me. And, yes, that hurt. That hurt, because I felt like I was starting to play second-fiddle to the two of them."

I didn't quite know what I wanted to do with Leland's "confession." So, Leland had some jealousy. So what? Unless he had it in him to kill Jackson, that meant exactly nothing.

"Were you angry enough to kill Jackson?"

What he said next was something that floored me.

"I don't know."

Chapter Seventeen

I PUT my head in my hands as Leland sat across from me. That was one thing I didn't want to hear.

"What do you mean, you don't know? That's the one thing you *should* know."

"I don't know. See, here's the problem. I've been seeing a shrink, right? And I've been telling him about what I remember about that night. And he's helped me uncover the fact that I really hate Jackson, deep down. That I had rage towards him. He's told me we all have it in us to kill. We just have to be presented with the right circumstances. He told me that when my defenses were down with the Ambien and the alcohol, I might have done it. My id, my inner core, is what was boiling at Jackson. In my every day life, I have these other things that keep me from acting on what is at my core. The superego and the ego. Taking the Ambien and the alcohol took all that away, and I just acted according to how I really felt. That's what my shrink told me."

"Leland, come on. You were that angry with Jackson

just because he has been calling Dill and showing Dill his new work before he shows you? I find that hard to believe." I did believe part of what Leland was saying was true. Intoxication *does* make your inner core come to the surface. Your hidden thoughts and feelings come out when you're intoxicated. The saying *In Vino Veritas* – "In wine is truth"- was the Latin term for that very phenomenon.

The fact that Leland's psychologist was telling him that he might have killed Dill worried me, to say the very least.

Leland paused and took another sip of his cocktail. He shook his head. "No, it's not just that. It's not just that. That's just one of the reasons why I was angry at Jackson. But there's more."

"Go on." I had the feeling this case was about to take a turn. I closed my eyes, imagining that I would possibly end up pleading Leland out by the time everything was said and done. "Tell me what else Jackson did that angered you."

He sat back in his chair and stared at the ceiling. Another sip of his drink. "I caught them," he said. "Dill and Jackson. I caught them together." He started to cry. "Dill told me it was just the one time but then he started to tell me he felt protective of Jackson. He told me that he was scared for Jackson because of what Mystic Anna was telling him about Jackson and how Jackson was in danger. How Jackson had so much darkness around him. Dill told me he wanted to save Jackson."

"You caught them? What do you mean, you caught them?"

He rolled his eyes. "Do I have to spell it out for you? I caught them that night. The night at the party, I walked in on them. They were up against the wall. Jackson was behind Dill and they were fucking. And Dill had been telling me for weeks that he felt protective of Jackson and he wanted to save him. That's why I hate Mystic Anna. That's why I despise her. She turned Dill towards Jackson. She gave Dill the idea that Jackson was a boy that he needed to save. Dill didn't even know Jackson but then he started to see Mystic Anna, and, suddenly, he was coming at me, telling me he felt the need to protect Jackson from his evil demons."

By this time, Leland was really crying. "Dill was going to leave me for Jackson. I know he was. I suspected it, anyhow, but when I caught them at the party, I knew. I found out that this wasn't the first time they had gotten together. I was sick that night, Damien, sick about what I saw. That's why I was going to stay there and sleep there that night. Then I take the Ambien and start drinking and wake up next to a dead Jackson. My knife is in his chest. My knife, Damien. Oh, God, I think I might've done it."

I swallowed hard. "Leland, now, come on. We can't get too far ahead of ourselves." I was seeing the entire case unraveling before my very eyes. "We can try for a plea agreement but I don't want to give up. You don't know if you killed Jackson. You're not sure about that. I admit, this whole scenario is looking pretty grim, but I don't want to plead you out unless I'm sure you're guilty."

Leland nodded. "Okay, you keep on looking. You keep on trying to figure out if somebody else did it. But I'm starting to think I was the one after all. I'm starting to think that, Damien." He took another huge sip of his drink and shook his head vigorously. "What if I did it? What if I did it? I'm going to die in prison. Oh my God…"

I sat there across from him, my heart sinking to my shoes. My gut was screaming at me not to plead Leland out. It was screaming at me to look further. I had to trust my gut.

I had always trusted my gut before and it rarely steered me wrong.

I finally stood up and put my hand on his shoulder. "Leland, uh, I have to go. I'm sorry. I'll be seeing you at the arraignment. 1:30, don't forget."

I hated to leave him there, sobbing and drinking, but I had to get away. I couldn't have his words in my headspace anymore. I couldn't let him influence me. I had to do my job and keep trying to find an alternative explanation for the murder. That was the only thing I could do. Leland was afraid he had done it.

I was still determined to show he didn't.

Chapter Eighteen

A COUPLE OF WEEKS LATER, I was starting to get to the end of my rope. But I had Garrett still working on it and he gave me some tidbits I could really chew on.

"Hey," he said when he called me. "I got a few things I found out. A few connections that could really help you."

"What are those connections?"

"Dr. Melber," he said. "You remember him, don't you?"

"Sure, sure. He started Jackson on prescription pills after his bicycle accident. Why do you ask about him?"

"Did you know he also was Leland's doctor back in the day? That he prescribed Leland's Ambien?"

I nodded. "That's interesting but not surprising. After all, Dr. Melber practices on the Upper West Side. That's where Leland had his old penthouse suite." I wrote that down. "Still, who knows? Maybe that's something."

"Yeah, who knows. Anyhow, that was just something I thought you might want to know."

"Thanks. Did you find out anything more about Alan

Taylor? Any mob ties, any way for him to get ahold of a professional hit man?"

"No, I didn't find out anything like that. As you know, he's a drug dealer and apparently owes other drug dealers. Or, at least, he owed other drug dealers. See, he got his drugs from the source. From Bolivia, Colombia and places like that. He dealt with the guys who brought those drugs from South America. These are some bad, rough dudes. I've been looking into their backgrounds, the guys Alan deals with, but there's nothing yet I can pinpoint. No transaction stands out to me as a smoking gun on the matter. I'll keep looking, though."

"Yeah, keep looking."

I had gone to the arraignment with Leland, and, by then, he had changed his tune. He took me aside before the court date and informed me I was to forget what he told me at his house.

"I didn't kill him," he said. "Keep looking for the person who did."

That meant that pleading him out would be out of the question. I would have to try the case, by hook or by crook, which was fine with me.

Yet, I felt like I had just hit a wall in my investigation. Nothing really was panning out for me.

I had gone through every piece of evidence, every witness statement, every single crumb, and nothing was turning up.

Yet something was calling me to go back to New York for more evidence. Once again, it was my gut giving me the direction to go in. Plus, I wanted to see Carina.

Carina and I had been in contact. I Zoomed her every evening. I helped the kids with their homework, and, when they were in their rooms, doing their thing on the computer or watching television, I would Zoom with her. And I knew I really couldn't deny it.

I was falling in love with her.

So, that was a part of why I wanted to go to New York – to see Carina. But I also felt there was something that I was overlooking. I felt that if I went up there again, I could find the missing puzzle piece.

THAT MONDAY, I dropped the kids off with Harper and headed up to New York again. I would only stay a few days. At least, that was the plan.

I was going by myself this time, leaving Garrett at home. And I would stay with Carina in her TriBeCa loft. Truth be told, I was quite excited by that one. I hadn't yet seen her place and felt if I got the chance to stay with her in her neighborhood, that could only bring us closer.

The plane touched down at JFK. I got my bags and met Carina outside by the curb. She was standing next to the curb, waving excitedly at me. She was even more beautiful than I remembered. She was dressed in a hot pink sweater that was tight in all the right places and slim black pants. Her blonde hair was in a ponytail and she didn't have barely any makeup on. She just seemed to glow from within.

I went to her, kissed her and held her in my arms. I couldn't deny it. As much as I wanted to just move on with my life, there was something bringing me back to her. I still didn't know how it would work between us, though. She had her job as a documentary filmmaker for NetFlix and I was established in Kansas City. My kids were in a private school and were really happy. I had no desire to live in a city as large as New York.

Kansas City was the right size for me – it was large enough that there was always plenty to do, from eating in great restaurants to sporting and cultural attractions. Their football team was world class, having won the Super Bowl twice and having hosted the AFC Championship game for many years in a row. It had the best player in the league, Patrick Mahomes. I caught my share of plays and concerts there, yet it wasn't so crowded that I was caught in traffic jams every single day.

Plus, if I moved to New York, I would have to start over. Take another Bar Exam, try to find my footing in the legal community, try to establish a reputation. I had already done all that in Kansas City. People knew and respected me there. I was getting quite a name in the legal community. I was kind of a big fish in a small pond and I liked it that way. In New York, I would be a guppy in a huge pond, and had no desire to be that.

In short, I couldn't move to New York. And I couldn't possibly ask her to quit her job and join me in Kansas City. So, we were stuck.

"Damien," she said after I held her for what seemed like hours. "God, it's so good to see you again. I know you're mainly here for business, but I hope I can give you a good share of pleasure, too."

"Oh, you will, you will," I said. "Starting in about a half hour, or as soon as you can get us to your place."

"I made dinner for us," she said. "It's in the oven as we speak. So, we better get to my place soon."

We called a cab, which took us to her place.

Her loft was in a building that had been built in the 1920s and had been renovated in the early 2000s. It had exposed brick, hardwood floors, and high ceilings. She told me her building also had a rooftop bar she was dying to show me.

"After dinner," she said. "And wine. We can't forget the wine."

I came up behind her as she chopped some vegetables for our salad. "And dessert. Let's go up there after dessert." I bit her ear so she knew just what dessert I was talking about.

"Oh, yes, dessert," she growled. "Oh, how I love your desserts."

She set the table and we sat down. "Now," she said. "Tell me about what's going on with your case."

I buttered a piece of bread and popped it into my mouth. It was warm and tasted like it was home-baked.

"You make this bread?" I asked her.

"Yeah. I mean, my bread maker made it, but yeah. I did."

I cocked my head. "Is that something you do?"

"Obviously. I mean, I baked it, so, yeah, that's something I do." She smiled. "But not often. I wanted to do something special for you. I also got this bottle of wine special. Taste it."

I took a sip, finding it full-bodied and smooth. "Delicious. Just like you."

"And you," she said, raising her glass. I clinked my own with hers and took another sip.

"Now, I'm sorry, what were you asking me again?" I asked.

"Oh, I was just asking how your case was going. I mean, you're here, so that must mean you're still trying to investigate everything."

"That's true, I am. I'm here for you, too, though."

She waved her hand at me dismissively. "Yeah, but if

you didn't have more business up here, you wouldn't be here. But that's okay, though. Any way I can get you, I'll take it."

"Now, I wouldn't be so sure," I said. "That I'm only here for business. I *am* here for business, that's for sure, but the pleasure is almost as important." I had the feeling she was unsure about how I felt about her. If she only knew how much I thought about her, she wouldn't be so insecure.

"Okay," she said. "Now, tell me what's going on with your case?"

"Well," I said, "things aren't going so well. I have a good suspect in mind. Alan Taylor. Circumstantial evidence looks really good for him. Really good. The only problem is, it's only circumstantial evidence. Yeah, I can sell it to the jury but would like something more solid."

"So, where are you going to look next?"

I leaned back. "I'm going to see George again." I nodded. "I don't know what I hope to find with him. I only know I still haven't really investigated him so much and think maybe I should."

"In what way?"

"He might point me in a different direction. By the way, did you ever figure out why Jackson lied about how he became addicted to drugs? I think that seems very odd, if you ask me."

"No. I still can't figure that out. Why? Do you think the fact that he lied about how he became addicted has anything to do with Dr. Melber?"

"I don't know. As far as I'm concerned, it's another piece of the puzzle. A small piece of the puzzle. Or maybe a large one. I don't really know. And how is your NetFlix documentary coming along?"

"Fine. I have most of the raw footage I need for it. It's

just a matter of putting it all together into a coherent narrative."

"You talk to George very much for this?"

She rolled her eyes. "Yeah. He's gotten even weirder, if that's even possible. Marie, Jackson's mother, thinks George has completely lost it. That he's officially ready for the rubber room. She's not joking about that, either."

"Marie's doctor is also Dr. Melber, right?"

"Right. That's correct. Why do you ask?"

I shook my head. "I'm talking to her tomorrow. I want to feel her out. She's still battling her own addictions, right?"

"Sure. Once you're addicted, it becomes a lifelong thing. That is if you're truly addicted and don't just have a problem. There's a difference, I think. Between having a drinking or drug problem and being truly addicted. Marie is the latter."

"And George is too, right?"

"No. He was, but he's gone into another realm. Marie thinks this, too – he's had a psychotic break."

"A psychotic break." I nodded my head. "A psychotic break. I wonder if I should skip my interview with Marie and just go straight to George again. Is he still living at his home or has he already been committed?"

"He's living in his home, ranting like a loon. At least, that's what Marie tells me. I'm trying to get his permission to be in the because he'll make a great character. I hate to say it, but if he's really gone outer-limits, it'll make for great movie-making. The film is already shaping up to where I think it's really good. Maybe even award-winning."

I nodded my head. "Award-winning," I said. My mind was a blank. There was a kernel in my brain, somewhere buried deep in there, and that kernel held the key to this whole thing. What was so frustrating was that I couldn't seem to access it, no matter what I did.

"Hey," she said. "Let's think about all this tomorrow. Tonight is for us." She came over to me and threw her arms around me from the back. "Only for us."

Chapter Nineteen

THE NEXT DAY, I went to see two people – Marie and George. I thought seeing these two people would clarify things for me, but, instead, they made me more confused. Especially George made me more confused.

I went over to his house in Connecticut. I rented a car to get us out there. Carina came with me as backup, plus she wanted to see George for herself to see if he was acting as crazy as Marie said he was.

I got there and realized he was acting even crazier. No matter how crazy Marie said he was, he was well beyond that.

The house was more of an estate than a house. It was one of those homes I always assumed was an apartment building when I used to see them. Or a Country Club. I was surprised we could just get in there, but I noticed that, when we got to the gate, it opened right up for us. There was no security, no lock, no need to know some kind of code. The gate just...opened.

Carina and I gave each other a look. "Well, maybe he didn't pay his bill for his security detail," I said.

"Yeah..." She looked dubious. "I guess."

We drove up through the winding driveway and finally got to his front door.

He charged out of the door with a shotgun in his hands. He had lost about 20 pounds since the last time I saw him and had grown out his hair, which was piled on top of his head in a man-bun. He had a full beard and mustache. He looked at us and waved the gun. "I told you to get the hell out of here and leave me alone," he shouted.

He stared at us with glazed eyes. He was looking at us yet not really seeing us. I wasn't sure what he was seeing but it wasn't us.

"Mr. Mason," Carina said. "It's me, Carina. You remember me."

"Who? I don't know anybody named Karen," he shouted. "I don't know anybody named Karen."

"Not Karen, Carina. Carina Maxwell. We've met several times."

"Get the hell out of here. I don't want any visitors. I told you that how many times?"

I stepped forward. "George, my name is Damien. I met you earlier. I-"

He finally looked at me, seeing me for the first time. "I remember you. You tried to pretend my stepson was alive when he wasn't. That was a sick joke and you're a sick fuck."

I looked over at Carina. I guess he had a period of lucidity. That was possibly a good thing. "Yes, that was me and I'm sorry about that."

"Yeah. You thought I did it. I know you did."

"Well, I was going to ask you a few questions, yes."

He shook his head rapidly and raised the gun at both of us. "No, no, no, no, no, leave me the fuck alone!" This time, he wasn't shouting at us but shouting behind him. He was evidently seeing somebody behind him and was shouting at this person. "Dammit, I said I know. I know."

"You know what? What do you know?" I asked him. He seemed to kind of know who I was, so I was hoping he would respond to me.

"I don't know anything," he said, addressing me. "At least not anything I'm going to tell you."

I spoke in a low voice, as calming as possible. "I need to talk to you about Jackson," I said. "I need to know what you know about him."

"I didn't know him. Not for the past few years. I divorced his mom and lost contact with him." He narrowed his eyes and looked at Carina. "You," he said, finally figuring out who she was. "You've been stalking me. You're always around here, asking questions. I told you I won't be in your film. I don't know why you keep pestering me."

Carina looked at me and shrugged. I had a feeling that getting George's permission was not something she was able to do. Not that I blamed him. His participation in the film would inevitably be something that wouldn't be good for him. To say the very least.

I took a deep breath. "I need to ask you some questions about Jackson," I repeated. "I'm trying to find out who might have killed him."

"Killed him." He shook his head. "Nobody killed him."

"Yes, somebody did," I said. "Somebody did."

"No, nobody did. He overdosed."

Chapter Twenty

WHAT HE SAID WAS strange to me, yet, at the same time, it made a certain kind of sense. At least, on one level, it made sense. That was the visceral level. The gut level.

But, on the other side, it made no sense whatsoever. I had reviewed the autopsy report. Yes, there were drugs found in Jackson's system, of course there was. But the cause of death was very clear – a stab to the heart with a very sharp knife. There was no way the Medical Examiner could find the stabbing caused Jackson's death if the cause of death was actually an overdose. That didn't make a lick of sense.

"Mr. Mason," I said. "I'm sorry, but you're not making any sense."

"Not making sense, not making sense," he said, in a little boy's voice. "Not making sense."

I inwardly groaned. The guy was not living in reality. He appeared to have moments of lucidity, but those were only moments.

"Mr. Mason," I said. "Your stepson was murdered. I

know you claimed not to have spoken with him for several years, but I still need to know if you are aware of anybody who might have wanted him dead."

"Listen to me," he said. "He wasn't murdered. He overdosed. That's all I can tell you."

I looked at Carina, who was staring back at me. She shook her head.

"Let's get out of here," she said. "This guy is creeping me out. I don't think he has any decent information, at least nothing you can use."

"Dr. Melber was his dad," George said. "He was his dad."

"Wait, what?" I asked George. "What do you mean by that? What do you mean, Dr. Melber was his dad? And what does that have to do with any of this?"

I looked over at Carina and her face had changed. She had a look that told me she had just solved a mystery.

"That's why, Damien," she said. "That's why he lied to me about how he got addicted. He was lying to protect his actual father."

"Carina, this guy is babbling like a loon," I said, "just like you said. I don't know if we can trust anything he's saying." I turned to George. "Why did you bring that up just now? About Dr. Melber being Jackson's actual father?"

"Because you need to know that," he said. "You need to know that. It will come in handy to you."

"Why do I need to know that? How is that piece of information relevant?"

"It is relevant. It is." He nodded. "And that's all you need to know."

"No, that's not all I need to know. I need to know how the fact that Dr. Melber is Jackson's father is relevant."

"That's all I'm going to say," he said. "All I'm going to

say. I you need me to come to your town and talk to the jury about it, I will. You don't need to subpoena me. I'll talk. That boy shouldn't have died. He shouldn't have died."

"I know he shouldn't have died. But-"

At that, he raised the gun on both of us. "Get out of here," he said. "Get the fuck out of here." He cocked the gun and my heart started to race. He was here, he was there, he was all over the place. He was maybe lucid in spots, maybe he wasn't. I couldn't really tell. What I did know was that, at that moment, he had lost touch with reality and was dangerous.

"You don't have to tell us twice," I said. "Carina, let's get out of here."

"You said it."

We both got into the car and drove off. I looked at the rear-view mirror and saw George was shouting at us and waving his rifle around. He was jumping up in the air and I heard him whoop and laugh while he shot his gun in our direction.

When we were out of his range, I looked at Carina. She looked stunned for a few seconds and then started to laugh. "What the hell was that?" she asked.

"I don't know," I said, then joined her in laughter. "Oh, God, I don't know. Was there anything I can take from what he was just saying?"

She shrugged. "Well, if Dr. Melber is really Jackson's natural father, that would explain one major thing. It would explain why Jackson lied to me about how he got addicted. But what was all that nonsense about how you would need to know that piece of information? As if Dr. Melber being Jackson's father would be relevant?"

"Not sure. But I think this means I'll have to speak with

Marie. I wanted to do that, anyhow, the last time I was here. It's now more important than ever."

"I've spoken with her several times. I can arrange for us to see her."

"Call her. See if we can go over there today. She might shed some light on all of this. With any luck she will, at least."

Carina called Marie and gestured to me that it was okay to see her. She hung up and looked at me. "She said to come on over," Carina said. "Marie rarely leaves her house these days. She's always out of it, though. Not as bad as George, but I need to give you a warning. She might not answer your questions coherently."

"That's okay. If she can at least answer the question on whether or not Dr. Melber is Damien's father, she'll be a great help. I think. I mean, I still don't know why Dr. Melber being Jackson's father means anything to this case. Maybe it does but I haven't yet figured it out."

We headed to Marie's apartment on the Upper West Side. It was a pre-war palace facing the Park. We took the elevator to her place, knocked on her door and waited.

Marie answered the door about ten minutes after we started to knock. She was a petite woman, only about 5'4", and probably didn't weigh 100 pounds. She had her hair cut in a short, neat bob, which surprised me, considering that Carina told me Marie rarely left the house. She was an attractive woman who looked younger than her years. Jackson was 27 when he was killed. This woman must have been in her early 50s, yet she could easily pass for a woman in her 30s.

"Come in," she said, her eyes vacant. She looked lost in her own world. She turned around and walked into her apartment, an enormous space elegantly decorated with murals all over the 30' feet walls. I didn't see that she had any of Jackson's paintings up on her walls, but I figured that was because Jackson's aesthetics wouldn't have gone with the vibe of her place. Her apartment was all white walls, black marble floors and chandeliers. Jackson's paintings were dark, foreboding, and disturbing. Especially his recent ones.

Marie saw me looking at one of the pictures on her wall. I didn't know the minutiae of art, but I could appreciate talent. Thus was painted by someone with a great deal of it. It was a picture of a young girl and a young boy. They were sitting outdoors on a hill with the city in the background. The use of light in this painting was what drew me in. In fact, everything about this painting drew me in.

I looked at all the other artwork. They were evidently painted by the same person. I could see themes and motifs and the technique was similar across all of them.

"I painted those," she said softly. "Back when I could get out of bed." She coughed lightly. I looked at her hand and saw she was shaking profusely. "Sorry," she said as she noticed me looking at her hand. Her voice was soft, so soft that I could barely understand her. "I've been very sick lately. Don't worry, though, it's not catching."

"I can see where Jackson got his talent," I said. I truly meant it. I wasn't saying that to be nice. Her paintings were that good.

Carina gave me a look and she nudged me. "Mrs. Michaelson," I said. "Thank you for seeing us on such short notice."

"Of course. You're investigating what happened to my son. Of course I will help you out." She gestured to two of her leather seats. "Please sit down."

We all sat and she lay down on the sofa. She pulled a

blanket over her body. Evidently, the woman was freezing, even though the temperature in the apartment was, if anything, slightly warm.

"Uh," I said, "we saw your ex-husband, George," I said.

"Yes. George. Such a tragedy. Such a shame. He's in his last months, you know. He destroyed his liver and now needs a transplant. That news sent him over the edge. George was always battling demons, mental health issues. Now he's dying. I can't bring myself to care that much about what happens to him, but he was my husband for a few years. I can't just ignore his plight."

"I'm very sorry to hear that."

"Don't be." She sighed. "I'm not much better than George. Carina has probably told you about my issues and they're all true. I've been addicted to painkillers for years. But when Jackson died, I decided to give them all up. I didn't want my boy to have died in vain. I wanted something good to come of it, so I kicked them all, cold turkey. I'm still going through withdrawal. That's why I look the way I do, why I haven't left the house in so long, why I'm so cold, feverish and sick. I just have to get through this period and get really clean. Then I can go out and face the world."

"Mrs. Michaelson, I wanted to ask you a couple of questions," I said.

"What are they?"

"Who is Jackson's father?"

"His name was Hugh Michaelson. A shipping heir. Very old money. He died in a plane crash when Jackson was only 9 years old. Why do you ask?"

I cleared my throat. "There's not a chance the father could have been Dr. Ashton Melber, could it?"

"That's my doctor," she said and then paused. She looked like she wanted to say something more, but something was keeping her from doing so. "Why do you think he was Jackson's father?"

"Two reasons. One is that, when Jackson was alive, he told Carina that he became addicted because his stepfather started him on hard drugs when he was very young. However, I got another story from Elise Hoffman, Jackson's best friend in prep school, and she said Jackson didn't even try drugs until he was hurt on his bicycle and was prescribed powerful painkillers."

"So he lied," Marie said. "What does that prove?"

"Nothing. But the other thing was that your ex-husband George told Carina and me that Dr. Melber was Jackson's father."

She sighed. "That's actually not true. And I know, because I did a DNA test when Jackson was born. It was true that I was having an affair with Ashton when I got pregnant with Jackson. I had to come clean to my husband about the affair because of my pregnancy. Trust me, that was the hardest thing I've ever had to do. The hardest thing I've ever had to do." She coughed. "Until now. Kicking these drugs is now, officially, the hardest thing I've had to do. I guess telling Hugh about Jackson's possible paternity issues is really the second hardest thing."

"I see," I said. "What kind of relationship has Jackson had with Dr. Melber over the years?"

"Well, it's like this. Ashton never had any children and was very much in love with me. He wanted Jackson to be his. He really did. And Jackson, well, when he was growing up, he had a hard time with things. He started to have a hard time after Hugh died in that plane crash. He was only 9 at the time. That changed him for the worst. Changed me for the worst, too."

"In what way did he change right at that time?"

"He started to get rebellious. Started skipping school, hanging out with the wrong kinds of kids. Started smoking cigarettes. Started drinking. At the age of 9. It terrified me, because I was so afraid I had passed on my terrible genes to him." She shook her head. "I've struggled with bi-polar disorder my entire life. For as long as I can remember, I've struggled. The last thing I wanted was to see my son struggle just as much."

"Did he get straightened out at that time?"

"For a time, yes he did. It was Ashton who straightened him out. After Hugh died, Ashton became Jackson's surrogate father. Jackson really took to him because it was the first time somebody took an interest. I'm ashamed to say that I wasn't really a mother to him. I've always had my problems. Bi-polar, depression, drug abuse, always out of it. And Hugh, well, he worked night and da. Day and night. He was a hedge fund manager, working for himself. Extremely successful. But he did nothing but work. Stayed at the office most nights. So, when Ashton took an interest in Jackson, that was the first time anybody ever did."

"But Ashton got Jackson hooked on drugs."

She sighed. "Yes, he did, accidentally. Jackson was in a lot of pain after his bicycle accident. A lot of pain. I didn't allow him to take painkillers. I didn't want to see him go the way I did. Told him he had to tough it out. So he went directly to Ashton and got a prescription. Ashton wasn't supposed to do that, of course, as Jackson was a minor. But he felt sorry for Jackson so he prescribed the pills for him. And kept prescribing them for Jackson for a couple of years. I didn't know any of this, of course. I was too out of it to notice that Jackson himself was hooked on painkillers."

"Why would a man who so cared about Jackson do

something like that? Continue to prescribe him painkillers long after Jackson needed them?"

"I don't. Jackson probably told Ashton that either he prescribes the pills to him or he would go to the street and get it." She nodded. "Come to think of it, that's what Ashton told me about his reasoning. He was afraid Jackson would get his drugs elsewhere. At any rate, Ashton finally cut off Jackson and that's when my son turned to street drugs."

"Were Ashton and Jackson still in contact when Jackson was killed?"

Her face looked blank. "Yes," she said. "Actually, Ashton always had somebody who went with Jackson whenever he went out of town. Kind of a handler, if you will. Somebody assigned to watch Jackson and make sure he didn't overdose." She drew a breath. "That was Ashton's biggest fear. He was always afraid that if Jackson overdosed, the investigation into my son's death would lead right back to him. He was terrified of that happening. If the investigation led to him, he would not only lose his physician's license but no doubt would end up in prison for prescribing drugs to a minor without permission of the minor's parents. So, he sent this guy, Wilson Raine, to accompany Jackson when he went out of town. Jackson and Wilson were good friends. I don't think Jackson ever put it together that Wilson was assigned to baby-sit."

"I see." I nodded. "So this Wilson Raine was Jackson's friend but also his handler. Unbeknownst to Jackson."

"Right. That's right."

As I stared at Marie, there was a kernel in my brain.

I asked more questions of Marie for the next few hours and she was more than cooperative. I felt sorry for her. She was trying to get her life together. I couldn't imagine what she was going through – struggling with lifelong bi-polar disorder, trying to come off a years-long addiction and losing her son. She probably didn't think she was strong, but I did. Just the fact that she didn't give up was testament to her strength.

I couldn't imagine losing either of my children. In Marie's case, Jackson was literally all she had left. If that had happened to me, I doubted that I could be as calm as she was.

Carina and I finally left after I asked question after question about Jackson.

By the time we left, I had an idea about what had happened.

And it was something I had never even considered before.

Chapter Twenty-One

November 1 - First Day of the Trial

"IT'S NOT TOO late to back out of this," I said to Ally, the prosecutor assigned to the Jackson Michaelson murder. "Seriously, you don't want to be humiliated, do you?"

We were both standing in the courtroom, waiting for Judge Reiner to take the bench. It was the first day of the trial and there were potential jury members swarming the hallways. I was a tad nervous about this trial, mainly because I had an out-there theory I didn't quite have the means to back up. It was a novel theory, to be sure, but, after I talked to Marie, the pieces started to come together nicely. I had enough documentation to somewhat make my theory fly. But, mainly, I had only circumstantial evidence.

Ally had actually forgiven me for what had happened before, when I basically dumped her to take up with Sarah. Once she was assigned the case, she and I ended up spending time together, trying to hash out deals for other cases we had together. But we could never come to any kind of agreement on this one. Not after I found out what I found out.

Carina, for her part, decided she didn't want to do the long-distance thing and broke my heart when she announced she would go to Venezuela with Frederico Cantalone. That wasn't the hard part. The hard part was when she also told me that Frederico Cantalone and she had become an item. That news hit me right in the solar plexus, and, I had to admit, I got depressed about it. Drank way too much, trying to drink her off my mind.

In the end, however, I knew it was all for the best. I was established here, she was established there, and her job as a documentary filmmaker took her all over the world. Far be it for me to convince her to give all that up and move to this town and do…something. I was never quite sure what kind of a job I could entice her with in Kansas City. After all, I loved this town, but it was not exactly the hub for international documentary filmmaking. I finally came to the conclusion that either I would have to uproot the kids and go to New York or we had to call it quits. The fact that Carina fell in love with Frederico Cantalone took the choice out of my hands and it was for the best.

Ally raised her eyebrows. "*I'll* be humiliated. *I'll* be humiliated." She snorted. "Nice try, Damien, but I hate to tell you there's no way I'll be humiliated. You're the one with the cock-eyed theory." She shook her head. "I mean, I've heard of some wild theories before, but never something like this."

"Okay, then," I said. "This is your last chance to get out of this in one piece. Going, going, gone."

She stood there, her arms crossed in front of her, a sly smile on her face. "Looks like I didn't take your wonderful offer, Damien. So sorry about that."

I took a deep breath. I hoped Ally really had forgiven me for dumping her before. Carina was in the past and Sarah and I were officially divorced. Sarah got a nice property settlement and the parenting plan called for her to see the kids every other weekend, every other school holiday and two months during the summer. However, she made it clear to me she wasn't interested in any visitation with the kids.

"It's time to move on, Damien," she had said, "and that means move on." Which she did. She moved out of state and stopped talking to any of us. Amelia was just fine with Sarah's cold treatment, but Nate was beyond devastated. He couldn't understand how a mother could do that.

Neither could I, but it happened. I couldn't force Sarah to see the kids so she was no longer a part of their lives.

"Ally, I…" I felt awkward, like I was asking a girl out for the first time. "I know you hated me in the past and I didn't blame you one bit. It was a very confusing time of my life, if you want to know the truth. But my divorce was finalized, and, well…" Damn, I felt embarrassed.

"You want to try again, don't you?" Ally asked me.

"I do."

She nodded her head. "I'll think about it. After I kick your ass in trial."

"Deal."

I was going into this with nothing but a theory. I had several witnesses lined up, including one expert, but Leland, who still couldn't remember what had happened that night, couldn't possibly help me. If I would put him on, it would be for one reason, and one reason only – because Leland's doctor was Dr. Melber. Dr. Melber prescribed Leland's medicines.

Harper was second-chairing this beast, and even she

thought I was absolutely insane to be approaching the case the way that I was approaching it. That is, until I convinced her there was mounting evidence that what I was about to argue was the truth. At that point, she declared me brilliant for having figured it out.

I only hoped she still thought I was brilliant at the end of the trial. The only way I could possibly prove my theory was the hope that both the Medical Examiner, Dr. Katy Moore, and Dr. Melber refused to lie under oath. That, and the fact that I found holes in the Medical Examiner's report big enough to drive a truck through, were my only hopes for acquittal.

Leland and Dill had worked to repair their relationship and their trust in each other, partially because Leland finally got Dill into some kind of rehab where he learned to quit Mystic Anna. I don't know how that happened, except that I knew Dill was not only doing a 12-Step program for addiction, but also was going through intensive psychotherapy in an effort to quit Mystic Anna for good. I didn't know a 12-step program would be beneficial to something like this, but, apparently, an addiction is an addiction, and the steps to overcome them are the same. The upshot was that Dill and Leland were solid, once again, and Dill was in the courtroom to support his husband.

Also in the courtroom was the media. That was one thing I didn't want, especially in this trial. Yet members of the media got together and sued for cameras to be allowed in the courtroom. *The Law News Network* would be streaming this trial live.

On top of that, media outlets from around the country were parked outside the courthouse steps. There was a CNN truck, a Fox News truck and and an MSNBC truck. There were trucks representing media websites and magazines. All of them struggling and straining to get a piece of the action.

No doubt about it, this particular trial would be one for the history books. And I would possibly fall right on my face.

Harper looked at all the news reporters around the courtroom and shook her head. "The trial of the century," she said. "I mean, I've been a part of high-profile trials before, but nothing like this. Nothing where there's a live feed streaming to people all around the country and news trucks parked outside. When I came up those courthouse steps, I was barraged by people with cameras and microphones. I can't believe this trial is drumming up this much attention, but I probably should have figured it would. After all, a mini-celebrity was murdered and the suspect is a billionaire. Put those two things together and you get instant media sensation."

"Yeah," I said, "and that's going to complicate jury selection that much more. I'd like you to take the lead on that, if you don't mind. Just don't forget to get to the bottom on who really has heard about this case and who hasn't been paying that much attention. Believe it or not, even in the most high-profile cases of the past few decades – Casey Anthony, Scott Peterson, the Menendez brothers and the big daddy of them all, OJ Simpson - there were quite a few people who didn't follow the facts. It was all background noise as they moved about with their lives. This case isn't like those other cases, thank God. I doubt it'll get to that level. But, nonetheless, it'll be tricky to find jurors who know little or nothing about this. And there's always the possibility that some prospective juror will lie and say that he or she doesn't know much about the case, when, in fact, they've been following every development and just want to be a part of it. I think you'll be better at weeding these people out than I would."

"I agree," Harper said. "And I agree that finding the right jury will be crucial on this one. We really need to find jurors open-minded about the possibility of corruption. That's the bottom line on this. We need jurors who don't have a high-minded attitude about doctors and medical examiners and realize doctors and MEs are just as susceptible to corruption as anybody else."

I took a deep breath as the jurors filed in, one by one. *Showtime.* We got the first batch of jurors, and Judge Reiner, who presided over my last murder case, gave them all instructions. Then it was time for us to choose who we wanted on our panel.

Ally went first, with her *voir dire* questions. She wanted to know not only if any juror knew anybody involved in the case, but also if any of the jurors had heard anything about the case. Almost everyone raised their hand when she asked that, confirming my suspicions that it would be next to impossible to find an impartial jury. Not that moving the case out of the jurisdiction would do anything – this case was so well-known that just about everyone in the country were following along at some point. The best I could do was find jurors who didn't really care about the case that much so they weren't hanging on every little event that happened.

After she asked her usual questions, it was Harper's turn. She would get into the meat of the *voir dire* to find out who would have some kind of a mental block with regards to this case.

"Ladies and gentlemen of the jury," Harper said. "You heard the questions that Ms. Hughes asked you and I would like to ask you a few more, if I may. Now, I would like to know if any one of you has a doctor in your family. If you do, please raise your hands."

A few hands went up so Harper asked some follow-up questions of those jurors. "Raise your hands if the doctor you know has been involved in adverse litigation, such as being on the wrong end of a medical malpractice lawsuit."

None of the people raised their hands, so Harper pressed on.

"Now, people know doctors are a good in our society. That's undoubtedly true. But they're also human and subject to the same temptations all of us are. If you believe doctors are always in the right and could never do anything deliberately to harm another human being, then I need to know this right now."

From there, quite a few people raised their hands and gave their opinions on the matter. Most of them said that, while they believed a doctor could make a mistake, they felt that since their oath was "First, do no harm," that meant a doctor would not deliberately hurt another human being. I made notes on the people who spoke most passionately about this subject and Harper went on.

She asked questions about their views on homosexuality, as Leland was openly gay, and looked to exclude those who seemed virulently anti-gay. There was only one guy who raised his hand and said that homosexuality should be outlawed, and I knew I didn't want that person on the jury.

A few more questions and Harper was finished. That group of potential jurors filed out and several more groups filed in. Same questions, same types of answers, and, by the end of the afternoon, we had our jury selected.

It was time to begin.

AFTER LUNCH, we gave our opening arguments. "Ladies and gentlemen of the jury," Ally began. "I would like you to focus on one person in this trial, and one person only. His name was Jackson Michaelson and he was a phenomenal artist. Absolutely phenomenal. He was only 27 and selling out gallery showings from here to Paris to Prague to Singapore. He was a true international sensation and his life was cut short far too young. If he would have lived, think about all the art to come."

She pointed dramatically at Leland. "But he will never realize his true potential because of this man. Leland Dewitt IV is a billionaire and he was, ironically enough, Jackson's greatest benefactor. Mr. Dewitt discovered Jackson when the artist was only 17 years old and living on the streets of New York. He considered Jackson to be his protégé, and was very jealous of anybody who he sensed would take Jackson away from him."

"Enter Leland's husband, Dill Dewitt. See, there is a real power imbalance between Leland and Dill Dewitt. Leland is a billionaire and Dill was, when Leland met him, working in a drag show. Mr. Dewitt felt Dill was his possession, the same as he thought Jackson was his possession. He lorded his money over both men so he expected them both to dance to his tune. He wanted them both to be at his beck and call."

"So imagine how Mr. Dewitt must have felt when he discovered Jackson and Dill were having an affair." She nodded. "That's right, ladies and gentlemen, that was happening right under Mr. Dewitt's nose. The two men were not only sleeping together, but, worst of all, Jackson Michaelson was cutting Mr Leland Dewitt off. When Mr. Michaelson was finished with a new painting, it was Dill Dewitt who received the text picture of the painting. Mr.

Michaelson used to always show Leland Dewitt first. After all, Leland Dewitt was responsible, in his mind at least, for Jackson getting to where he was. He demanded absolute loyalty and fealty, and, for all these years, that was what he got. At least that was what he got until Mr. Michaelson's attention and affection turned to Dill Dewitt."

"Leland Dewitt could not tolerate the fact that his protégé, the man he made, turned on him. Turned his loyalties to somebody else and that somebody else was his own husband Dill. So he killed Mr. Michaelson in cold blood."

"There is the motive, ladies and gentlemen. Plain, old-fashioned jealousy. The evidence will show Dill Dewitt received numerous text messages from Jackson Michaelson. Jackson mainly sent these texts to show Dill Dewitt his latest masterpieces, but there were also plenty of text messages that were sexual in nature."

"The evidence will show Dill Dewitt and Jackson Michaelson were caught having sex by Leland Dewitt on the night of the murder. Mr. Dewitt literally walked in on the two of them. The evidence will also show that a knife belonging to Mr. Dewitt, with Mr. Dewitt's fingerprints all over it, was used to stab Jackson Michaelson in the heart."

"There you have it, ladies and gentlemen. Motive, means and opportunity. Mr. Dewitt definitely had motive – he was insanely jealous and enraged that his protégé turned on him and stabbed him in the back by having sex with his husband. Worse, Mr. Michaelson was having an emotional affair with Dill Dewitt as well. Means – Mr. Dewitt owned the knife found in Jackson Michaelson. His fingerprints were on this knife and only his fingerprints were on the knife. Opportunity – Mr. Michaelson was murdered in the back of Mr. Dewitt's art gallery. Mr. Dewitt was in the art gallery at the time in question. He definitely had the opportunity to murder Jackson Michaelson."

"I submit to you, ladies and gentlemen of the jury that, by the time the state has carefully presented the evidence in this case, you will have no choice but to find Mr. Dewitt guilty of murder in the first degree. I ask for a guilty verdict in advance. Thank you very much."

She sat down and I stood up.

I would have to make this wild, implausible theory sound plausible. And then I would have to pray it all panned out on the stand. My career was on the line with this, but, more than that, my reputation. I was pursuing a high-risk, high-reward strategy.

If it worked, I would look like a genius.

If it didn't, I would look like an idiot. And, worse still, my client would serve life in prison. For something he didn't do.

No pressure.

Chapter Twenty-Two

I APPROACHED the jury and looked all of them in the face – one by one. I stared into each of their eyes. And then I closed my own eyes.

"Ladies and gentlemen of the jury," I began. "I submit to you there was not a murder at all. None whatsoever. In fact, there was not even a crime committed."

I looked at all of them to see if I got their attention and, sure enough, they were all looking at me quizzically. "No crime was committed." I nodded and then looked away. "Well, no, scratch that, there was a crime committed. But it wasn't murder. It was obstruction of justice and extortion. You've heard the old canard that it's always the cover up? Well, that's what happened here."

"You see, Jackson Michaelson had a drug problem. A serious drug problem. This drug problem started when he was 16 years old because a doctor overprescribed pain meds to young Jackson after he got into a bicycle accident on the streets of New York City and broke his arm. That's not even the criminal part – the criminal part was that Mr. Michaelson was prescribed these drugs, as a minor, without written permission of either of his parents. This is clearly against the law of any state, including New York State."

"The doctor who started prescribing these drugs is named Dr. Ashton Melber. He's a prominent physician with a practice on the Upper West Side of Manhattan. He maintains a very exclusive clientele and has become very wealthy in his own right. He has a lot to lose if something ever happened to Jackson that would possibly lead the authorities back to him. If ever there was an investigation into his conduct it could become known about how he prescribed powerful pain meds to a minor and how he continued to prescribe these meds for two more years. Two more years, ladies and gentlemen. He prescribed these pain meds to Jackson for two years. In other words, he continued to prescribe pain meds to Jackson long after his broken arm healed."

"What happened next was predictable. Dr. Melber finally cut young Jackson off, but, by that time, Jackson was absolutely addicted. Dr. Melber knew Jackson's family history, too. Jackson's mother is addicted to prescription drugs and has been for years. Dr. Melber knew that, so he should have known Jackson was also susceptible to addiction. Yet he prescribed these meds and continued prescribing them, which eventually led Jackson into a heroin addiction. Jackson was addicted to heroin from the age of 19 until his death. This heroin addiction was the result of his initial addiction to prescription pain meds."

I paced back and forth. "And what would have happened if Jackson died of an overdose? I'll tell you what would have happened. He was a prominent artist, a celebrity, and the media would have covered that extensively. Sooner or later, probably sooner, the road would lead back to Dr. Melber. After all, that was how Jackson's addiction began. That whole story would fit so neatly into the current narrative of addiction in this country. Opioid addiction is such a problem in this country that some believe it needs to be declared a national emergency."

"So, imagine if you will, the media swarming Dr. Melber in the event of Jackson's overdose. Dr. Melber would lose his practice, his medical license and most likely would be facing criminal charges." I didn't mention that last part probably wasn't true, as the Statute of Limitations had run out on his crimes. But it certainly was true that he would lose his medical license if it ever got out he was prescribing drugs to a minor long after said minor needed them. "Imagine if you will what would happen. The opioid addiction narrative would have a very public face, Jackson Michaelson, and there would be a very convenient villain in this story – Dr. Ashton Melber."

"What happened, ladies and gentlemen, was that Jackson overdosed on heroin the night of April 9. Evidence will show Jackson had a handler that went with him on all his trips. The handler's job was to make sure Jackson didn't overdose. The handler was actually an employee of Dr. Ashton Melber. That handler, Wilson Raine, was with Jackson the night of the overdose. He got distracted that night because he was flirting with a young female at Mr. Dewitt's art gallery. Tragically, he was distracted just long enough that he was unable to prevent Jackson's accidental overdose. He found Jackson lying in the back of the art gallery. He panicked."

"Here's what happened next. My client, Leland Dewitt, was also in the back of the art gallery, but was passed out. He was drinking that night and taking Ambien and has been known to do activities while on that popular sleep drug. That's a common side effect – some people drive while on Ambien and don't even know it. Others eat, others carry on a conversation. Wilson Raine knew my client was on Ambien. The reason why he knew this was because Dr. Melber was Mr. Dewitt's physician as well."

"From there, it was a simple plan. Plunge a knife into Jackson's dead body, making sure the knife belonged to Leland Dewitt, and make Leland Dewitt think he killed Jackson while under the effects of the Ambien. A brilliant plan, really. Make the overdose look like a murder. That way, nobody would be asking Dr. Melber questions about Jackson's drug habit. If Jackson died as the result of murder, the fact that he was addicted to drugs becomes less relevant."

"Then there was the cover-up about this. Of course, the Medical Examiner will rule the death was an accidental overdose. They're trained to figure that out. Unless blackmail is involved. I will present evidence on what this blackmail was. I will present evidence that Dr. Melber blackmailed the Medical Examiner, Dr. Katy Moore, and forced her to present findings on the autopsy report that Jackson died as the result of the stabbing, not as the result of a drug overdose."

"Now, I know this whole scenario sounds pretty far out to most if not all of you. I'm sure you all have heard of people trying to cover up a murder by making it look like an overdose. I'll bet none of you have heard of somebody trying to cover up an overdose to make it look like murder. Yet, that's exactly what happened here. The evidence will show this."

"Once I have presented my evidence, you will have no choice but to decide there was never a murder committed, and I will ask you find my client not guilty. Thank you very much."

There. I did it. I wrapped it all up neatly in a bow. My theory was now out there and it was up to me to prove it.

This would be the challenge of my life.

Chapter Twenty-Three

AFTER ALLY and I presented our opening arguments, it was time to take a break.

"Okay, ladies and gentlemen of the jury," Judge Reiner said, "you've heard both sides' opening arguments. It's time to take a short break." He looked at the clock. "It is now 2:15, please be back in the courtroom at 2:30. Thank you."

The jury filed out and I was immediately besieged by reporters who were dying to get my story. They couldn't come back behind the bar, though, so I simply walked away, as opposed to answering their questions. I was way too nervous to do anything else.

I could just imagine the headlines if this thing went sideways. I would look like a fucking clown. But I knew in my gut that what I said happened was the truth. I would just have to prove it. That was all there was to it. I just had to work and do my best to prove it.

Ally walked over. "The plea offer is still good, you know. 20 years in prison, your client is eligible for parole in 17.

He's 32 now. He'll be out of prison before he's 50. For what he did, it's a steal."

"Yeah, a steal," I said. "I wonder why you were authorized to offer such a light sentence for murder one. Perhaps it's because you know my theory is correct."

"Oh, come on now, if I thought for a second you were right about this, I would drop the charges in a heartbeat. No skin off my nose. We'd be pursuing the good doctor for obstruction of justice and extortion."

"Oh, but obstruction of justice and extortion are so less sexy than murder one, isn't it?" I was half-joking and half-serious but didn't want to push her too far. I wanted to try again with her, so I didn't want to piss her off.

"In this case, obstruction of justice and extortion would be pretty damned sexy," she said. "But I don't believe you, not for a minute."

"Well, you'll just have to see." I nodded. "I noticed on your Exhibit list that you don't plan on introducing the death photos. Why is that? You guys always love to show the jury those death photos. Love to blow them up, let the jury see the dead body, make them hate my client even more than they do. Love to prejudice the jury against my client, because when they see those photos, they want somebody to pay for the murder, by God. But you won't show the death photos this time. Why is that?"

Ally crossed her arms in front of her. "I'm just not going to show the photos, that's all." She looked down at the floor. "No other reason. I don't have to justify my every strategic decision to you. I've made the decision not to show them and that's that."

"Could it be because there was very little blood on the body when it was found?" I saw the crime scene photos, and that was one of the things that struck me about them.

There was a small pool of blood in the chest area, where the knife had been stuck, but the amount of blood on the body was *very* small. I knew it could be explained away by the prosecution – after all, Jackson had allegedly been stabbed right in the heart, so he wouldn't have bled that much. His heart would have stopped instantly.

I initially was surprised there was blood on the body at all. Then I eventually found out why there was blood on the body, and it was one of the most astounding aspects of this case.

I had spoken with Wilson Raine several times before the trial and he was no help. He did nothing but lie. My only hope was that he didn't continue to lie on the stand. He knew the penalty for perjury and I hoped he would heed that. He shouldn't be willing to go to prison for his boss, Dr. Melber. That didn't mean he *wasn't* willing to go to prison for Dr. Melber. It just meant that he *shouldn't* want to go to prison for him.

"No, that's not the reason why I am not showing the jury the crime scene photos," Ally said.

"Huh. Well, okay, then, if that's how you want to play it."

"That's how I'm playing it."

I looked up and saw the jury was filing back in.

I was looking forward to grilling the cops on the scene and the Medical Examiner. They both were on Ally's witness list, along with the fingerprint analyst. I didn't have any questions for the fingerprint analyst. The fingerprints on the knife were that of my client. After all, my client actually owned the knife. It was handy for Wilson Raine to use as Leland had an entire small living area in the back of his art gallery. It was like a small studio, really, with a couch that came out to a bed, a small dining room table and a kitchenette. The knife was taken from the kitchenette. Leland had explained to me that sometimes, when he was getting ready for a large show, he moved into the gallery for a week or more. This was why he had the small living area in the back.

Unfortunately, there was only one set of fingerprints on that knife, and those belonged only to Leland. Not that that meant anything – Wilson could have easily picked up the knife with a napkin and plunged it in.

Ally also had Dill on her list. Dill freaked out when I told him he would have to take the stand, but I reassured him that the fact he and Jackson were having a brief affair wasn't something fatal to the case. He was more upset that he and Leland had finally gotten to a good place again, with the help of counseling and didn't want to re-open old wounds. I didn't blame him there. Leland was a forgiving sort, however, and he, too, reassured Dill that everything would be okay.

The jury all took their seats and the judge was back on the bench. "Okay," Judge Reiner said. "That was the last break of the day for you folks, so settle in and try to make it all the way to 5 PM. I promise you, we'll be out of here by that time." That was the truth, too. Judge Reiner was never one to dilly-dally. He scheduled his trials, most trials anyhow, rapidly. He kept things moving along in the courtroom, too. Attorneys in Jackson County didn't call his courtroom the "rocket docket" for nothing.

"Counselor," Judge Reiner said, addressing Ally, "please call your first witness."

"The state calls Officer Steven Wyler," Ally announced. Steven Wyler was the first responder and was one of the people I most wanted to grill.

Officer Wyler was a straight-shooter as far as I knew. No

bullshit with him, no games. I hoped to draw out of him that he had some suspicions about the body when he came up on it.

"Please state your name for the record," Ally said.

"Officer Steven Wyler," he said.

"And Officer Wyler, as I understand it, you were the first responder to the scene of Jackson Michaelson's murder, is that correct?"

"That is correct."

"Can you please tell the court why you were called to the Dewitt Gallery, located in the Crossroads District of Kansas City, Missouri?"

"Yes. I was dispatched because there was an emergency 911 call that was placed stating a man was deceased in the back part of that gallery. I was the closest squad car in the area so I took that call and went directly to the gallery."

"What time was it when you were called?"

"It was a little after 2 AM on the morning of April 9. It was 2:30 AM, to be exact."

"And what did you find when you arrived at the gallery?"

"I found a deceased white male, along with Mr. Dewitt, who was sitting on his couch, just staring at the body of the deceased. I asked Mr. Dewitt what had happened and he said he didn't know. I had a conversation with him and he answered my questions. He indicated he wasn't aware of what had transpired just before I arrived. I later found out he claimed not to remember speaking with me. He later claimed he did not have a memory of being arrested and taken downtown to speak with the interrogation officers."

"He claims he had no knowledge of these conversations? Do you know why he claims that?"

"Yes. He apparently has been prescribed Ambien for

sleep issues and claims he routinely has lucid conversations with people even though he doesn't remember these conversations the next day."

"I see. But he had a conversation with you?"

"Yes. He did. But it was not a productive one. He kept reiterating to me that he had no knowledge of how the deceased passed away. He also told me he was a good friend of the deceased and that he was one of the strongest benefactors of the deceased. It was at this time that I learned the identity of the deceased, Jackson Michaelson."

"I have nothing further." Ally looked at me and sat down.

I stood up. "Officer Wyler," I said, "you explained on direct that the reason why you went to the Dewitt Gallery was because you were dispatched there due to an individual calling 911, correct?"

"Yes that's correct."

"Do you know who that person was who called?"

"No I do not."

"Oh, I see. Then it was an anonymous call, then?"

"Yes."

"It wasn't my client who called 911, then?"

"No. It wasn't your client who called."

"Okay. So, you get to the Dewitt Gallery shortly after 2 AM on the morning of April 9 and you found the deceased lying on the floor and my client sitting on the couch. Correct?"

"Correct."

"Was there anybody else around? Anybody else in the gallery or in the studio apartment located in the back of the gallery?"

"No."

"No." I nodded my head. "Nobody else around. Did you ask my client who might have called 911?"

"I did."

"And what did he say?"

"He didn't know who called 911."

"Did you think it was at all odd that somebody anonymously called 911 when there wasn't anybody in the gallery who might have placed that call?"

"No."

"No. You didn't find that odd."

"No."

"You didn't say to yourself, hmmm, I got a 911 phone call about this body, yet nobody in this gallery called it in? You didn't question why the person who called 911 didn't bother to stick around and speak with you?"

"No. Anonymous phone calls are not an unusual occurrence."

"But wasn't this particular situation unusual? It's 2:30 AM, nobody is around the gallery, let alone in the gallery, and the only people still at the gallery were my client and Mr. Michaelson. That's not an unusual occurrence?"

"Well, I guess that's somewhat unusual."

"To me, it's very unusual. What happened to the mystery person who dialed 911?"

"I don't know."

"And you're sure it wasn't my client who called?"

"I'm positive. He gave me his phone and there wasn't a call made to emergency services."

"And he didn't use Mr. Michaelson's phones to call it in?"

"No. I recovered Mr. Michaelson's cell phone at the scene and there wasn't a call from that phone, either."

I was satisfied I had drawn blood with this exchange, so I moved on.

"Now, you saw the body on the floor. How much blood was pooled around Mr. Michaelson's chest?"

"The blood on his chest measured about the size of a half dollar."

"A half dollar. So, it was like this." I used my forefinger and thumb to approximate the size of a half dollar. "Is that correct?"

"That is correct."

"So not much blood."

"No. But that's not unusual, either. The knife was plunged directly into the heart which caused death instantaneously. There wouldn't be a large amount of blood in a case like this."

"I understand that, but there's a difference between not a large amount of blood and blood that only measured the circumference of a half dollar, isn't there?"

"I guess," he said. "But I'm not a medical doctor so I can't speak to that."

"You're not a medical doctor, but you are an officer, aren't you? You routinely get called to homicide cases, correct?"

"That's correct."

"Then that makes you experienced in the amount of blood that should be present for any given homicide, correct? You could generally know how much blood would be present when somebody is stabbed in, say, the jugular, versus the amount of blood that might be present when somebody is stabbed in the leg or in the chest or abdomen. Right?"

"That's right."

"And you're telling the court that, if somebody is

stabbed in the heart, the amount of blood that will be noticeable at the scene would be only the size of a half dollar?"

"I've seen other bodies who have been stabbed through the heart, and usually there is more blood on the body. But it's not unheard of for there to be such little blood."

"Not unheard of. In all the homicide cases you've done, have you ever seen a heart stabbing where there was as little blood as what you found on Mr. Michaelson?"

"No."

"I have nothing further for this witness."

I sat down. I did a pretty good job with the officer. I knew Ally would ask some follow-up questions, so I was prepared for that.

"Counselor," Judge Reiner addressed Ally. "Your witness."

"Thank you, your honor." Ally approached the Officer Wyler. "Officer Wyler, just for the record, you have been to crime scenes where the person who called 911 was not present, correct?"

"Correct."

"What might be some reasons why an individual who called 911 not want to be present at the scene?"

"Objection," I said, "calls for speculation."

"Sustained. Counselor, please re-phrase the question."

"In your experience, what have been some reasons why an individual who called 911 would not want to be present at the scene?"

"Well, in my experience, it's usually because the person was a witness not seen by the perpetrator and they fear reprisal if they gave their name. They naturally would not be on the scene when the officers arrived. And that's actually why some people call 911 anonymously - they don't want to get involved in the case."

"I have nothing further."

"Mr. Harrington," Judge Reiner said, "do you have anything more for this witness?"

"No, your honor."

"Officer Wyler, you may be excused."

Officer Wyler stepped down and Ally was invited by the judge to call her next witness.

She called Dill to the stand.

Chapter Twenty-Four

I LOOKED OVER AT DILL, who looked like he was going to face an execution. He walked very, very slowly, and, when he passed our table, he and Leland locked eyes. Leland nodded his head and smiled and Dill gave a half-hearted smile back.

Then he took the stand and was sworn in.

"Dill Dewitt," he said when Ally asked him to state his name.

"Mr. Dewitt, are you the legal husband of Mr. Leland Dewitt, the defendant in this case?"

"Yes I am."

"And were you present in the Dewitt Gallery on the night of April 8 of this year?"

"I was."

"Was there any kind of a conflict between you and Mr. Leland Dewitt that evening?"

He looked at Leland, his eyes getting big and terrified. "Yes," he said softly. "There was."

"And what kind of conflict happened that night?"

He took a deep breath. "I'm ashamed of it, but Jackson, Mr. Michaelson, and I were having sex in the studio apartment in the back of the gallery. Leland came back and caught us in the act."

Ally smiled. "Caught you in the act." She looked like the cat who had eaten the canary. "And what happened after Mr. Dewitt caught the two of you in the act?"

Dill cleared his throat. "He screamed at both of us. He cried and started saying, over and over, 'how could you do this to me, how could you do this to me, how could you do this to me?'" Dill shook his head. "I can't forgive myself for doing that."

"So he started yelling at the two of you," Ally said. "Is that all he did?"

"No. He wasn't drinking when he caught us but started drinking right after that. Which is bad. He had taken his Ambien pill right before he caught us and knew he wasn't supposed to be drinking when taking the Ambien. When he has problems with Ambien it's usually because he was drinking with the medicine."

"When you say 'he has problems with Ambien,' what do you mean by that?"

"He sometimes has incidents where he's having a conversation with me and has no memory of it the next day. Other times, he gets up and eats a whole meal while he's on the Ambien and has no idea he's even doing it. One time, he drove to a convenience store and back and had no memory of it the next day. But usually this happens when he takes his Ambien while drinking."

"And you say he was drinking and taking Ambien that night, correct?"

"Right." Dill took a deep breath and then slunk down in his chair. His body language said *please make this stop. Make it stop.*

"Now you and Mr. Michaelson were having sex and Mr. Dewitt caught you. Have you been in contact with Mr. Michaelson prior to this incident?"

"Well, yes. He was a good friend of Leland's and was definitely Leland's most important sponsored artist."

"By sponsored, you mean?"

"I mean Leland has this gallery and also has many other galleries in New York City. He always has exhibits and gallery showings featuring Jackson's work. He also has many friends in the art world and has made sure his friends also show Jackson's work. Plus he gave Jackson a monthly stipend when Jackson was first starting out. He also got him an apartment in New York."

"He did all that for Jackson?" Ally said. "Impressive."

"Well he believed in Jackson, that's all. He knew talent when he saw it. Leland is very good at recognizing somebody who has, as he calls it, a powerful and unique voice. Jackson definitely had that. If Leland didn't come along to sponsor him, somebody would've."

"But somebody didn't sponsor him. Leland sponsored him. Leland was his main benefactor. Would it be safe to say Leland expected a degree of loyalty from Jackson? After all, he gave Jackson his start and continued to promote him. Leland Dewitt is a billionaire with billionaire friends. I don't believe it would be overstepping my bounds to say that, without Leland's largesse, Jackson would not be the superstar he was when he died."

"Objection," I said, "Counselor is testifying and speculating while she does it. She doesn't know if Jackson would or wouldn't be a superstar without Leland, so I move to strike the last part of her statement from the record."

"Sustained," Judge Reiner said. "Counselor, you know better than to editorialize. This is my warning. That part of your question will be stricken from the record. Now please rephrase the question, this time without commentary."

"Sure," Ally said. "Mr. Dewitt, is it fair to say that Leland Dewitt expected loyalty from Jackson Michaelson?"

"Of course he did." Dill nodded.

"But he wasn't loyal, was he? In fact, he was extremely disloyal. Wouldn't you say?"

"Well…"

"Well, what? Did he or didn't he have sex with you and are you or are you not the husband of Leland Dewitt?"

"Well, yes."

"The answer is yes and you equivocate on whether or not Jackson was loyal to your husband?"

"I mean, we didn't mean anything by it, having sex like that. We both were inebriated – he was on drugs and I was drunk. And it just happened. It didn't mean anything to either of us, though."

"I see. So, in your book, having sex isn't being disloyal unless the two parties mean it?"

"Yeah. I guess so."

Ally rolled her eyes and sighed. "Okay. But wasn't Jackson texting you for months before this incident?'

"Yes." Dill shifted uncomfortably in his seat.

"Yes. And wasn't Jackson texting you photos of his latest paintings?"

"Yes."

"And weren't these photos texted to you before they were texted to Leland?"

"Yes."

"In fact, there were times when Jackson didn't even bother to text Leland these photos of his artwork, right? He would exclusively text you and not him, right?"

"Well, right. I mean, I got him more than Leland ever did. I understood what he was trying to do with his art. What message he was trying to convey. Leland more saw him as a money-maker. He knew Jackson was talented, but he really wasn't on the same wave-length as Jackson, as far as Jackson's art is concerned. I *was* on that wave-length."

"But Leland was very hurt that Jackson showed you his art work before he showed him, right?"

"Well, right…"

"And he had expressed to you how hurt he was about that, correct?"

"Right. But-"

"So Leland didn't buy the argument that you 'got' Jackson more than he did, did he?"

"No. But that was why Jackson preferred to deal with me. I could critique him better because I understood him more than Leland did. He wanted my feedback."

"That's not the issue here, is it? The issue is how your relationship with Jackson made Leland feel and you just told the court that Leland was very hurt by what you and Jackson had with one another, right?"

"Right."

"And, in fact, Jackson had sexted you a time or two, didn't he?"

"Well, yes, usually when he was totally high, though."

"Again with the intoxicated excuse." Ally shook her head. "Leland found out about the sexting at the same time he found out about the art texting, right?"

"That's right."

"And how did he react when he found out?"

"He was angry and hurt. He called Jackson and chewed him out."

"He chewed Jackson out?" Ally said. "What kind of words did he express to Jackson when he chewed him out?"

"He screamed at Jackson about doing that and said he was hurt that, after everything he did for him, he would prefer me over him. But he never threatened to kill him or anything like that."

I inwardly groaned. Dill's testimony was going a long way towards making the jury think Leland was guilty and I once again questioned Dill's motives. Maybe he really was trying to get rid of Leland so he could live high on the hog on Leland's money without having to put up with the hassle of Leland himself. It certainly was a possibility.

Then again, he had to tell the truth. He was telling his truth and it just so happened to make my client look really, really bad.

"He never threatened to kill him, but he had words with him, right?"

"Right."

"Mr. Dewitt, has the defendant ever gotten violent with you while under the influence of Ambien?"

More uncomfortable shifting in his seat. "No."

"Has he ever gotten violent in front of you while under the influence of Ambien?"

He sighed. "Yes. Yes, he has." He shook his head.

I looked over at Leland and wrote a note. "What the hell?" I asked him in my note.

Leland just shook his head and looked down at the table.

Great. Just great. These two idiots didn't bother to tell me about this. I sat up straight and listened for what was about to come next.

"He got violent while under the influence of Ambien?"

"Yes, he did." Dill shook his head.

"Please enlighten me," Ally said. She looked over at Leland accusingly. "When did Leland show violence while taking Ambien?"

"Well, it was only the one time," Dill said with an uncertain tone in his voice. "We were at a party and a guy was hitting on me all night. Leland had taken his Ambien because he does that sometimes – he takes it an hour before bedtime and wanted to leave the party early, so he took his Ambien early. He figured he would be in bed in an hour but we stayed later than he wanted to."

"You stayed later than he wanted to. And what happened when Leland saw this guy hitting on you at the party?"

"He got very angry and started to beat on the guy. But that's all it was – he beat on him. The guy didn't fight back because he was too drunk, and that was that. The fight was over before it started, really."

Ally nodded. "And Leland hasn't been violent with anybody when he *wasn't* taking Ambien, right?"

"Right."

"Perhaps Ambien brings out his rage?"

"Objection," I said, rising to my feet. "Calls for speculation and expert testimony. This witness is not qualified to speak on what the side effects are for Ambien."

"Sustained."

Ally took a deep breath, knowing she had drawn blood. Lots of it. She glared at me and sat down. "I have nothing further for this witness."

Great. This was just great. I would have to clean up this mess. I would have to somehow, someway, rehabilitate Dill. I was so angry that Leland and Dill told me nothing about

Leland's little violent episode while on Ambien. I also didn't know about how Leland would drive while on Ambien. It was pretty clear that Leland's problem with the drug was more extensive than he was willing to tell me. That pissed me off.

I hated when my clients hid things and lied. It was always so stupid when they do so, too, because it always came out in the most inopportune times. Usually in the middle of trial, as was happening right now.

I approached Dill, who was looking like he wanted the floor to open him up and swallow him whole.

"Mr. Dewitt," I began. "You're privy to the relationship between Leland and Jackson, correct?"

"Yes," he said uncertainly. "That's correct."

"To your knowledge, has Leland ever threatened Jackson?"

"Threatened him how?"

"Threatened his life. Or threatened him in general – threatened to cut him off financially, threatened to ruin his career somehow, threatened to start pulling his works from his gallery. Any kind of threats."

"No, I never heard about any kind of threats that Leland made to Jackson."

"So, is it fair to say that Leland wasn't angry enough with Jackson to threaten him?"

"Yes, that's fair to say."

I paced back and forth. "And Leland never actually brandished a weapon against anybody while under the influence of Ambien, did he?"

"No, he never did."

"He just got into a fist fight that one time, correct?"

"Correct."

"Was anybody hurt in that fist fight?"

"No, nobody was hurt."

"Did you fear somebody would be hurt in that fist fight?"

"No, I wasn't afraid that somebody would be hurt."

"So, is it fair to say that you've never actually witnessed Leland express any kind of life-threatening violence while under the influence of Ambien?"

"Definitely fair to say," Dill said, nodding. "Definitely fair to say."

"Now," I said, "how would you characterize Leland's interest in Jackson?"

"Well, it was an ego boost."

"In what way?"

"Leland looked pretty hip and cool to his friends because he was such good friends with such a hot young cutting-edge artist. You know, his best friend is this art superstar known all over the world. That was a definite feather in his cap."

I nodded. "So knowing Jackson was an ego boost for Leland, then?"

"Yes, a definite ego boost."

"Then is it fair to say that Leland cares about his social standing?"

"Oh, definitely, definitely," Dill nodded. "He cares very much about what his circle of friends thinks about him. He very much likes to keep up with the Joneses."

"And how do his friends treat him now that he's been accused of Jackson's murder?"

"Well, he definitely doesn't get too many invites to parties anymore. His friends have mostly stopped returning his phone calls. His dance card is definitely not as full as it once was." Dill shook his head sadly. "It's been difficult to watch him trying to get in contact with all his friends. They don't answer the phone. When he calls them at their office, their secretary tells him they're busy. I know it hurts his feelings to be shunned like this."

"And it's important to him that the people in his social circle look up to him, correct?"

"Very correct."

"Mr. Dewitt, do you believe your husband killed Jackson Michaelson?"

"Oh, no," he shook his head adamantly. "No I don't."

"And why don't you think he killed Jackson?"

"Well, as I was saying, Leland got a lot out of his connection to Jackson. Even if he weren't accused of Jackson's murder, he still would have found himself shunned by many of his friends. Sad to say that many of them only wanted to be friends with Leland because they wanted contact with Jackson. Everybody wanted a piece of that boy."

"Is that the only reason why you believe Leland didn't kill Jackson?"

"Well, that and the fact that I don't think he has it in him. Even when he's under the influence of Ambien, he would never do something like that to another human being. He's just too kind and gentle."

I took a deep breath. It wasn't the best exchange in the world but would have to do. I didn't feel that I completely rehabilitated him, but it was what it was. I would have to live to fight another day and hope I got Leland's story out through other witnesses. "I have nothing further."

"Counselor," Judge Reiner said to Ally. "You have any follow-up questions?"

Ally appeared to think about it but finally stood up. "No, your honor."

"Mr. Dewitt, you may step down. Ms. Hughes, call your next witness."

"The state calls Dr. Richard Hyman," Ally said.

Dr. Richard Hyman was the expert witness who would establish what the Ambien effects were. Dr. Hyman would testify that it was certainly possible for somebody to kill another person while taking Ambien and not remember it. He had a patient where this occurred and would testify about it. This was one witness who could very well sink my case and I knew it.

Dr. Hyman was an older gentleman with white hair, blue eyes and a bulbous nose. He walked slowly with a cane as he approached the witness stand. Nevertheless, I knew he would be an astute expert and I would have to cross-examine him hard.

He raised his right hand and swore to the tell the truth, stated his name, and Ally got right down to business.

"Dr. Hyman, could you please state your title?" Ally asked him.

"I am a medical doctor and board certified as a sleep specialist."

"And, as a sleep specialist, what do you do?"

"I treat individuals with sleep disorders, including sleep apnea and chronic insomnia."

"Do you sometimes prescribe the drug Zolpidem, commonly known as Ambien?"

"No I don't. Not anymore."

"You don't prescribe it anymore. And why is that?"

"I have had several patients who complained to me about driving while on Ambien and I even had one patient murder his mother while on Ambien. I decided this was a drug that can have dangerous side effects and I have refused to prescribe it to my patients."

"Okay." Ally nodded. "You said you had a patient murder his mother while taking Ambien. Can you tell me a little bit about that particular case?"

"Yes. It was two years ago. His name was Bradley Spencer. I treated him for insomnia for several months. We did a sleep study where I studied his biorhythms while he slept and I counseled him on proper sleep hygiene. There are things that everyone can do to help them sleep better at night. Go to bed at the same time each night, only use your bed for sleep and not for electronics, and not eat past a certain point. Lifestyle changes. These didn't work, so I prescribed Ambien."

"And were you prescribing Ambien on a regular basis at this time?"

"Yes, I was."

"Tell me about what happened with Bradley Spencer."

"He was taking Ambien on a regular basis and has no history of violence or mental illness. He murdered his mother one night while on Ambien and did not remember the crime when he woke up. I spoke with him while he was in jail, awaiting trial, and spoke with the officers at the scene. They said that when they arrived at his home, he was sitting next to his mother's body, completely in a daze. He had a conversation with the officers and the officers took him downtown. Gradually, the effects of the Ambien wore off and he became lucid. He did not remember killing his mother nor did he remember speaking with the officers. He didn't remember the trip to the police station nor did he remember speaking with the officers at the station."

"I see. And did you do research on this?"

"Yes. After this incident occurred, I started reading medical journals. Turns out there had been several 'Ambien murders' that have occurred through the years. That was when I decided Ambien was too dangerous to prescribe to my patients and I stopped prescribing it."

"When a person is under the influence of Ambien and they do something while under the influence – it could be something as innocuous as having a conversation with one's roommate or it could be something as serious as committing a crime – what is their state at the time they're doing this action?"

"They are, for all practical purposes, still asleep. Their brain waves are identical to somebody in a deep sleep. Yet they're talking, eating, or driving – I have researched cases where people on Ambien have killed people while driving. Since they were asleep at the time of the action, they won't have any memory of what happened. They won't have a memory of it any more than you would have a memory of being in the middle of a deep, restorative sleep."

"So the defendant in this case, Leland Dewitt, is accused of killing a man while under the influence of Ambien. In your professional opinion, is it possible he could have done this?"

"Well, of course, I have to make one caveat to my answer on this, and that is that I have not treated Mr. Dewitt personally. But, yes, it is possible, especially if he was taking the Ambien in conjunction with alcohol."

"I have nothing further."

I scratched my head, wondering if I should cross-examine him. He was a solid witness – he was able to speak in layman's terms in words that everyone could understand. He was an expert in his field and it was certainly true there had been several "Ambien murders" throughout the years. Leland fit the bill on this.

"Counselor," Judge Reiner addressed me. "Do you have any questions for this witness?"

"Yes, your honor," I said, standing up.

I approached him. "Now, Dr. Hyman, you said you stopped prescribing Ambien after one of your patients murdered his mother while on the effects of the drug, correct?"

"Correct."

"I know about that case. I read about it. It turned out you prescribed the maximum of 10 mg, yet he admitted he was routinely taking 20 mg or more of the medicine, isn't that right?"

"Yes, that is correct. He was definitely using the medicine in dosages well above the maximum."

"In fact, in the other cases involving Ambien murders, there were always some kind of mitigating factor, wasn't there?"

"Such as?"

"Such as taking too much of the medicine or taking other drugs in conjunction with the medicine. Typically, the patients who have murdered somebody while taking Ambien took dosages over two times the maximum legal limit. Several of them were also on anti-depressants at the time, isn't that right?"

"Yes, that's right."

"Now, you have the result of my client's tox screening taken on the date of his arrest. It was taken as soon as he got to the police station. Can you tell the court if my client's blood work showed he took a higher-than-maximum dosage of the drug?"

"Yes."

"And did he take a higher-than-maximum dosage?"

"According to my analysis, no he did not."

"And he wasn't on other drugs at the time, was he? Like

anti-depressants, blood pressure meds, street drugs or anything like that, was he?"

"No, he wasn't. He was drinking alcohol, however."

"Yes, he admittedly was. However, have you run across any cases of Ambien murders where the individual took under the maximum dosage, or right at the maximum, and killed somebody, even if that person was also drinking at the time?"

"No, I have not."

"In fact, there was a case where a man was drinking whiskey with his Ambien and he murdered his housemate, but he had taken five times the maximum dosage, isn't that right?"

"Yes, that is correct."

"But that was the only case where alcohol played a part, correct?"

"Correct."

"So if my client took the maximum dosage, but not above the maximum dosage, it would be unlikely he could kill somebody and not remember it, even if he was also drinking, isn't that right?"

"Well, it's highly unlikely that any patient will kill somebody, even if they are taking more than the maximum dosage."

"Then it's even more unlikely that somebody like my client, who did not take over the maximum dosage, would kill somebody and not remember it?"

"Yes, that is very unlikely."

"In fact, that has never happened, has it?"

"You mean, it has never happened that somebody who has not taken over the maximum dosage killed somebody while under the influence of Ambien?"

"Right."

"No, that has never happened."

"Nothing further."

I sat down and smiled. I felt that exchange went quite well. I glanced over at Leland and I could see he thought so, too.

This was shaping up to be a decent trial after all.

And I hadn't even gotten to cross-examine the one person I really wanted to get my hands on.

The Medical Examiner.

Chapter Twenty-Five

UNFORTUNATELY, I didn't get the chance to cross-examine Dr. Katy Moore, the Medical Examiner in this case, that day. After Dr. Hyman was finished with his testimony, Judge Reiner announced that the time was 4:30 and we were calling it quits for the day.

"Be here bright and early tomorrow morning at 9 sharp," he called out to the jury members, who filed out of the courtroom.

I gathered my belongings, stepped out of the courtroom and immediately had microphones shoved in my face. I sighed. "Look, guys, you know I can't comment on this case, so why do you keep asking?" I shoved my way through the throng and made my way to the elevator, with Leland right behind me.

"That went well," Leland said. "As well as could be expected. I think you really schooled some of those witnesses."

"Thanks," I said, "but tomorrow is our make-or-break. And Dill did us some harm. I think he did us a lot of damage. I know he had to tell the truth and all, but the truth really didn't help us, did it?"

"No, I guess it didn't," Leland said. "But his testimony wasn't fatal, was it?"

"No. I think I rehabilitated him pretty well on cross-examination. Tomorrow, the Medical Examiner cross will be crucial. That, coupled with my putting Dr. Melber on the stand, should seal the deal. Although I have a feeling Wilson Raine will be the weak link in all of this."

I had dug up what I needed to on Dr. Moore, and found the link she possibly had with Dr. Ashton Melber. I had this information and would use it against her to break her down on the stand. I already had my cross-examination perfectly lined up. By the time I got through with her, I could probably get a directed verdict out of the deal.

At least, that was my hope. A directed verdict meant I wouldn't even have to put my witnesses on. It meant the state didn't meet their burden of proof. When a judge directed a verdict, it took the entire thing out of the jury's hands, because it meant automatic acquittal. I had never in my professional career managed to get a directed verdict, but I just might this time.

I went home that night and found something I didn't really plan on seeing.

My mother was standing on my front porch.

Chapter Twenty-Six

"HEY, MOM," I said, unlocking my door. "Why didn't you just go in? I got my nanny, Gretchen, in there watching the kids."

"I didn't want to barge on in there. I don't know that girl from Eve."

"Okay, then," I said. "Well, don't just stand there, come on in. You're welcome to stay for dinner, too."

"I don't want to be a pain in the ass," she said. "But if you're making it, I guess I'll be eating it."

"It looks like you could use a good meal, to be honest with you." Mom was always super skinny, but she'd lost about 10 pounds since even the last time I saw her.

"Are you eating enough, Mom?"

"Son, I'm never eating enough. But that's not why I'm here, to mooch food off you."

We walked in the door. The kids saw my mother and they got up off the floor, where they were sitting and watching TV, and ran over to her. "Grandma!" Amelia said excitedly. She threw her arms around my mom's waist and beamed.

For Nate's part, he was standing behind his sister, waiting to give Mom a hug. Mom reached out her arms and gave Nate a hug while Amelia was still holding onto her. "Group hug," she announced.

The kids finally let go and went back to sit in front of the TV. I paid Gretchen, who thanked me and left. "Okay, Mom," I said. "What's going on?"

"What do you mean, what's going on? Can't I see my only son and my only grandkids without you thinking I got something up my sleeve?"

"Actually…" I shook my head. I had seen Mom once a month for the past few months, going over to her trailer home every time. But she had never once come to my home. I naturally thought something was probably up.

"I mean, I'm happy to see you, Mom, but, yes, I am curious about what brought you here."

"Eh, you got me. Yeah, I gotta reason to be here."

"Go ahead."

"Well, I don't know how to say this, so I'm just gonna come out and say it. I told your dad about you. He wants to meet you."

I raised an eyebrow. "Excuse me? Why would you do that?" After I found out who my father was, I chose not to get in touch with him. My mom made it clear she didn't want me getting involved with Josh Roland, and I didn't want to, anyhow. I had no interest in getting to know the man who raped my mother, even if said man was my dad. I had lived this long without knowing the bastard. I could keep going without knowing him.

Yet my mom chose to tell my father about me. I wondered why she would do that.

"Listen, I don't know what happened, what kind of birdie got into his ear, but he showed up at my house one day. You won't believe this, but he showed up wanting to apologize. After all these years, he's on my stoop apologizing for raping me. Well, I told him he knocked me up all those years ago and told him about you. He said he didn't have any children anymore, because his own son died of an overdose, and he wants to get to know you. His own son was your age."

"Oh? And what happened to you saying you didn't want me getting involved with that crazy-ass family?"

She shrugged. "Well, I don't know what to tell ya except for that things seem to be different with him. He's not quite as nutty and violent as I remembered him. He told me losing his son changed him, and, who knows, maybe people can change. He's gonna come and visit you here, but he's gonna call first."

I sighed. "Mom, I'm in the middle of this huge murder trial right now," I said. "The last thing I want to do is visit with my long-lost rapist father."

"Then he'll come on over after your trial," she said. "Listen, you're not gonna get out of this. I know, I know, I shouldn't have thrown you under the bus like that, but you really should know your father. He was a bastard back then but I don't think he is anymore."

I hung my head and stared at my hands. "You really don't know why he decided to seek you out after all these years? That's weird, isn't it?"

"Yeah, well, I might have lied about that, sorry." She sighed. "Listen, it's been eating at me ever since you saw me and I told you about what happened with Josh. So, I went to his office and demanded he see me. You could have knocked me over with a feather when he agreed to talk to me.

Turned out that he got himself into AA several years ago and wanted to make amends for raping me all those years ago. He was glad to see me for that reason. We talked, I told him about you, he said 'are you sure,' I said 'I'm positive,' and that was that. He wants to see you."

I felt myself getting pissed at her, first because she lied and second because she talked to my father without telling me she would do it.

"Okay, fine," I said. "I'll meet with him after the trial. But when I say after the trial, I mean after the trial. Tomorrow will be pivotal in this trial. So, after dinner, you can hang out here and play with the kids if you want, but I'm going into my office to prepare for tomorrow."

"Do what you want, I don't give a crap," Mom said. "As long as you feed me."

I got the food on the table and we all sat down to eat.

"Man, Nate," Mom said as she watched him wolfing down his food. "Slow down, you're gonna explode like Creosote in *The Meaning of Life*." She pointed at me with her fork. "You remember that scene, don't you, Damien? When that big fat man kept puking into a bucket while he ate, and then he finally exploded all over everyone in the restaurant?" She started to laugh. "Ooo, boy, I love that movie."

I smiled. I got the reference, but not really. Nate was skinny as a reed. You wouldn't know it by looking at him, but I had never seen anybody eat at much as him.

"Yep, Mom, I remember. The wafer thin mint was the last straw."

"Yeah," she said. "And you, Amelia, you're just picking at that food." She looked at me. "You better look out, Damien, she might end up with anorexia. Amelia, you're a beautiful girl, I don't know why you don't want to eat. You won't get fat, I promise."

"Mom," I said, "Amelia just happens to not like Shepherd's Pie so much," I said. "That's all."

"What the hell is wrong with Shepherd's Pie?" Mom asked. "Man, this is good Shepherd's Pie. I eat this stuff at my friend's house all the time and she doesn't drain her hamburger."

After dinner, I went upstairs and got right to work. I went over the autopsy report and reviewed my other evidence I had about Dr. Moore. I would break her down hard.

My grilling of her would be the turning point of this case. Either I would draw blood tomorrow or I wouldn't. If I did, the trial was over. I won. But if she held firm, I would have to rely on the possibility I could break somebody else down.

The stakes in cross-examining her couldn't be higher.

Chapter Twenty-Seven

THE NEXT DAY, I got to the courthouse early. I sometimes liked to get to the courthouse early so I could just relax. I didn't like to rush in the morning. I preferred just to come into the courtroom with my cup of coffee and just…relax. It was so early that even the media hadn't yet arrived. That was another reason why I wanted to get there early – I didn't want to face the media bullshit.

Leland got there a little before nine and sat down next to me. He clasped his hands in front of him.

"Are you ready for this?" he asked me.

I shrugged. "I guess so," I said. "I mean, yes. Yes, I am ready for this."

Harper was next to arrive. She looked harried, which she sometimes did. Harper was somebody who tended to run a little late. She seemed out of breath.

"Sorry I'm late," she said to me, "traffic was a bitch."

"Not a biggie," I said, "the judge isn't here yet, neither is the jury. Just relax."

She took a deep breath. "I will. It's just that..." She shook her head. "I just hope this works."

"It will. By hook or by crook, it will. I got this."

"I hope." She looked around. "The media has been on this like white on rice, haven't they?"

"Yeah," I said. "They keep asking me for a comment, as if I tell them anything at all about the case. They should know better than to ask a lawyer to comment on a pending case. One would think."

"One would think," Harper agreed.

The judge got on the bench and the jury was seated. Ally took her place, along with her second-chair, Ronald Todd. It wasn't quite time to start, so Ally came over to where I was sitting.

"I think you're buying me dinner," she said, "because you're going down."

"Don't be so sure," I said. "I have an Ace up my sleeve. You'll see and then you'll wish you dismissed the case when I asked you to."

That was something that happened once I started putting the pieces of the puzzle together. I went to Ally and asked her to drop the charges against my client. She laughed me out of the office.

I would end up laughing. At least, I hoped so.

"My next witness, Dr. Moore, will be my last witness," she said. "After that, I guess I cede the floor to you."

"I figured she would be your last witness," I said. "You know the people I have lined up. But I wouldn't be surprised if I get a directed verdict on this one."

"You're trying to mind-fuck me," Ally said, "but it won't work. I don't intimidate easily."

"We'll see if you intimidate easily."

"Okay," Judge Reiner said, banging his gavel. "The case

of State v. Dewitt has come to order. Ladies and gentlemen of the jury, the state is still presenting evidence. Counselor, call your next witness."

"The State calls Dr. Katy Moore."

Dr. Moore approached the bench. She was a tall lady, about 50 years old, with grey hair tied back. She walked rapidly and with purpose. She sat down, took her oath, stated her name, and Ally got right to it.

"Dr. Moore," Ally said, "you are the Medical Examiner on this case, are you not?"

"I am," she said. "I am the medical examiner for this case."

"And you examined the body of Jackson Michaelson, did you not?"

"I did. I did the autopsy of Jackson Michaelson."

"What were your conclusions?"

"I concluded that Jackson Michaelson died from a stab wound to the heart."

"What caused you to draw that conclusion?"

"I examined the body and noted there was a tear in the left ventricle of the heart. There was also a laceration on the chest where the knife made contact with the deceased. I examined the body and found that, other than the tear in the chest and the laceration in the chest, the body was unremarkable. There were no other injuries present in the body and, while the toxicology screening showed the deceased had large amounts of heroin in his system, I concluded the stab wound to the heart was the primary cause of death."

"Can you tell the court your qualifications to make these judgments?"

"Yes. I am board certified in forensic pathology and graduated from Harvard Medical School with a medical degree in 1979. I completed four years of training in forensic pathology, along with a forensic pathology fellowship. I have been a medical examiner in Jackson County for 27 years."

"I have nothing further."

I stood up, relishing the chance to put her on the spot, yet, at the same time, strangely dreading it. She had her reasons for doing what she did and they were good reasons to her. I felt a bit of pity for her, because, if this cross-examination went the way I wanted, she would possibly lose her career.

Yet, I had to do what I had to do.

I approached her. "Dr. Moore, you stated the cause of death for Jackson Michaelson was a stab to his heart, correct?"

"Yes, that was my conclusion."

"It didn't concern you that the amount of blood around the chest wound was so minimal?"

"No. It is not unusual for there to be minimal bleeding when the stabbing is directly into the heart. The heart stops beating immediately, which means the blood stops pumping at the point of impact. I did not find it unusual at all that there was minimal bleeding with this wound."

I nodded my head. "Are you the mother of Landon Moore?"

She shifted in her seat uncomfortably. "Yes, that is my son."

"Is it true that Landon Moore has been convicted for possession with intent to distribute three times and has served time in state prison for these crimes all three times?"

"Objection," Ally said, standing on her feet. "Relevance."

"Counselor," Judge Reiner said, "what is the relevance

of whether or not her son has been convicted of drug possession with intent to distribute?"

"May I approach?" I asked.

Judge Reiner motioned to me and I went up to the bench with Ally.

"The crux of the defense is that Dr. Moore was subject to blackmail. I'll show she was blackmailed by Dr. Melber into changing her findings on the cause of Jackson's death. Her son, who has been convicted several times of possession with intent to distribute and who would have been arrested a fourth time, if not for the intervention of Dr. Melber on her son's behalf, is at the heart of the blackmail scheme."

Judge Reiner shook his head. "I'll allow it, but if you get over your skis, counselor, I will shut it down. And your line of questioning on this matter better come to something, because if it ends up looking like a fishing expedition, I will have the entire exchange stricken from the record. And I won't give you any quarter whatsoever in your case in chief if this thing goes sideways. Fair warning."

I nodded, feeling the pressure to produce. I knew how impatient Judge Reiner could be and knew there was an excellent chance that, if I didn't produce anything in this witness, he probably would shut me down with my witnesses. That meant that either Dr. Moore confessed to being a part of the blackmail scheme or I would end up losing this case.

No pressure.

Ally sat down and I approached Dr. Moore again. "Okay, the last question I asked was about your son, Landon Moore. As I understand it, he has been convicted three times for possession with intent to distribute, is that right?"

She cleared her throat. "Yes, that is correct." She shifted

in her seat uncomfortably and I could see terror in her eyes. She tried to hide it, but I could see it. She wasn't one to hide her emotions, that much I could tell.

"Now, as I understand it, you did not release your findings of Mr. Michaelson's death for six weeks, is that correct?"

"Yes, that is correct."

"And why were the findings so delayed?"

"I saw there was a large amount of heroin in the deceased's system and was concerned that perhaps Mr. Michaelson had actually died before he was stabbed in the heart. I wanted to get the result of the toxicology screening before I made my final findings."

I smiled, seeing this was going well. Very well.

"You thought it possible that Mr. Michaelson had died of a drug overdose before he was stabbed in the heart. Yet, you found this was not the case. Why did you end up making those findings?"

"I made those findings because the amount of drugs in his system was not sufficient to have killed him. Plus, I found there was blood on the chest at the time Mr. Michaelson expired and that would not be the case if Mr. Michaelson had passed before he was stabbed in the chest. There would not be any blood around the wound in that case."

"Oh? Even if somebody had stabbed Mr. Michaelson right after his heart stopped beating?"

"It would have to have been instantaneous. The stabbing would have to have come right after the heart stopped beating, within 30 seconds to a minute."

I nodded. "You tested the blood around that wound, did you not?"

"Yes, I did," she said, nodding. "I tested that blood."

"Why did you test that blood? I mean, is that part of your routine when you examine a body?"

"No, that is not a part of my routine."

"Then why did you test it this time?"

She cleared her throat. "I tested the blood because I was concerned the blood pooled around the wound on the deceased's chest did not belong to him."

"I see. And why did you suspect that?"

"Because I initially thought the deceased had expired before he was stabbed. My initial thought was there was a cover-up of some sort. That perhaps the deceased had overdosed and somebody made it look like a murder."

I nodded my head. "And, in fact, you did a DNA analysis of the blood on the deceased's chest, did you not?"

She swallowed hard. "No, I did not. I simply tested to see if the blood type was the same as the deceased. O positive. The blood around the wound was the same blood type as the deceased, so I was satisfied with this."

I nodded. I knew that she was lying. She *did* order a DNA analysis of the blood, because she knew there was something rotten in the state of Denmark on this one. The results of the DNA analysis clearly showed the blood around the knife wound *did not* match Jackson, which ultimately meant Wilson Raine must have been ordered to make the whole thing look like a murder. He most likely plunged the knife into Jackson's chest, panicked when he saw no blood drawn, and then deliberately sliced his own hand or wrist or some part of his body that would bleed well and dripped it around the knife. That was my theory, and, if the Medical Examiner would have been honest and included the true results of her DNA analysis, which showed the blood on the chest didn't belong to Jackson, this whole case would've been long over.

I had presented the results of the secret DNA test to Ally and she still didn't drop the charges. She stood by the Medical Examiner's findings, even though the blood on the body didn't match Jackson's blood. I couldn't understand why that didn't convince her but it didn't. She had accused me of fabricating the DNA evidence and said it was obtained illegally, which it admittedly was. Harper's hacker, Anna, somehow got her hands on it. That girl was amazing. Because the results were obtained illegally, Ally thought I had somehow created the results from whole cloth and refused to believe my theory.

Her loss.

Dr. Moore didn't include that secret DNA analysis in her findings. She lied on her final report on Jackson's cause of death and I knew exactly why.

I cleared my throat. "Are you familiar with a Dr. Ashton Melber in New York City?"

She started to squirm. "I am."

"And are you aware that Dr. Ashton Melber enticed your son, Landon Moore, into distributing OxyContin to 18 people in and around the Kansas City area on his behalf?"

"He did." She wouldn't elaborate, because, at this point, she had to know where I was going.

"And your son did, in fact, distribute these drugs illegally for Dr. Melber, did he not? In exchange for $100,000, he distributed these drugs for Dr. Melber, correct?"

"Yes, that is correct." She looked like she wanted to be anywhere but where she was, answering questions that would possibly lead to criminal charges against her and would definitely result in some kind of serious discipline against her medical license. The woman worked hard all her life to get where she was, and, just like that, it would all be lost.

"And isn't it correct that Dr. Melber enticed your son into distributing illicit drugs because Dr. Melber specifically wanted blackmail to make you change your findings about Jackson Michaelson's cause of death?"

She cleared her throat. "Yes, that is why he recruited my son to distribute drugs."

"Of course that was why," I said. "I mean, the man paid your son $100,000 to distribute drugs to 18 people. That was all profit to your son, too. There was obviously a reason Dr. Melber wanted to use Landon. And isn't it true that Dr. Melber called you and said that, unless you changed the results of your autopsy report to reflect that Jackson Michaelson died of a stab wound, not of an overdose, he would report your son to the authorities anonymously?"

Dr. Moore hung her head. Her hand flew up to her throat and she found her necklace. She took the charm of her necklace in her hand and played with it.

"Yes, he called and threatened that. But that's not why I found Jackson died of his stab wound. That had nothing to do with it."

"It had nothing to do with it?" I shook my head. "Nothing to do with it?" I paced around. I shook my head. "Dr. Moore, how many people in the United States have type O positive blood?"

"Around 37% of the US population has type O positive blood," she said.

"37% of the United States population has that type blood type. That's what, 99 million people in the United States with the same blood type?"

"Yes, that is correct."

"So, what was the point of testing that blood if you just wanted to match up blood types? If there are almost 100 million people in the United States with the same blood type, what was would the testing tell you? It certainly wouldn't tell you the blood found on Jackson's body was different than Jackson's own would it?"

"I wanted to do a preliminary analysis," she began.

"Dr. Moore, isn't it true you did a DNA analysis of the blood found on Jackson's body and found this blood did not, in fact, match Jackson's own body?"

"No."

"I'll remind you that you're under oath."

Dr. Moore sat there, just staring at me. She was an animal caught in a trap with no place to go and was freaking out. It was in her eyes. I could see her wheels turning. She knew that I didn't have the documentation about the DNA test. If I did, I would have presented the findings to her on the stand. I didn't have the test, because I obtained it illegally and there was no way I could use it. So, I just had to hope she would tell the truth.

But if she told the truth, her life would be destroyed. As it was, it was possible that she could continue to lie and get out of it. It looked bad for her that she admitted Dr. Melber recruited her son because he wanted to blackmail her, but she didn't quite admit the blackmail caused her to change her findings about Jackson's death.

Then again, if she continued to lie and there was an investigation into her actions, and the truth came out about the DNA test, she would not only have an obstruction of justice and falsifying an official report to contend with but a perjury charge on top of it.

She had to know an investigation would come after this trial. She had to know that. The media was taking down our exchange with bated breath. I knew this. There was no way out for her. She had to tell the truth. Only by telling the truth would the potential damages against her be mitigated.

She finally hung her head. "Yes," she said softly. "Yes, I did a DNA analysis on the blood on Jackson Michaelson's body, and no, the blood on his body did not match the DNA analysis."

I heard a collective gasp from the jury and smiled. "In fact, you changed the results of your autopsy report to reflect Jackson died from being stabbed when you actually concluded Jackson overdosed, isn't that right?"

She sighed. "Dr. Melber told me if I didn't change the results of the autopsy, he would put in an anonymous tip on my son," she said. "What was I to do? My son would have been facing federal charges. He'd been convicted three other times. He would be facing 27 years in prison. I talked to a defense attorney and that's what he told me. 27 years in prison for my son. Mandatory minimum, he said. I had no choice but to do what Dr. Melber asked me." She hung her head and started to cry. "I was wrong for doing what I did. I know I was wrong. But what would you do? You would protect your child, no matter what."

I nodded. My work was done. I destroyed a woman's career in the process, so I couldn't feel good about it. But my work was done.

"I have nothing further for this witness."

Judge Reiner looked over at Ally. "Ms. Hughes, do you have any follow-up?"

"No, your honor." She looked over at me and I could see how embarrassed she was.

"The witness is excused."

She hung her head, tears in her eyes, and scurried rapidly out the door. Once she was on the other side of the door, I heard a loud sob coming from the hallway. I was gutted. I didn't want to do that to her. She didn't deserve it. She had the bad luck to have a no-good son and a corrupt doctor blackmailing her. I didn't blame her for doing what she did. She was as much of a victim as my client was.

Judge Reiner cleared his throat and looked at me and then to Ally. "Ms. Hughes, do you have any additional evidence to present?"

"No, your honor."

He looked at me. "Mr. Harrington do you have a motion to present?"

I knew what he was getting at. He was inviting me to move for a directed verdict. "I do, your honor. In light of Dr. Moore's testimony, I would like to move for a directed verdict of not guilty."

"Any objections to this motion, Ms. Hughes?" Judge Reiner asked Ally.

"None, your honor."

"Very well then. Defendant's motion for a directed verdict of not guilty is sustained. The defendant is free to go." He then looked over at the jury. "Ladies and gentlemen of the jury, I thank you for your service. What just happened is that the defendant moved for a directed verdict of not guilty, which is my prerogative to grant if I have found the state did not present sufficient evidence to meet its burden of proof. I have found that, in light of the testimony of the medical examiner, which proved to me that Mr. Michaelson passed away as the result of a drug overdose and not because he was stabbed, the state did not meet its burden of proof. Therefore, I have directed that the verdict in this case is not guilty. That takes the decision of guilt or innocence out of your hands. I apologize for that and I apologize your time has been wasted. Unfortunately, once in a great while, this kind of thing happens and it is bad for everyone involved. Once again, I thank you for your service. The jury is free to go."

Everyone in the jury was looking at one another in a daze. They were talking quietly amongst themselves, and I heard a lot of them saying things like "what the hell just happened?"

I gathered my documents and looked at Leland. Leland didn't look terribly excited, probably because he was pretty sure this outcome was pre-ordained. Once he knew just what had happened, he put his faith in me to prove it.

"Well, I guess I'll go home," he said. "Thank you so much for helping me out. You're as brilliant as I heard you were and even more handsome." He smiled and got up. "I have to find Dill and tell him the good news. He was so depressed last night after his testimony. He was so afraid all the bad memories would come up again. But we're good."

"You're welcome," I said. Then I looked and saw the throngs of reporters dying to get a comment from me. As I walked towards them on my way out the door, I just shook my head.

"Still no comment," I said. "You saw for yourself what happened. You don't need me spouting off cliches to make this story any more interesting than it already is."

I pushed my way through them and found myself on the elevator.

Another case down. I had to smile at how it all went. It was even smoother than I thought it would be.

Ally got on the elevator too, opening up the doors at the last minute.

"Guess I'm buying after all," she said with a smile.

"Guess so."

Chapter Twenty-Eight

April 8 - Dewitt Gallery, Kansas City, Missouri

WILSON RAINE WAS SUPPOSED to be watching Jackson Michaelson. That was his one job. Ashton Melber paid him very well to travel with Jackson all over the world and basically make sure Jackson didn't overdose. He was very careful to make sure Jackson didn't show signs of doing too much heroin. He was also very well trained to revive Jackson if something happened and his heart stopped. This was something he had done on several occasions – he traveled with electric paddles and had to restart Jackson's heart three times in the past year. Every time Jackson "coded", Wilson was there with the paddles and the Narcan to literally bring him back from the dead.

But that night was different. He was at the party Leland Dewitt had held for Jackson and was having a great time. He had caught the eye of a 6' tall blonde bombshell, the type of girl always out of his league, and was salivating on her all night. He couldn't believe his good fortune – a girl like that never gave a guy like him a second look. Yet, here she was, hanging onto his every word. She didn't even know who Jackson Michaelson was, so it wasn't like she was only flirting with him to get to Jackson. That was what usually happened – he would get to know a girl only to find out that she was only interested in meeting Jackson. But that wasn't the case with Gisela that night – she genuinely was flirting with him because she liked him. Guess she was one of the rare supermodel types who liked the skinny nerdy guys with glasses and shaggy hair.

He ended up meeting her in the bathroom and having sex with her right then and there. He still couldn't believe he could get such a goddess attracted to him. Having sex with her was like nothing he had ever felt before in his life. He felt like an important stud. The sex was primal and animalistic and she was really into it. So into it that she gave Wilson her number and asked him to meet her for drinks the next evening. Wilson was excited about this, even though he knew Jackson would have to come along on the date. That was the stipulation and the reason why Dr. Melber paid him $150,000 a year – he could never lose sight of Jackson.

After he and Gisela were finished, he knew that it was time to check on his charge. It was almost 2:30 AM and the gallery had already closed by this time. Only he and Gisela were in the gallery and he presumed Jackson was in the living space in the back of the gallery. That was the last time he saw him, anyhow.

"I'll see you tomorrow," he said to Gisela, kissing her luscious red lips one last time.

"Tomorrow," she said with a smile and a wink. "Can't wait."

He was whistling as he went to the living quarters and turned on the light.

Then he stopped.

Jackson was lying on the floor, not moving.

"Oh, shit, not again," Wilson said as he went to his bag and got out his paddles and Narcan.

He went over to Jackson, checked for a pulse, found none, and then proceeded to paddle him several times. Nothing. He turned the paddles up. Nothing. He felt Jackson's skin. It was cold to the touch.

It was then Wilson knew there was nothing that could be done. Jackson was dead and had been for some time. It was too late to do anything about it.

He went to the bathroom and threw up. And then he called Ashton Melber.

"Why are you waking me up at this time?" Ashton demanded. "Do you know what time it is? It's after 3 in the morning here in New York."

"I have to wake you," Wilson said breathlessly. "Something has happened."

"What has happened?"

"It's Jackson. He's dead."

Silence. "Did you try the paddles? The Narcan?"

"Yes. He's been dead for too long. He can't be revived this time."

Ashton exploded. "What do you mean, he's been dead for too long? You're supposed to watch him at every moment. That's your job. That's what I'm paying you a hundred and fifty grand a year to do. Your only job. How did Jackson die without your knowing about it?"

Wilson started to cry. "Well, I..." He had to come clean. "I met somebody at the party tonight. I wasn't talking to her long. I guess it was just horrible timing." He was lying, of course. He had been macking on Gisela for several hours, not even paying attention to Jackson during that time.

"Well, then, you know what to do."

"I do." Wilson nodded. "I'll find a knife and make it look like a murder."

"Go and do that. I'll wait on the line."

Wilson went to the kitchenette and found a knife. Using a paper napkin, he picked up that knife, went over to Jackson and plunged it right into his heart.

He didn't even think about the fact that there wouldn't be blood when he did that.

He went back to the phone. "I did it, but there's no blood. No blood. What can I do? The cops will come as soon as I call 911 and they'll see a body with no blood. Oh my God, they'll know something is up. What can I do?"

"Slice yourself in an area that will bleed well but not too well. Slice yourself and drip that blood on Jackson's shirt, around the knife."

"That will never fly. The Medical Examiner will know what happened."

"I'll take care of the Medical Examiner. Just do as I say."

Wilson found another knife and cut into his forearm as he stood over Jackson's body. He dripped his blood onto Jackson's shirt, just enough that an officer on the scene wouldn't be suspicious.

It was then that he saw a man. Leland. He was sitting at the dining room table, his face a complete daze. His eyes were open, however.

"Leland," Wilson said. "Did you see what happened here? You were in this room when this happened. Why didn't you find me immediately? I told you I have emergency training and can revive Jackson if something like this happened. Why didn't you find me?"

Leland's eyes were glazed over, like he was in a trance. He just shook his head as he looked at Wilson. "I don't know what you're talking about."

"Jackson. He's dead. Were you here with him the whole time?"

Leland just shook his head again, his eyes completely glazed over.

Wilson knew it was time to get out of there and call 911. He was fairly certain if there was a murder investigation, Leland would be the target. He was in the room with Jackson, after all. Plus, Wilson knew Leland was on prescription Ambien. Dr. Melber prescribed it to Leland. Wilson knew that was probably why Leland was acting so dazed – he was on Ambien right at that moment. His eyes were open but his brain was sleeping.

That was perfect, actually. Wilson had read about Ambien murders. The cops would think Leland did the murder while under the influence of Ambien and Leland wouldn't know if he did it or not. That would solve Wilson's main problem with the whole murder scenario, which was that he himself might be a suspect in the murder, just because it was known he was always with Jackson.

In a way, Wilson felt shitty about doing this. But he had to save his own hide. If he didn't do this, Dr. Melber would make sure he went to prison. Dr. Melber had evidence that Wilson was into kiddy porn, evidence that he had held in abeyance on the condition that Wilson handle Jackson and not screw up. That was why Wilson was so anxious to make sure this whole thing looked like Leland murdered Jackson.

He didn't quite know how the Medical Examiner would get on board, but Wilson knew Dr. Melber had something up his sleeve to make that happen.

He always did.

Chapter Twenty-Nine

ALLY and I didn't go out that night. I was too bushed but we made plans for the next night.

I got home and flipped on the lights. "Nate, Amelia," I called. The house was completely dark. "Where are you guys?"

My heart started to race. They were supposed to be home. It was 6 PM. It was already dark, because the time had changed.

"Nate, Amelia," I called.

And then, all at once, a bunch of people jumped out at me. "Surprise!" they shouted.

"What the fuck?" I asked. "It's not my birth-"

It was then that I saw who was in the crowd. Leland was there. So was Dill. Garrett was there. Harper was there with her kids and so was Tammy, Harper's law partner and Harper's assistant Pearl. My mom was also there.

But then I saw the people who mattered the most to me in that crowd, and I suddenly realized why the party was happening. Connor, Jack, Nick and Tommy. My boys. I knew they were getting out of prison at any moment, but I wasn't quite sure when it was.

My mouth dropped open and nothing came out.

Then the four guys came up to me and we all embraced in a group hug.

And I was doing something I hadn't done in a long, long, time.

I was crying.

―――――

WINNING that case was a good thing. It made me happy to see justice done for my client, even if a life, that of Dr. Moore, was ruined in the process. But seeing the guys free…there were no words.

The party went on until the wee hours of the morning and then most everybody left but the guys. They stayed the night and the five of us talked until seven the next morning. Just talked, caught up on one another's life, reminisced and laughed a lot.

"Oh my God," Tommy said. "Remember that one night when we went to that party out in the woods? We couldn't find it for hours and we all were drinking so much that Connor got sick in the back of the pickup."

"That's because you made me drink all that nasty homemade hooch you made, Jack," Connor said.

"Nasty? That was some fine shit," Jack said. "Some damn fine shit."

"Some damn fine shit, my ass," Connor said. "Rat piss probably tasted better."

"You would know, Connor," Nick said. "You were the one living with so many rats in your bedroom."

"Yeah, I felt sorry for the rats I found around the house and made them into pets. So what of it?"

We all laughed.

"Hey, Damien," Connor said. "I still can't believe that Governor commuted my sentence. I still think you had something to do with that, man, but you'll never tell me. But whatever happened, all I can say is thank you."

I had seen him in prison after I blackmailed the governor into commuting his sentence. He knew I had something to do with it but I would never tell him the truth. Nobody knew the truth except me, the Governor and maybe Leland.

"I had nothing to do with it," I lied. "But man, I'm so glad you're out."

We clinked our beer bottles and told more stories and laughed some more.

That night and the next morning was the best of my entire life.

Which was good, because I didn't know it at the time, but I was about to enter the most trying part of my life.

TWO WEEKS LATER, I found that Dr. Ashton Melber lost his license to practice medicine and was brought up on charges that included obstruction of justice and extortion. He was facing up to 20 years in prison for his crimes. I felt his fate was just.

What wasn't just was what happened to Dr. Moore. She, too, lost her medical license. It was suspended pending an investigation. The only good thing was that her son didn't actually get arrested for his distribution of OxyContin to people, so I guess she probably felt her complicity in this whole charade was for the greater good. I felt badly for her, but it couldn't be helped. I had to expose her to get my client off. What was done was done.

I also finally saw my father. I went to see him at the headquarters of his company. He was the fourth generation of his family and was currently the CEO of an international bio-tech company headquartered downtown. He was a bastard, to be sure, but my mother was right – he seemed contrite about what had happened. She forgave him, so I guess I needed to as well.

Unfortunately, I didn't get the chance to really know my dad. One week after I visited him, he was found murdered in his office.

And, somehow, I was under investigation for his murder.

Next in the Kansas City
Legal Thrillers series

vinci-books.com/theaccused

A shocking accusation. A partnership tested. A race against time to uncover the truth.

Harper Ross faces her toughest challenge yet when her law partner, Damien Harrington, is arrested for the murder of his birth father. Convinced of Damien's innocence, Harper delves into the case, only to uncover shocking secrets from Damien's past that shake the very foundation of their partnership.

Turn the page for a free preview…

The Accused: Chapter One

HARPER

"WAIT, WHAT?" I asked on the phone. Damien was calling me and I couldn't really understand what he was saying. It sounded like he was telling me he was arrested for the murder of his father, but I was sure I was hearing him wrong. "Damien, I can't understand you. I must not be hearing you right."

"Harper, did you just hear me tell you I've been arrested for killing my father?"

"Yes."

"Then you're hearing me right. I'm at the station. They're trying to grill me, but I'm not talking. Please come down here. It goes without saying I want you to represent me."

"I'm leaving now," I said as I found my winter coat. It was November, and freezing outside. I had stayed late at the office yet again, as I tried to close out some files that had been sitting on my desk for far too long.

I went to my car, scraping the windshield, as it had begun to snow and I had parked my car on the street in front of my Plaza Office. I wrapped my coat around me tighter and put on my hood. I hated winters in Kansas City, even though I loved the holiday season.

As I drove towards the police station, which was downtown, so it was about a ten minute drive, my mind was racing. I had heard on the news that Josh Roland was dead, and I felt bad for Damien when I heard about it. Damien had just found out Josh was his father and was trying to give the guy the benefit of the doubt even though Josh raped his mother. I had lived through my own rape and never could forgive my rapist. Yet Damien's mother had forgiven him and Damien was trying to get to know him.

Now this. The poor guy couldn't catch a break when it came to his father.

I called the girls from my car. Abby picked up. "Yeah, Mom," she said. "What's going on?"

I took a deep breath. "Abby, I know I promised to be home for dinner tonight," I said, "but it looks like that won't happen. Better bring out that emergency pizza out of the freezer. Make sure Rina gets that essay done for her English class tomorrow and I know you have a quiz tomorrow in Algebra. Goes without saying, but the two of you need to get all your stuff done."

"Mom," Abby whined. "You promised."

"I know," I said, feeling guilty. She was right. I *did* promise to be home early that evening. They counted on me to be home when I said I would be home. I tried hard to be home on time to have dinner with them, but when I couldn't, I let them know ahead of time. They were 13, so I didn't always have to have a sitter with them. I could rely on them to either heat up a frozen pizza or order something off of GrubHub or UberEats, and I usually could rely on Abby getting her homework done and her flute practice in. Rina was usually hit or miss as far as that was concerned, but I tried to light a fire under her whenever I was around, so even her grades weren't suffering that much.

"You know, Mom, but what?" Abby demanded.

I sighed. "I have a very important client," I said. "I'll tell you about it when I see you tonight."

"Who is so important, Mom? Who is more important than your promise to us you'll be home tonight?"

"Damien," I blurted out. I didn't want to talk about this over the phone, but I figured she would find out sooner or later. "Damien is so important. He's down at the police station right now. He was arrested for killing his father." I saw the police station coming up, and I pulled into a spot on the street right in front of the building. "Now, I'm here at the station and need to get in there and see him. I'm sorry, really I am, and, believe me, if it were anybody else but Damien, I would be home right now."

Abby sighed. "I'm sorry, Mom," she said, sweet Abby returning. "I should have known you really did have an emergency. Don't worry about me and Rina. I don't really want that pizza, so I'll just order something from UberEats if you don't mind."

"Go for it, Buttercup," I said. "I'll be home as soon as I can."

"Okay." She was quiet for a few seconds. "Will he be okay? Uncle Damien?" Her voice sounded anxious.

"I don't know," I said truthfully. "I wish I did, Buttercup. I hate to say it, but I don't know any more about this whole thing than you do, which isn't much. All I know is he just called me from the station. I saw shis father was murdered, but I just couldn't imagine Damien being behind it all."

I talked to Abby as I approached the building. I went in,

gave my ID to the woman behind the glass. She nodded and buzzed me into the area where I could talk to Damien.

"I'll tell Rina," Abby said. "She'll be upset."

"I know." I drew a breath. "Not to mention his kids. Oh, God, I hope they're okay. I know they have a sitter, Gretchen, but I might have to take them if Damien doesn't make bail." I shook my head. "I'll burn that bridge when I come to it. Bye, Buttercup. Have to go."

I hung up the phone and followed the officer to the interrogation room. Damien was sitting at a table, his arms crossed in front of him, glaring at the officer standing above him. I put my briefcase down on the table and sat down next to him.

"Hey, Harper," Damien said, his glare trained on the officer. "Glad you could make it."

I crossed my hands. "Okay, get me up to speed here," I said. "What's going on?"

"My father was found in his office, bludgeoned by a table lamp. There were signs of a struggle – the floor lamp in that office was knocked over and papers were strewn all over the floor. My fingerprints were apparently on the lamp base." He glared again at the officer. "Of course my fingerprints were on that lamp base. I'd been in the office and touched that lamp while I talked to my dad. I was nervous when I met him. I have a nervous tic that makes me want to touch things on people's desks. Paper weights, lamp stands, statuettes, whatever. I touch things when I don't know what to say to somebody."

I whipped out a yellow pad of paper. "Okay," I said to the officer, whose name was Officer Leeds, "you have my client's fingerprints on the lamp base. What else do you have on him? I'm listening and I don't hear anything that gives you guys probable cause to arrest him. I better hear something more than the fact that Damien's fingerprints were on the murder weapon or I'm going to demand you release him."

Officer Leeds narrowed his eyes at me. "His fingerprints were the only prints on the lamp base except for the victim's. This was a brand-new table lamp, just bought today. If there was some other person who used that lamp as a weapon, there would be some sort of other fingerprints on it. There was none."

I cleared my throat. "Well, I still don't believe you have enough evidence to hold him. It's November. Somebody could have come into the office wearing gloves and done this."

I had to admit it looked bad that only Damien's fingerprints were on the murder weapon, especially since it was a lamp. Because the lamp was used as a murder weapon, it could reasonably be assumed the murder wasn't premeditated. Therefore, it could reasonably be assumed the perpetrator wouldn't have been using rubber gloves or some other method of concealing his or her fingerprints. But it was a possibility that somebody was wearing winter gloves when he or she did this.

Either that or somebody clearly framed Damien for this. That was the only other explanation I could think of for why Damien's fingerprints were on the lamp and nobody else's fingerprints were.

"We have probable cause to arrest him because his fingerprints were on the murder weapon. You're the lawyer. You know very well that something as simple as that can be enough to charge somebody." Officer Leeds glared at Damien. "Plus, your client has not exactly been a choir boy. He has quite a juvenile record."

"A juvenile record? A juvenile record? You're using his juvenile record against him? That stuff is sealed."

"It's been unsealed," Officer Leeds said. "By the governor himself."

"Governor Weston went through the trouble of unsealing Mr. Harrington's juvenile record?" I was dumbfounded about that one. "Why would he do something like that?"

Office Leeds shrugged. "Ask Governor Weston that question. I obviously can't answer that for you. I can only state that happened. Because Governor Weston unsealed your client's record, I can also tell you that Mr. Harrington will go in front of the Missouri Bar soon. He lied on his Bar application when he said he had no adjudications. He clearly did. But that's neither here nor there."

I cocked my head at Damien, who was having a problem meeting my eyes. "Okay, well, I understand Mr. Harrington probably had some issues in his youth. I don't know what they have to do with this charge, though."

"He has a charge from when he was 15 years old. He beat up a 21-year-old guy named Julian Wise. He used brass knuckles. The guy went into the hospital for three days because of it. He has also stolen three cars. He was involved with an underground gambling operation and served as the enforcer for this underground group. Your client was lucky he was put into prison when he was 18. It seemed to have straightened him out." He looked over at Damien, who now was hanging his head down. "Seemed is the operative word."

"Well," I said, feeling at a loss for words. Inwardly, I was seething at Damien. He never told me any of these things. He told me he was wrongfully imprisoned at 18, but he never bothered to tell me about his juvenile crimes. I was completely blind-sided by this officer. "I don't think *seemed* is the operative word here. Ever since my client has lived a stellar life since being released from prison. He's highly respected in the legal community. He has no adult criminal record. Besides, you know as well as I do you can't base probable cause on a person's record. Especially a juvenile record."

"No, but we can base probable cause on the fact that your client's fingerprints were on the murder weapon and he had motive for killing Mr. Roland."

"What motive?"

"The victim raped his mother. That's your motive right there. That would be enough for Mr. Harrington to want Mr. Roland dead, but that's not even the most compelling reason Mr. Harrington had to kill Mr. Roland."

"Oh? What other motive did my client have for killing Mr. Roland?"

"Mr. Roland had confidential information that could have sent his best friend, Nick Savante, back to prison."

The Accused: Chapter Two

I SIGHED. There was one thing I knew about Damien - he would do anything to protect his best friends. I didn't think killing somebody would be in his wheelhouse, but one never knew. It depended on what Josh Roland had on his friend, Nick, and how good this piece of information was.

"What piece of information did this guy have about Nick?" I asked Officer Leeds. "That would send Nick to prison?"

"Nick is apparently already violating his parole," Officer Leeds said. "Damien got Nick a job with Mr. Roland. Damien's first mistake. He should have figured Nick would get sticky fingers. That's what allegedly happened. We have found, through our preliminary investigation, that Nick was stealing from Mr. Roland's company. He was inflating invoices and pocketing the money. Mr. Roland was on top of this. He fired him and called Mr. Harrington into his office to read him the riot act about introducing Nick to him. That was when Mr. Harrington killed Mr. Roland."

I looked over at Damien. He wasn't looking at me. Then

he looked at me, shook his head and rolled his eyes. I gave him a look that told him not to speak and he got it. He shook his head again and looked away. I could see burning hatred in his eyes.

"Will Nick back to prison?" I asked Officer Leeds. "Is there an arrest warrant out for him?"

"At the moment, no, there's not, but there soon will be."

"Okay." I nodded. "Will you charge my client in his father's murder?"

"We are. He hasn't spoken to us because he knows better, being a lawyer himself, but, yes, we have enough evidence to charge him. I anticipate we will. I just need to get word from my superior about this, but I think he'll be charged by the end of the night."

I took a deep breath. "Do you mind if I have a word alone with my client?"

"No, not at all," he said. "Maybe you can talk him into doing the right thing and confess."

Damien rolled his eyes and glared at Officer Leeds as he got up and went outside the door.

I looked at the window, knowing we were being watched and listened to the entire time. Therefore, I wouldn't talk to Damien about anything of substance. "Damien," I said, "how are you holding up?"

He shrugged and said nothing.

"Well, I guess you'll be charged and booked," I said, "I'll be there for your initial appearance. I don't anticipate a problem getting bail for you."

"I don't know about that," Damien said, his voice seething. "I pissed off somebody pretty high up on the food chain. He's getting his revenge. I fully anticipate I'll be denied bail. I wouldn't be surprised if that's the case."

"Damien, it's your first offense," I said.

"No, it's not. My juvenile record has been unsealed. I have a record now, Harper, and not a great one. Plus, Harper, I'm telling you, this one goes all the way up to the top. You have a handful on your hands, Harper, a handful."

"Damien, you're not making any sense."

"I know I'm not," he said, "but I will. We just need to get to a place where you and I can speak privately. When we're not being watched through a two-way mirror. I need you see me tomorrow morning in the jail. A professional visit. I'll tell you everything."

"Okay," I said. "In the meantime, your kids..."

"Yeah. I hate to ask this of you, but do you mind taking them?"

"No, no, of course not," I said. "I'll pick up Nate and Amelia after I leave here. I'll pack a bag and bring them over to my house tonight."

"Thanks." Damien hung his head. "I have a story to tell. This whole thing reeks of a setup and I have a good idea on who's behind this. And, Harper, when you find out who's behind this, you'll be stunned. Absolutely stunned."

At that, the officer came back in. "Time's up," he said. "We're going to charge your client with the murder of his father." At that, he put the handcuffs on Damien and read him his Miranda Rights. "Mr. Harrington, you are under arrest for the murder of Joshua Roland. You have a right to remain silent..."

After they read Damien his rights, they took him out of the room to be processed. He looked back towards me as he was being marched out and I felt for him. He was 35-years-old and a well-respected attorney. He'd won some really amazing cases. But yet, here he was, looking like a scared kid. That was the look on his face – that of a terrified kid.

He knew something. I could tell. He knew something and his look told me things were dire.

Very dire.

As I left the police station, I was filled with a feeling of dread.

Something told me this case would be one of the most challenging of my entire life.

I hoped and prayed I was wrong.

The Accused: Chapter Three

THE NEXT DAY, I met Damien for his initial appearance. I saw him coming out in his orange jumpsuit and my heart went out to him. I knew how humiliated he felt. I had been where he was. I was in court for my kidnapping charge back in the day when I was determined to protect my kids at all cost. I was also in court for a DWI when I was framed by the cop in the Darnell Williams case. Both times, I knew my colleagues were whispering about me behind my back. I shouldn't have cared about that, but I really did. Nobody wanted to be humiliated in front of their peers.

I went over to him and put my arm around his shoulders. "It'll be fine," I whispered. "I talked to the prosecutor and they're against giving you a bond. I'd like to talk to Ally about this, though, and see if she can pull some strings so I can get you a bond review with little opposition."

Damien shook his head. "You can try, Harper, but trust me when I tell you I won't be granted a bond. I'm being accused of murdering one of the richest men in the city.

Credibly accused of murdering him, I might add. I'll be very surprised if I'm granted a bond."

"We'll see," I said. "It's worth a shot."

"I guess."

"I think we have a shot, but if you're not granted a bond, you probably need me care for Nate and Amelia. Right?"

"Right." He put his hand on my shoulder. "Harper, I wanted to tell you how much I appreciate your support." He hung his head. "Man, I'm in the middle of a nightmare. A complete nightmare." He looked at me. "Harper, I'd like you to do something else for me, if you don't mind."

"Sure, what do you need?"

"Find out what happened with Nick. I just can't believe he would violate his parole like that. I'm telling you, I think there's something rotten going on. Really rotten. I haven't quite figured it out, but I have a good feeling about what's happening. I have a feeling all the guys will be in trouble, sooner or later." He shook his head. "I've made a very powerful enemy, Harper. Nobody will be safe until you and I come up with a plan to stop this."

I was intrigued. He still didn't feel comfortable telling me everything. I knew why. He knew as well as I did that attorney-client privilege only applied when he and I were one-on-one. Anything he told me right at that point wouldn't be covered by privilege. I was therefore anxious to visit him in jail or, hopefully, at his home, assuming he could make bail.

The judge got on the bench and started to call his cases. "I'll take the inmates represented by private counsel first," he announced, and then he called several cases, all of whom pled "not guilty," before he got to our case.

"State verses Harrington," he said and then looked

surprised when Damien came up to the bench. "Mr. Harrington," he began and then he shook his head. "You've been charged by the State of Missouri in one count of Murder in the First Degree. How do you plead?"

"Not guilty, your honor," he said.

"I would like a bond review," I said. "At the moment, Mr. Harrington is held without bond. He's not a flight risk. He's also a respected member of the bar." I leaned forward. "Please, your honor. You've seen Mr. Harrington in court, time after time. He's one of us."

He shook his head and studied the file in front of him. "Let's see..." He carefully read the charges and evidence. I knew this judge, Judge Kenner, typically didn't see the file before he got on the bench for the initial appearances. There were just too many files and defendants on any given docket for him to have studied every single file beforehand. But this was Damien, one of our own. That gave him pause. "You've been charged with the murder of one our most prominent citizens, Josh Roland."

I knew his dilemma. This was a case the media was covering extensively. Josh Roland, for all his problems, was a billionaire and a prominent CEO of a major corporation. He had his issues with drugs and sexual harassment and apparently raped at least one woman, Damien's mother. But these issues were swept under the rug. Josh had a handler charged with covering up all his misdeeds, a professional whose only job was to pay off anybody who needed to be paid off or blackmailed whoever could be blackmailed, so all of Josh's crimes and misdemeanors were never covered in the newspaper.

So, for all intents and purposes, Josh Roland was an upstanding citizen. A philanthropic billionaire who funded hospital wings and had entire university halls named after him. Children's Mercy, the children's hospital that relied on philanthropic funding because it provided so much indigent care, was kept afloat because of Josh Roland's efforts. His annual charity balls for Children's Mercy were legendary and raised billions over the years. He also was a part of the investors who funded the Kansas City Chiefs. If there was one thing Kansas Citians passionately loved, it was the Super Bowl-winning Chiefs. Patrick Mahomes and the Chiefs were Gods in this town, rightfully so.

Plus, Josh Roland's firm, Aragon International, was on the cutting edge of bio-technology. While he did come from old money – his great-grandfather made his money in diamonds while his grandfather got into shipping and lumber – Josh made his own path, using his inherited fortune to found an internationally well-respected company that locally employed thousands of people.

I wasn't hopeful bail would be granted to Damien, but I had to pray this judge would see past who the victim was.

Judge Kenner looked at Steven Harper, the prosecutor assigned to this docket. "Mr. Harper, do you have any objections to Mr. Harrington being assigned bail?"

Steve looked like he was put on the spot. I knew his dilemma – Damien was a colleague, a respected member of the legal community. The criminal bar was close-knit. Prosecutors and defense attorneys were generally friendly with one another. Especially a defense attorney like Damien, who worked in the Public Defender's Office for several years, which meant he got to know almost everybody in the prosecutor's office, even Steve.

Yet Steve had a job to do.

"I do object, your honor," Steve said. "Mr. Harrington has been accused of a very serious crime. Murder One." That was all he said, however. He couldn't say much more.

"Ms. Ross," Judge Kenner said, "What say you?"

"My client is not a flight risk. He's a well-respected member of the bar and has two small children at his home. He doesn't own a passport, so there's no chance he can leave the country. I understand he's been accused of a very serious crime, but that's not a sufficient reason to deny bail to my client, your honor."

Judge Kenner studied the file some more. "Okay, here's what I'll do. I'll set bail at $3 million cash. The terms and conditions of the bail are the defendant shall not have contact with anybody working for Aragon International, he cannot leave the jurisdiction, he will be monitored electronically, he cannot leave his house unless he is going to work and he cannot have contact with known felons. I understand Mr. Harrington is an attorney, but I must restrict his movements. I'm very sorry, Mr. Harrington. I know you most likely have cases in far-flung places like Harrisonville and Bonner Springs, but, for now, I need you to stay in Kansas City proper. If you have cases in those other suburbs, I'm afraid you'll have to reassign them. I'm sorry, Mr. Harrington, but that's the best I can do."

Damien looked surprised he was getting bail. Granted, $3 million was very steep, and, in order for Damien to make that bail, he would have to drain all of his savings, but he would get out of jail. That was important.

All I could think of was that it was a great blessing Damien won that major wrongful death case. If he didn't, he probably wouldn't have had the money to get out of jail.

"Thank you, your honor," Damien said, looking at me in wonder.

The guard led him away and he looked back at me. "Meet me at my home this evening at 7," he said over his shoulder.

"I'll be there."

I left the courthouse feeling pretty good. It definitely could have been worse. Considering how important and wealthy the victim was, I was prepared that Damien would be denied bail. He wasn't, so that was a good sign.

At least I hoped it was.

Grab your copy...
vinci-books.com/theaccused

About the Author

Rachel Sinclair was a criminal defense attorney for eleven years, so she doesn't scare easily. She graduated from the University of Missouri-Kansas City School of Law in 1998, and worked for the Public Defender's Office for several years before striking out on her own. She currently lives in San Diego, California, with her boyfriend, Joey, and her two fur babies, Annie and Toby. In her spare time, she likes to read, bicycle all over town, Boogie Board at the beach, and watch trashy television.

www.ingramcontent.com/pod-product-compliance
Lightning Source LLC
LaVergne TN
LVHW030241250326
834688LV00047B/1747